THE ANGEL JOPHIEL

by

GERALD BRENNAN

ಬಐಛ

DreamStreet
Press
Ann Arbor, MI USA
www.DreamStreetPress.com

to

my little sister Peggy

MARGARET JOAN BRENNAN

(1961-2022)

THE ANGEL
JOPHIEL

The current habit of desecrating beauty suggests that people are as aware as they ever were of the presence of sacred things. Desecration is a kind of defense against the sacred, an attempt to destroy its claims. In the presence of sacred things, our lives are judged, and to escape that judgment, we destroy the thing that seems to accuse us.

Beauty cannot be ignored, so it must be vandalized…

– Roger Scruton

Angus Fairbairn has to leave the delivery room because he knows that, despite his promises and best efforts, he will not be able to watch his wife give birth. The noble picture he forced into his head these past few months – standing next to Emma, holding her hand with the babe pushing at life's door, all easy smiles and calm encouragement – this is not going to happen.

He pushes out through the double doors, ripping the little mask from his face and takes deep breaths as he lumbers down the hallway, now stopping and bending, hands on his knees, panting hard but relieved that the urge to vomit is fading. He needs a real drink but for now, water will do. He unbends, spies the fountain on the wall, steps to it and gulps greedily from it. Angus straightens and wipes at his wet mouth with the cuff of his workshirt, careful to avoid the greasemark, sighs heavily and looks about.

The nurses at the desk down the hall are looking at him. *Let them look.* One breaks free and starts toward him, a forced smile on her old face. He closes his eyes, trapped, and waits. *I'm fine for chrissakes just let me the hell alone it's hard enough without-*

"Mr. Fairbairn? Everything okay?" She touches his shoulder. He flinches and opens his eyes. Her smile is genuine.

He feels like a jerk. "Yeah… I'm all right. I just got a little…"

"People think it's easy in there, but it isn't," she says gently. "My husband couldn't do it either." This is a lie, she's childless, but her magic works and Angus begins to relax.

"I'm okay now. Thanks." He lets himself be guided to a small chair in a row against the wall. "I just got a little…"

"I know, Mr. Fairbairn. It happens all the time. Would you like some coffee?"

"Coffee… yeah. Coffee would be good. Thank you."

Emma cannot just walk away. This is her first baby and she is 18 and afraid.

But as the moment grows close and her anxiety peaks, something happens to her. She unexpectedly feels the woman in her overcome the girl. She senses being filled with a strength and resolution that makes her feel oddly masterful. The baby's head appears, and with one more determined cry and shove her babe is born. (She will cherish this feeling, that unanticipated well of strength and high-spirits that she will draw to her rescue many more times in her long life to come.)

Emma's baby does not make a sound, and with concerned looks the attendants cut the cord, wrap the infant, and the new baby is whisked out of the delivery room by the obstetrician himself in the lead. Emma, a bit foggy, witnesses all this and it dawns on her that something is not right.

"My baby didn't cry!" She begins to panic through her fog.

The anesthetist touches her arm. "That's okay. Not all babies cry. Your baby is breathing normally and appears bright-eyed and healthy. Don't worry about that."

"But where is he? Or she? Is my baby a boy or a girl?"

The attendants search one another's faces for an answer to Emma's question. No one responds.

Emma loses it. *"WHAT'S WRONG!?"*

I remember coming out. It was slushy, then cold. My birth is not my earliest memory of this earthly life. I remember Emma's womb. I remember dreaming and the dreams becoming what I am now obliged to call 'real.' When I came out from Emma's body I sensed a great joyful presence in the bright, green-tiled room, turning almost at once to confusion and anguish. I remember being bundled up and moments later I recall Emma crying out in distress though I was by then in a different room. It was not my ears that registered her agony, but I heard her as clearly as if I were still inside of her. I write of this eight years after it happened. It is out of

order in my journal because, as I explained, I
have from the beginning been ordered to write,
but I had yet to chronicle this event. My mission
is clear. I am to find three people and guide them
on their path, which is essential for the flowering
of humanity: Sam Morgan, Bran Englander,
and Alma Pierce. All three must be activated
or my earthly mission will fail.

– from *Chronicles of Jophiel, Vol. I*

Under some sedation now, lying tearful in a private room apart from the recovery room, a fearful Angus stands beside Emma and strokes her hair, as the couple wait in quiet torment for the obstetrician to come and finally tell them exactly what this is all about. Angus is an impatient man in the best of circumstances, but the minutes crawl over him now like fire ants and he can wait no longer for answers. He storms to the door, which opens before he reaches it, and there stands their Dr. Salinger, face to face with fiery Angus.

"It's about goddam time!" Angus growls at him, immediately regretting it. Salinger ignores this outburst, is calm, but obviously troubled. Angus steps back, contrite. "Sorry," he whispers. "You have news for us?"

The doctor steps in, greets Emma and asks that Angus be seated next to her while he closes the door and sits in the corner chair.

"Is my baby okay?" Emma asks as she pushes the button to raise herself to a seating position.

"You baby is as healthy as I have ever seen. But there-"

"Where is he?" Emma demands. "Or she? *Do we have a baby boy or girl?*

"That's… that's what we're going to talk about."

Angus stands and runs a calloused hand through his greying red hair, frustrated. "Jesus Christ, it's a simple enough question!"

"It's not a simple answer!" Salinger barks and calms himself at once. (Angus is only a little younger than the doctor, and wiry, but Salinger is a much larger man and will not be intimidated.) "Now *please*. Sit back down and I'll tell you everything we know about what's going on."

Angus sits, looks up at Salinger and nods, bracing for the news. He takes Emma's hand.

"Babies are almost always born male or female, with obvious genitalia that makes it all very clear." He pauses, thoughtful. "When there are anomalies, these are called 'intersex states.' Sometimes more male characteristics are most obvious, sometimes female characteristics."

"Are you sayin' our baby's one of them?" Angus asks.

"No. See, it's always either one or the other, or else it's a blend of the two. But this is different."

"Different how?"

Salinger takes a deep breath and lets it out noisily. "There is no genitalia present." Angus and Emma both close their eyes, trying to assimilate all this. The doctor continues. "But the baby is urinating fine. Your baby has, an aperture…"

"A hole," Angus says.

"Correct. Anatomically, it's as correctly placed as one would guess, and there seems to be no problem with urination. We're testing the urine now, but the color and volume is good, and the baby suffers no distress."

Emma speaks. "So… no sex organs? No he or she?"

"Well, only *externally*," the doctor replies. "We don't know what's going on inside. We'd like to do an MRI."

"What's that?" Angus asks. "I heard of it but what is it?"

"It's a computerized image of radio signals emitted by the body. It's safe. No radiation. From this, we can tell if the baby has ovaries inside, or a prostate, or related structures that have some degree of presence or lack thereof. See… there has never been an instance, a medically *verified* instance, of a child born without *any* sexual characteristics. Always - either, or, or a blend. Never just… none. So, I urge you to let us proceed with the MRI."

"Then you'll know? Boy or girl?" Angus asks.

The doctor looks frustrated. "Then we'll know more."

Emma puts her face in her hands and starts to cry.

The baby had the MRI that very noon and was kept under observation while Emma was formally released, though she naturally stayed at the facility through the ordeal, holding the baby whenever she was allowed and staying as close by as she could manage when she was not. She has calmed considerably since the birth and is actually most upset at Angus's unabated wrath at the situation. He would not stay with her, deciding instead to "go the hell back to work" until there was some news. Emma wondered if he were angry at *her*, at what she has brought into the world.

Her baby is beautiful. All moms think that, but Emma has never seen such a baby. The eyes, the smile… She is totally in love with her child and was playing with names in her new-mom mind, but always skidding back to the fact that names are essentially sex-based, and the cycle of worry would renew.

The nurse alerts her that the radiologist and obstetrician are nearing the end of their conference and that Emma should call Angus back to the hospital to hear the summation of the report.

When Angus arrives, he is ushered to a conference room, greeted there by Emma holding the baby and pacing, patting her infant on the back. "I just fed… the baby," she says with a big smile, avoiding all the personal pronouns – 'him' or 'her' for obvious reasons, also the word 'it'… well, that is simply *out* of the question.

Angus has not softened during his time away. "Yeah," he says. "That's swell." He has yet to so much as look at the child.

"Wanna hold the baby?" Emma offers shyly.

"What?" He finally glances over at them, quickly looking away again. "Nah. I'm good." He sits, crosses his arms, and sniffs. Emma sighs and takes the chair next to him, snuggling the baby in the crook of her shoulder, the little head next to her own, gently rubbing the baby's back. A polite peck on the door and it swings open revealing a slightly rattled-looking Dr. Salinger. He nods his greeting and closes the door.

He turns to look at the trio and sighs. "I'm gonna sit if you don't mind."

"We don't mind," Angus says. "Whaddaya got?"

Salinger gets to the point. "Your baby is spectacularly healthy but has no sexual characteristics."

Angus sighs and nods. "Go on."

"We have been unable to find a clinical discussion that describes the baby's condition because it has never been known to exist in humans."

He struggles to communicate his findings in an elementary way. "You might remember from high school that the female provides the X chromosome, the male, either X or Y. The combination of XX is a girl, XY is a boy."

"Yeah. Okay. So?"

"See... embryologically, and developmentally, the default position is to develop female reproductive organs and characteristics. But if the male adds a Y-chromosome then the embryo develops into the male sex. Even conditions which result in a missing X-chromosome – just one 'X,' what we call Turner's Syndrome – still have the female appearance though with undeveloped or nearly-absent sex organs and *lots* of other problems. So, the idea that a 'normal' human could be born but with no sexual organs and no secondary sexual characteristics has just never occurred. There's just nothing in medical history that is recorded that we can cite as another case like this."

"But the baby is healthy," Emma says.

"Yes. Very! See, that's the thing. Always, genetic muta-tions or chromosomal changes that induce what we have here with your baby would certainly cause numerous other changes in many organs in the body that would be terribly obvious and *lethal*, so such a fetus would be most unlikely to be born alive or survive past birth. Yet your child is as healthy and content and alert as any I have ever seen. And the MRI reveals about the most perfect set of infant innards *any* of us have ever seen!"

At that the baby belches loudly, causing Emma and the doctor to chuckle. Angus, not so much.

"So, what do we do? What's going to happen?" Angus stands, agitated, with no room for pacing. He clenches his fists. "How do we know the baby's not gonna fall over dead in a week? And not a he and… not a she? What the hell are we gonna do?" He looks beseechingly at Emma. *"What are we gonna do?"*

"Mr. Fairbairn… Angus," the doctor says. "There are plenty of he's and she's out there with all *sorts* of terrible problems." He bows his head. "I've seen so *many*…" He looks up and into Angus's face, but Angus is far away and will not meet the physician's eyes. "But your baby appears to be the picture of health. We took some other tests, the results from which we won't have for a little while, but the blood is perfect. The urine is fine, all the organs fit for living are where they need to be and functioning beautifully. The baby is bright-eyed and full of smiles, and a real beauty. Is all that not something?"

Angus stares off into space, as if he has not heard a word, but instead seems to be attending to some terrible scene he cannot break away from.

"Angus, listen to me. I'm not an expert in this sort of thing. No one is. I *can't* guarantee your baby won't fall over dead in a week – but for the life of me, I don't know what it would possibly be *from!* And since we can't put a biological sex on the child, you might… just pick one and go with it. It would be a relief to pick a sex, pick a name, and raise your baby as best you can. Keep in mind that children are amazingly resilient if treated with just simple kindness. The big issues that may lie ahead won't really surface until puberty, and we don't know how your child's body or mind will respond to puberty. We also don't know what medical advances might occur relevant to the child's situation 15 years from now. Things may be much different in 2030 than they are now."

Angus is looking at the doctor but not hearing him. "Can we go?"

The doctor shakes his head and looks at the floor in mute frustration. He cannot break through Angus's wall. "Yes. You can all go home," he sighs. "We'd like to see the baby in a couple weeks, if…" Angus shuffles to the door, opens it and walks out into the hallway, paying no attention to the doctor's words. Emma stands with the child and takes the doctor's hand in her own. Salinger continues. "And, umm… counseling. Yes. No one has any experience in this line, but I can still recommend a couple good people to help you get settled in. If you're interested."

Emma smiles at the doctor. "We'll see. You've been very helpful. I imagine this was quite the ordeal for you, too."

Salinger brightens and nods, squeezing Emma's hand gratefully. "It was, indeed, Ms. Fairbairn. Thank you. And your baby is beautiful." He pauses and smiles. "Everyone seems to note that. That's… unusual around here. So many babies…" She frees her hand and with the grace that shall always define her, joins her troubled soul of a husband in the hallway and together the three of them make their slow, sad way toward the elevators.

I remember what took the place of my mother's womb: it was a blue and lacy bassinette. I would lie for hours within, enjoying the whirling, shifting geometries of the colorful mobile my mother had affixed above. My mother worried that I never cried. I never needed to cry nor wanted to, save for twice – I made tears in my life two times – so far. My father I rarely encountered. I sensed his presence more than I saw or even heard it. He did not hate me. I know hate; it wasn't that. But something was growing inside him that would be a danger to me. That would not be permitted, and this made me sad for my father. He wanted a boy, so they decided to call me a boy's name that could be

8

turned into a girl's name should "a miracle
happen," or if puberty compelled me to that pole.
They therefore named me Jesse.
But Jesse is not my name.

– from *Chronicles of Jophiel, Vol. I*

2

Out of the rain at last, Matt Fischer and his fiancée Janet are taking their seats in the middle of the restaurant that Janet's little sister, Emma, had hand-picked for them as a place to celebrate Matt's proposal. It's their first visit to Ann Arbor as a couple. This city is Emma's home, and she has not seen her sister Janet in many months. And Emma has never even met Matt, a situation to be remedied first thing tomorrow, when the couple will have breakfast with Emma and Angus and spend the day with them.

"I can't wait to see the baby," Janet says as the *maître d'* inches Janet's chair into position as she sits.

Matt leans his umbrella against the wall and looks about him. The restaurant is swank and small, and almost full. The diners are mostly quiet and to themselves, except for the male foursome nearby who are drunk and celebratory though not obnoxiously so. Matt nods to them; a couple of them nod in return. A waiter places two small glasses of water, each sporting a thin, perfect lemon slice and two clear ice cubes, in front of Matt and Janet.

"I said, I can't wait to see the *baby,*" Janet repeats.

"Yep, I hear you. We'll see them tomorrow," Matt says. "Emma won't tell you what's wrong, though, huh?"

"She wants to see me, us, in person. And I guess Angus is acting weird."

Matt furrows his brown and sighs, looking away. "Yeah… great."

"Don't get upset. Don't *you* get weird. I know meeting people annoys you but he's our brother-in-law. Or will be yours soon enough. And you've never met him so don't pre-judge."

"Okay, but," Matt points at his ears, "I *hear* things."

"I know, but…"

"Good evening, my name is Jordi. May I interest you in something to drink?"

Ah. Matt thinks, *saved by the sommelier!* "You sure can," Matt pipes. "Janet?"

"You're making my new resolve difficult," she says. Then reconsiders the occasion. "Okay. The usual?"

Matt says to the lad, "Something white and crisp from the Loire. You pick." The wine steward smiles and is off. The table next door is getting boisterous. *They are really right on the edge there,* thinks Matt.

Matt and Janet peruse the menu. *Appetizers. Maybe just,* Janet muses. They read until the wine comes, and the steward pours. It's good. They toast their love.

"Hey! Garçon!" the big guy at the next table hollers out to his server, a young woman. Cute with a ponytail. She gives him an annoyed look and heads toward the kitchen.

Matt tenses, *What a boob. That's the wrong word he's throwing around there.*

Now the big guy holds up his empty martini glass and shouts again after the woman who has now reappeared with four bowls of soup on a tray for the big guy's table. "Hey! Garçon!" A table nearby shushes him, but he ignores. "Bring another martini with them soups!"

The server is at the table and distributes the soup. "Yes, sir. Right away. Anyone else?" she asks. No takers.

"Good!" Big guy says. "Just keep 'em comin', garçon."

The server folds her hands and looks at the man. "Sir, 'garçon' means 'boy' in French."

"So? How do you say 'tip' in French?" and the big fella laughs and laughs. Even his tablemates look uneasy. He sips at his drink as the offended server heads back to the kitchen, then he tries the soup. "God DAMN that's hot!" and he slams down his spoon and takes an emergency gulp at his drink (the martini, not the water), now almost gone.

Matt's shoulders are tense, and he has a bad feeling about all this, but Janet calms him with her cool smooth hand on his. "Forget them," she coos. "This is our night." And they toast again.

The waiter appears, introduces himself and takes Janet's appetizer order. Nothing for Matt. "Wait. Bread?" he asks and is told it's on the way. They'll order dinner later, Janet tells the server.

Things seem to be quieting down, but after a few minutes the big guy needs yet another martini. "They need bigger glasses in this joint," he opines to all.

One of his tablemates chuckles. "I dunno about that. You know what they say about martinis, right?"

The big guy belches. "No. What? They make you burp?"

"Two is too many; three are not enough."

Big guy doesn't laugh but the others do. He twists himself in his chair trying to locate his server. He sees her talking with patrons at a far table. "Hey!" he yells. "Garçon!"

Matt quietly snaps. "Hey pal," he says to the big man at the next table. "You call that girl 'garçon' again and you'll be eating soup out of your lap."

The big guy sizes Matt up. Much smaller guy. "Fuck you," he says to Matt, and turns to call again, louder, "Hey! Gar-"

Before big guy gets the offensive word out of his mouth Matt had snatched his umbrella, reached over and deftly tips the soup bowl into the big man's lap. He howls "FUCK!" and springs to his feet, bunching his fists at his side. He makes the mistake of advancing on Matt.

Matt springs up and with the heel of his open palm strikes the big man in the nose in a deft snap. Big boy stumbles back and falls flat on his ass, blood spewing from his nostrils. A huge mess. He sits for a moment in a daze with the blood sheeting down from his nose. One of the shushers from before is on his cellphone. *Cops,* Matt thinks. *Ah well…*

11

A few of the staff members come over to help the guy but they seem unenthusiastic. The other diners are mostly nonplussed. A few clap, some are smiling. The women look a little spooked. Janet is annoyed.

"Did you have to do that?" she moans, exasperated. Matt sits back down and sips his wine.

"He's fine. It's the most blood with the least injury," Matt explains.

"You mean the most *embarrassment.*"

"With the least injury," Matt repeats softly.

"What about the hot soup?" she says.

"He'll be fine," he tries to reassure her. "He had it coming. He knows that. He just never thought it would happen."

The big fella has come around and is helped to his chair. He makes a fuss over all the blood, stanching the stream with napkins and upturned head, but won't look at Matt. The manager is trying to calm him. Matt just hears mumbles. He sips his wine and toasts Janet. She's resigned and lifts her glass to his. They drink.

The bread, good bread, along with Janet's appetizer, crab cakes, arrives at the same moment as Ann Arbor's finest. Two of each, in fact, cops and cakes. The manager and the young woman server fill the cops in. An elderly couple looks on and the old gent says to the cops, "If I were younger I would have done the same thing! Shame on that slob! He hurt a girl's feelings." The old missus pats his hand.

By the time the cops get around to the big guy his nose is still bleeding and there is blood on him, the floor, his shirt, the tablecloth… The police are not sympathetic to the man. They have heard enough from staff and diners.

"They look good," Matt says to Janet.

"What?" Janet is confused. "What are you even *talking* about?"

"Your crab cakes," he says. "They look good. Eat them before they get cold."

"O… Yeah. Okay." And she digs in with as much enthusiasm as she can muster. Matt smiles and shakes his head.

"And if you think I'm paying for any of this you're out of your goddam minds!" big boy hisses as he stands unsteadily and starts toward the door with the aid of his associates.

Matt stands and calls out "Hey, pal." The big guy stops and turns hatefully toward Matt. Matt takes out his wallet, flashes a hundred dollar bill at him and throws it on the big guy's table. "My treat. Have a nice night."

One of the cops tools by Matt's table as he resumes his seat. He touches the rim of his cap to Janet, "Ma'am." She smiles back. "He can press charges, you know," the cop says to Matt.

"He'll be too embarrassed," Matt replies.

The cop stifles a laugh and fixes Matt with an appraising look. "Are you in the business?"

Matt smiles. "Not exactly. Not anymore."

"Well, I need your I.D. anyway." Matt takes the wallet back out, removes his license along with his concealed pistol permit and surrenders these to the cop. He does what he needs to do and in a few minutes the cops are gone, the bloody linen replaced, the stained floor wiped spotless and all back to near-normal.

Janet looks over at her dear Matt. "Don't tell me."

"I'm *starving,*" he chuckles.

"You would be!" she laughs and shakes her head in mock disbelief.

At the close of their otherwise enjoyable dinner, the young lady makes a point of thanking Matt and the manager would not take his money for their meal.

3

The young candidate for Senate is almost finished with his speech but the crowd is getting unruly. He tries to focus on the teleprompter and not on the bottle that just missed the lectern. Two burly agents move in front of the lectern, one on either side, eyes studying the crowd behind dark glasses.

He was warned this could happen, but he feels he must take his case "to the people."

"And I say, in conclusion, that the only way we can continue in the ways of freedom that our founders had envisioned, is to-"

What sounds like a gunshot ends the festivities abruptly. The crowd on the fairgrounds scatter in all directions as the two agents force the future Senator to the floor of the platform and cover his body with their own. When the coast is deemed clear, the two men hustled the young candidate backstage and into the bulletproof BMW parked behind the rear of the amphitheater. The car zooms away, the future Senator in back sandwiched between the two agents. Up front there is an amazingly skilled driver, blasting through the twists and turns to get to the highway, and next to him, holding on for dear life, is Phil, the number one man to the Senator-to-be.

"Law and order, sir," Phil calls to his boss in the back seat. "It will be an easy sell. Especially after what just happened. It's unfortunate, but we can use this to our advantage."

Phil is good at this sort of thing – manipulating a crisis to his advantage. Especially since he had set the whole thing up.

4

It's not really what you'd call a nice house.

Matt parks the car in front and notes the dilapidated state of the home that Emma and Angus call their own. The whole neighborhood has a run-down look.

"I thought Ann Arbor was a big-ticket town," Matt says, shutting the car off.

"Well… Emma keeps it nice inside," Janet replies.

They exit the car and head up the walkway. Matt stops and looks back at the car. Janet knows he's feeling a little queasy. Matt drives a new Land Cruiser, worth more than most of the other cars he sees on the block totaled together. He doesn't feel guilty exactly, he feels… ostentatious, not a problem in his usual surroundings.

Angus is at the door. He misinterprets Matt's anguish. "Don't worry," he calls at Matt, jokingly, "no one's gonna steal it."

Matt laughs and Angus holds the door for them to enter. Matt notes, *she does keep it nice inside.*

Once inside, smiling Angus sees Janet, "Hey, you." pecks her on the cheek, then turns to Matt, holding out his hand. "So, I'm Angus. I guess I'm your future brother-in-law."

"I guess you are. Glad to meet you." Matt is surprised at how old Angus is, guessing almost 50 compared to teenage Emma.

"And that's Emma," Angus points down the hall and as if on cue, Emma comes dashing out from the baby's bedroom. Fifteen years younger than Janet, obviously her sister, but smaller, slimmer, and rosy. She gives Janet a huge hug and turns to greet Matt. Emma looks at him and smiles and he takes a step back, looking as though someone had just slapped him.

Emma is alarmed. "Matt? Are you okay?"

"Honey, what's wrong?" Janet asks.

Matt has recovered. "I'm okay… I need to sit down," he says and Angus points to a big leather chair.

"Have a seat. Wanna drink of water or something?" he asks Matt.

"No… thanks… I don't know what that was all about."

Janet kneels next to him and takes his hand. She gives him a questioning look; he shrugs. He has no clue. Emma is anxiously standing near, a hand over her mouth.

Angus wants to be a good host. "Maybe a beer?"

Matt laughs. "That would be the thing. Thanks, Angus." The room lightens.

Angus calls from the kitchen, "Anyone else?"

Beer for four. They sit and chat for a few minutes, then Emma rises and says, "I think Jesse is awake! I'll go get him."

"Huh," Janet says. "I didn't hear him in there."

"The baby don't cry," Angus says. "She just knows when he's awake." He gives a 'what the hell' gesture and Janet and Matt laugh nervously.

"How old now?" Janet asks.

"Two months," Angus says.

Emma comes back with the babe, little Jesse, wrapped up in a blue blanket. Janet rushes to see 'him,' but Matt sits awestruck at the vision of mom and baby. The glow of it. Her glow. Matt recovers and anxiously glances over at Angus, who to Matt's relief is not paying attention.

Janet's face has a wondrous aspect. She looks up at her little sister. "I know people say this sort of thing all the time but… this is the most beautiful baby I have ever seen in my life."

"I know, right?" Emma says with a laugh. "I mean, what's up with that?"

Matt rises and walks over to meet his future nephew for the first time. At first he can't take his eyes away from Emma's face, and he notes her blush and recovers himself, and looks at the baby.

"My god… you know, I usually don't notice…"

"Isn't he adorable?" Janet says.

"He's just as you say," Matt stammers. He looks over at Angus in his chair. "He's amazing."

Angus nods, looks away and takes a hit of his longneck Bud.

"You must have good genes, brother," Matt quips.

Angus darkens and drains the beer. "Not good enough, I'm afraid."

A pall hangs over the room for an agonizing ten seconds. Emma sighs and speaks. "Why don't we all sit down, and I'll tell you what's going on with our little Jesse."

And so they sit and wait until Emma can find the words. But the words will not come so easily, and it is Angus who finally speaks. He is bitter but restrained.

"Our baby is the only baby in medical history to have been born without any sexual characteristics of any kind." And the words hang in the air.

"Really…" Janet whispers.

"Yeah. Really," Angus returns. "Not a male, not a female, not some combination. Just… Not."

"Overall health?" Janet asks cautiously.

"Top of the charts," Angus says. "Not a blemish. The whole medical community has its panties in a bunch over all this because of no other cases ever anywhere. They wanna do *studies.*" He hits the beer. "Offered us money, even. We told 'em shove it. I mean, it's bad enough, right?" Emma bows her head over this and looks hurt.

Angus sighs deeply and concludes. "We're raising him as a boy. We call him Jesse."

After a pause, Matt raises his beer. "To Jesse," he says. Two of them return the toast.

Angus holds up his empty bottle. "I need another beer," he says, and heads to the kitchen. He opens a new longneck and stands, out of sight of the others, next to the refrigerator, brooding.

A couple minutes pass this way, in silence, and Matt hears, "Honey. Matt! *Hey!*" Janet has been calling to him. He jerks to alertness, realizing he has been staring at Emma the entire time. "Are you okay?" she asks him, a bit annoyed, Matt detects.

He blushes, and Emma has an odd, questioning look on her face. *Such a lovely face,* Matt thinks. *Like from an old painting.*

There is no more discussion about the baby for the rest of the morning. There was a certain finality in Angus's summary that seemed to inhibit any elaboration. They talk of many things in those few hours, as families will. Emma and her sister are gabbing happily, and she takes Janet outside to look at her garden, of which she is very proud, leaving the menfolk to chat.

They've each had a few beers. Angus is more relaxed, and Matt is tired from little sleep.

"So, Angus, what do you do?" Matt asks.

"I fix motorcycles."

"Really. Do you ride?"

"Hell, yeah," Angus lights up. "That's my Triumph in front of the carport. I fix Harleys all day, but I got a thing for English bikes. My Harley pals make fun of me. Sixties and seventies, mainly. Just sold a restored Norton for 15 grand. Good money but I regret it already."

"Where's your place?"

"I got a shop next town over, in Ypsilanti. Very busy. Long waits."

"So, people must think you're worth it."

"We do good work." Angus takes a long, satisfying hit on his Budweiser. "How about you? What do you do?"

"Nothing." And they both laugh. Matt elaborates. "I used to own a company that trained what we called 'defense agents.' We were lucky, and success came fast." Matt sips at his beer. "I had it for about ten years and sold it last year. Now I consult. Rarely. I'm a little tired of it."

"Dangerous?" Angus asks.

Matt yawns. "Yeah, sometimes." He thinks a space and huffs. "But for what, you know? I was glad to get out."

"The way the country's headed… probably a good idea to get out," Angus says. "Things seem to be falling apart. Country's goin' to hell."

"You asked *him*!?" Emma is astonished.

"I know!" Janet says. "Can you believe that?"

"I guess…" Emma is on her knees planting basil near her tomatoes. "But still no date set?"

Janet is a little annoyed. "We'll decide soon." She stands on the lawn, so her shoes don't get dirty and wet. "Do you think he's handsome?"

Emma stands up, brushes at her knees, and gives Janet a big smile. "I think he's amazing. I think he's *rich*, too!"

18

They both laugh. "He sold his company for like 50 million dollars," Janet says.

"Yeah… he's just got that look about him. So, then what does he *do* all day?"

Janet sighs and looks sad. "He's bored! He does some consulting stuff, but he hates it, I think. He goes to the shooting range and the gym a lot… reads a lot…"

"Is he happy?" Emma gets to the point.

"I *think* so," Janet says. "I think he's happy about marrying me. The having children thing I thought would be a big thing. He told me he wanted them, and he knows I can't give him any, but he swears he wants to marry me anyway – that it makes him happy."

Emma puts her arm around her sister's waist and smiles. "How could he *not* be," she whispers. They laugh gaily and stroll up the back walk into the house. There they find the men talking and drinking. This is no big deal for Angus at 2 p.m. on a Saturday, but Matt is not used to beery daytimes and knows he will pay for this with a nap later in the day.

The two visitors soon take their leave of Emma and Angus. Everyone had fun, and for a couple of hours, even Angus got outside of himself enough to forget his troubles. He thinks of taking the Triumph for a spin but, no – too many beers. One more DUI and that would ice him for a long time.

Emma tends to little Jesse and as the beer buzz loses its grip over Angus he reverts to the dark and miserable mood that has become the default since the birth of his child. He is more resolute now than ever that only he can deal with the situation as it needs to be dealt with. He decides to take a walk to clear his head.

> *I knew what was in my father's heart. My grief*
> *about his thoughts and plans was so vivid, but*
> *my little body could not then so much as make*
> *an intelligent sound that I might have counseled*
> *him or consoled him. My grief was doubled by*

the thoughts of my mother, toward whom I was
as powerless in the same way. This was all very
hard, much more difficult
than I was prepared for.

– from *Chronicles of Jophiel, Vol. I*

Though Angus had planned to wake at 2:30 a.m., he has had no sleep this night from which to rise. Emma is snoring softly. Angus slips silently from the bed and, avoiding the squeaky part of the hallway flooring, enters little Jesse's room, a nearby streetlight lends the room a soft glow. Jesse lay in his little shell of a bed, wide awake, regarding his anguished Dad standing next to him.

"I'm… I'm sorry, little Jesse," he whispers, and starts to cry. "I'm so sorry." He puts his hand on Jesse's little head and tries to stop crying but cannot. "This is the best I can do for you, and for your mom." After a few moments, he pulls his hand from the baby's head to his wipe tears away. He calms himself and looks again into the eyes of his baby, who has not once broken his gaze into Angus's eyes.

"Forgive me…" he whispers. "God forgive me."

And Angus bends and pinches the infant's nose closed with his left hand, and with his right covers the baby's mouth with his palm. And his shoulders shake as he weeps again, and waits…

Emma wakes early, up with the sun, and Angus is not lying next to her. She calls out to him. *The baby. Something feels wrong about the baby.* Emma jumps naked from her bed and rushes to little Jesse's room to find Angus dead on the floor, and her precious Jesse noiselessly crying his first, and so far, only, tears.

I could not breathe. My father was at once
weeping and trying to suffocate me. But there
came intercession as I knew there would, for as
soon as I began to feel uncomfortable, another set

20

*of arms and hands appeared atop my father's.
They were made of light, and I knew whose they
must be. My father's hands opened, and he
gasped and spun to face the apparition. It was
Metatron (as called here below), as I knew it
would be, and my father was held fast in an iron
grip around both his upper arms. My father's
aspect was of terror, his eyes bulging from their
hollows, yet he spoke clearly. "Who are you! Let
me go! I must do this!" but he could not budge
from the iron grasp. Metatron's aspect was gentle
and loving, and Metatron said to my father,
"You may not do this. But know now and
forever that you are forgiven." My father's terror
deepened but he slackened and resisted no more.
With a gracious smile, Metatron touched my
father at a space between his eyes, and my father
fell to the floor. We heard his soul flee, eager to
be away from us. Metatron! That smiling gaze
turned to me, and tears trickled from my eyes
down the sides of my face. My poor father! My
mother's sadness! Metatron bent and put that
great forehead of light against my small face and
thus we remained for a long space. Such comfort
and bottomless well of strength! I sensed my
mother stirring in her room, and Metatron, my
companion of ages, vanished into the aether.*

– from *Chronicles of Jophiel, Vol. I*

5

It's the evening after Angus's funeral and Emma is a
wreck. Her head is still aching from the miserable rigors of
the day and the day-long roar of dozens of motorcycles – it

seems that every acquaintance Angus had was an avid rider and that every rider in town knew Angus.

After the funeral, the mourners all shared a brunch at the Holiday Inn. There were a few friends and acquaintances, but no family members save the three because there simply are no more.

Everyone was nice to Emma, especially the bikers and their consorts, many of them hairy and huge and menacingly attired, yet weeping freely and blubbering as they told tales of capers back in the day involving the late and evidently much-beloved Angus. Every once in a while, one of the men would start to tell a story and one of his colleagues would give him a swift cuff or a kick, then nod over at Emma, and the story-teller would clam up, realizing that Emma might best be spared *that* particular tale. Emma knew that Angus had a long and separate life with all these people, but really, she had no idea…

The food was a notch above, the drinks flowed freely and expensively (there were few teetotalers among the riders), and Matt picked up the tab for the entire event, including the funeral and cremation. Janet was fine with that, and Emma's gratitude was immense but quiet. "You are a godsend," she whispered when Matt had insisted how things would be. For Emma has no savings, and if it weren't for Matt and Janet's timely visit whatever would she have done?

She has a rare object in her hand, for her: an adult beverage, specifically, a can of hard cider. Her sister, Janet, and Janet's fiancé, Matt, flank Emma on the couch in her home. They have been at her side since the death of Angus, staying with her here at Emma's home.

Now home safe at last after a most trying day, the baby (perfectly behaved and a joy to all, especially bewitching the motorcycle mamas) is safe and sleeping. The hard cider is do-ing its trick. Emma likes the odd drink, but she never drank at home because it encouraged Angus to be more of a drunk than he normally was. She is relaxing now, for the first time since seeing her husband dead on the baby's floor three mornings ago. Her eyelids flutter, her head lists and she snuggles a bit into the crook of her loving sister's neck, who strokes Emma's hair until she falls asleep, a state finally permitted her as a blesséd sense of closure at last dawns inside her.

The next morning, after coffee for three, Matt wants to talk to the ladies. His aspect is insistent and dead serious, and Janet has never seen him quite like this. Emma has been a little unnerved by Matt's quiet gazing upon her when he thinks she isn't aware. (Like most men, he doesn't really understand how naturally women are tuned in to this sort of thing.) She's not offended; she likes Matt and is profoundly grateful. She's just… wary.

He sits in Angus's tattered La-Z-Boy and the ladies sit across from him on the old threadbare couch. "I have…" he pauses for a big sigh, "a bunch of suggestions."

Janet giggles. "Honey, I've never seen you like this." Emma raises her eyebrows and just smiles.

Matt returns the small laugh, trying to make this lighter. He rubs his nose, and continues carefully, looking at Emma. "I'm very concerned about your well-being for the future, and for the baby. You are our only family. Janet has told me of your circumstances, umm… regarding your lack of savings and the fact that Angus brought home the bacon, and that… well… he's *gone*. And I know if I feel this way, that Janet is at least as concerned as I am for the both of you."

Janet takes Emma's hand as Emma meets Matt's gaze. "Thank you, Matt."

Matt clears his throat and continues. "So, I've done a lot of thinking these past couple of days, and… well, I have a plan."

"To do what, hon?" Janet asks. "You never said a word to me about this. Just sort of *brooding* for the past couple days."

Matt holds up a hand. "I know, I know… but this seemed to be the way to do it. So bear with me, okay?"

"Okay. So… what's your plan?"

23

"Well, I would like you to consider quitting your job back home."

"Really?" Janet is more surprised than affronted.

"Yeah. We don't need your income, and with your credentials you can walk into any hospital or health center in Ann Arbor and write your own ticket if you want to work."

Janet considers this. "Yeah, maybe."

"Baltimore was nice 20 years ago, but it's going to hell now – there and all the big cities. We should get out of there anyway. The riots and the robberies alone are enough to make any sane person flee." Matt delivers the punch line. "And I want to buy a house. Around here. I was once at a client's home in, umm… Barton's Hill?"

"Barton Hills," Emma corrects.

"Right. What *you* said. And I want us to live there."

"Us?" Janet ventures.

"Yes. Here's what we do." Matt leans forward and starts gesturing with his hands. "See, we find the place, then work on it, you know – split it in half. A common space in the middle, maybe share a nice kitchen, too, but a separate living space for you and me," he's looking at Janet now, "and another for Emma and Jesse. *Lots* of space, *huge* spacious estate with maybe a… a… stream or pond and *hundreds* of trees!"

Emma's jaw hangs low, and she is gaping at Matt imbecilically. Janet is shaking her head back and forth in a daze. Matt laughs heartily.

"Your *laughing?*" Janet is incredulous. "Matt, this is serious! What about you? What will *you* do?"

"I'm not doing anything *now!*" he roars and laughs again. "But this would be one *hell* of a project!" Matt pops up from the chair and begins pacing the room, gesturing grandly. "It would keep me busy for a long time. It would be fun, and it would look out for the only family either of us have." Matt points to Emma. "They'll be safe and provided for and they won't have to worry about money." Matt is getting upset. "God *damn* worrying about money. There is *nothing* so soul-sucking and debilitating as that – *and I will not allow it!*" He

24

looks at Emma, barely recovered. "Do you understand? *I will not permit you and your baby to suffer that way!*"

Emma is frightened at Matt's ferocity, bends low and breaks into tears, her face in her hands. "I think you upset her," Janet says to Matt as she leans to caress her sister.

"No!" Emma says, sitting up suddenly. "Well, I mean, yes. But… I'm just overwhelmed."

"Good!" Matt pronounces with authority.

Janet is jarred. *"Good?"*

"Yes. She *ought* to be overwhelmed. It's an overwhelming prospect. It's outrageous and wonderful and… *liberating.*"

Emma laughs as she wipes tears with her sleeve. "Matt, I won't pretend that this isn't the most wonderful thing that was ever presented to me, next to my sweet Jesse. But I need to know what Janet thinks about all this." She looks at her sister. "This idea must be like an earthquake for you! And if you have the smallest objection I'd rather be in a homeless shelter than in such a fine place."

Matt looks upon Emma with wonder in his face. "Well said," he whispers.

Janet looks at him, and she begins to realize how deeply he… what? She lovingly regards him and thinks about the right word for how he feels about Emma. It comes to her. How deeply Matt *honors* her. He would lift her sister, her oldest friend, from the pending agonies of a penniless, unemployed single-mom with the snap of his finger. Janet speaks to him. "I think I love you more right now than I ever have."

Matt offers a hand to each of the ladies and they rise, then the three clumsily but affectionately embrace. "Tomorrow we find a house to make into a home," Matt says, feeling hungry as he always does after a big decision. "Let's get lunch!"

My Dad has come. My Father had to die so that he would come. He loves my mother so intensely and he loves me. He is my guardian and will be a rock for me and my mother. In her soul, my mother is preparing to take him into her heart, but she knows it not yet. Her pain was so deep,

and now that the hurt is lifting she is confounded
by the vistas opening before her. My heart aches
for her sister, for she loves my new Dad and my
mother very much, and though now her love is
pure, I sense this shall change.

– from *Chronicles of Jophiel, Vol. I*

6

It has been almost six months since the home in Barton Hills was purchased and most of the work on the main living space has been finished, or practically so. Matt is busy with the project and has never been happier. He's constantly under foot of the workmen and they dislike him for this, but Matt cares not. His new wealth has given him a new philosophy on life: he's paying them; he'll do as he pleases. The months of constant noise and dust is driving Janet and Emma crazy, but they are careful not to let Matt know this.

The house is by any definition a mansion, and the estate is ten acres, wooded and seemingly isolated. They are amazed at the way the community is laid out: there are neighbors, many of them, but they can't *see* them, so spacious are the various environs and all so carefully landscaped that the illusion of seclusion is complete; yet the bustling center of Ann Arbor is but minutes away across the Huron River.

The front door opens on a large, high-ceilinged room with many comfortable seating areas and a splendid fireplace. They decided on a single kitchen, and the one that came with was quite fine and needed little alteration, but all new appliances, natch, and weren't the ladies in a happy tizzy over sorting all *that* out. There is a large dining room that they decided to share, with a long table, custom-made.

Most of the new construction is being done to create the two separate living spaces. Each area has a large multi-purpose room (both being used as media rooms with giant

26

TVs and amazing audio piped into the nooks and crannies of the separate living spaces), an office suite, a master bedroom and two smaller rooms to be used however deemed desirable, and three baths.

Attached on the side is a four-car garage, just enough to accommodate. The ladies each have a car, and though Matt offered to lease a new car for Emma, she thought that was "just too over the top" considering everything in context. So, she drives her battered Corolla, hilariously out of place in her new environs. Matt has the Land Cruiser and an Austin Healy 3000 which he likes way too much. His mood often depends on how well that car is running, and it breaks a lot.

Out back runs a large deck patio the length of the home, with a pro charcoal grilling area – an outdoor kitchen, really – complete with the furnishings necessary to make it all just right.

There would also be a magnificent garden area (both the ladies very much into this), but fall is in the air and the most they can do is plan for the new season.

Matt and Janet have still not set a date for their nuptials. Matt is blissfully unconcerned about all this, citing what a busy time it is and that the house should be finished before they even consider setting the date in stone. Janet sees the logic but is starting to feel uneasy.

She has never glimpsed or had reason to suspect the slightest impropriety between Matt and her sister, and she feels ashamed even *thinking* about such a thing, but something is starting to seem wrong about their situation. *Why couldn't Matt have bought her a nice little bungalow in the city,* she thinks to herself at times, *or taken Emma and the child back east with us?* Then guiltily dismissed the thought as she realizes how her sister needs the help, and how much she loves Emma and Jesse, and how she so enjoys helping and all the fun the four of them have together. *But we would be married by now if it weren't for this crazy setup we have.*

And though there has been nothing untoward observed between Janet's fiancé and her little sister, she is not fool enough to let the obvious fondness between the two go un-noticed. *What kind of love is it,* Janet often wonders, *that is so natural yet so chaste? Are they really as brother and sister?* She has not spoken to Matt about this and has no idea how to broach the subject or even whether she ought to. And the worm in the back of her mind is this: she always knew Matt wanted children, though she herself is incapable of having any. Matt always says it doesn't matter, but…

Another half-year passes, and progress continues on the house, but the end is at last in sight. Still no date has been set for Janet's marriage to Matt, but the house and grounds are almost finished, and Janet is confident that they will set the date soon after. She is busy enough at her new job, which she enjoys, as a nurse-anesthetist at the University Hospital. It was like Matt said – all she had to do was apply and the offer they made her was more than she was ready to ask for.

Emma is happy and healthy and has started playing the piano again – something she has not done since she was a girl (which wasn't really terribly long ago). She is naturally musical and plucks patiently away on the new little Yamaha studio piano in her music room. Matt wanted to buy her a grand piano, but she refused the offer, considering herself unworthy. She is the type who sticks well to a task so her daily practice routine pays off, and her training as a girl has all come back to her.

And little Jesse? He is still an oddly perfect child. Beautiful and good-natured and completely cooperative with his loving Mom. He's over 11-months now, big birthday coming up. He has been walking for the last couple of months. His health has been perfect, and he eats almost anything with great gusto. Except meat. Can't even keep it in his mouth. They think it's a 'stage.' It isn't.

"Can you believe this little guy's gonna be a year old tomorrow?" Matt is holding the grinning baby up to the ladies as if he is Exhibit A, and the two women laugh. He hands

28

the baby to Emma, who puts him in his highchair. Time for a baby's dinner.

Emma affixes a bib and wipes his mouth. Jesse recoils at the gesture as any baby does but is eager to eat. Emma looks at him adoringly.

"My little Jesse," she says.

"*Jofi*, mama," Jesse says. Emma is stunned. Jesse has never before said a single word. These are his first words, and they are clearly annunciated and expressive of, what? *impatience?*

Emma just stares. The other two adults are out of earshot and don't know what's going on here. She's freaked out. "What did you say to mama?" she asks, wondering if she has just imagined what she heard.

"*Jofi*, mama," Jesse repeats.

Emma laughs. "Sweetheart! You're trying to say your name!" She calls over excitedly to Matt and Janet, who come see what her fuss is all about.

"Watch this!" she says to the two and turns back to Jesse. "Say it now, honey. Jesse! Say Jesse."

Jesse looks annoyed. *"Jofi,* mama."

The two gasp, hearing little Jesse speaking for the first time. And so clearly!

"Jesse," Emma enunciates slowly with exaggeration

"No!" Jesse says. "Not Jesse. *Jofi!*" There is a slight lisp and much spraying of baby spittle, and his voice is very small, but he's doing as well as he can with his undeveloped physique.

Emma laughs nervously. Matt and Janet look at one another. "Honey," she tries again. "Try to say Jesse."

"Jesse is not my name!" he insists to shocked Emma. "My name is *Jofi*. J-O-F-I." The toddler spells it out for all to take careful note in case there is some misunderstanding.

The trio is slack-jawed and spellbound until Matt breaks the charm. "Well, I gotta tell you – that's sure as hell good enough for me. Jofi it is." And he pokes Jofi on the bud of his little nose, "boink!" and Jofi blinks and smiles.

The ladies comically gawk at one another, dazed and be-fuddled. And… wait… did the baby just *laugh?* At *them?*

So, they call him Jofi. If they forget he acts upset and never lets an opportunity for correction slip by.

> *I am called a better name now, in my happy*
> *home, less noisy and dusty now. My mother no*
> *longer gives me her milk, and this irritates me*
> *more than I was prepared for. I loved those*
> *blissful encounters, for my mother and myself,*
> *more than anything else that I have experienced*
> *here so far. We were as one when she fed me*
> *from her breast. I could touch most keenly then*
> *the goodness of her heart. Now they try to put*
> *animals in my mouth! I spit them out instantly,*
> *but the trace remains, and I taste it for hours.*
> *Most distressing, but I live in a home full of love*
> *and the distress can never last long.*
> *It shall not be so very much longer.*

– from *Chronicles of Jophiel, Vol. I*

7

The young priest reaches out to take the hand of the Senator's right hand man. "Mr. Powell."

"Call me Phil," He releases the priest's hand and guides him to a comfortable chair facing Phil's desk. Phil takes his seat and smiles. "Father Holt, do you mind if I call you Preston? I'm not too comfortable with the 'father' thing."

"I wish you would," the young priest says. "I'm not espe-cially comfortable with it myself."

This surprises Phil. There's something odd about this priest…

"Well then, what can I do for you?"

Fr. Holt starts to speak but is distracted by an item on the desktop. "A chess board?" The priest takes it all in. "An interesting position. From Fischer vs. Spassky. Do you play with the Senator?"

Phil laughs. "Ahh… no. He's not the deep thinking sort. His virtues lie elsewhere."

"I see," says Preston.

"So, what *can* I do for you, Preston?"

Preston takes a deep breath and says, simply, "Safety through Sacrifice."

Phil is caught a bit off-guard but recovers quickly. He looks away, thoughtful. "Huh," he says. "Catchy."

"I want you to know that, out there in flyover country, many of us support what the Senator seems to be about." The priest speaks slowly and sincerely. "We're tired of the rot, the decay. We want change and we know it will be painful to bring about. There are many millions of us willing to make the sacrifices necessary to bring safety back to our cities and our homes."

Fr. Holt stands, as if in ceremony. Phil rises in response and the two men behold one another from across the desk.

"Your star is starting to shine, Phil. You are almost as well known as the Senator. We hope great things will come from you." And at that the priest extends his hand and Phil takes it. Preston squeezes firmly. "Safety through Sacrifice."

Phil is genuinely overwhelmed. He squeezes back. "I can't tell you how… how pleased I am that you've honored me with your visit."

Preston withdraws his hand, almost reluctantly, and smiles sincerely. "The honor is mine, Phil. I know you're busy. We shall continue to speak well of you and your mission."

And at that Fr. Holt takes his leave, closing the door after him. Phil stands, musing.

"Safety through Sacrifice," he whispers. "That's good. That's *very* good."

8

Another year has passed at the Fischer estate. It's been a warm autumn and Matt is sitting in the great room having a whiskey with a cool breeze blowing in from the back windows. He decides it's time for bed, lugs himself from his chair and heads for the stairs.

Matt enters his bedroom. Janet's face is red and soaked in tears. She's sitting in front of her mirror in her nightgown. It's 10 p.m. He thought she was asleep. He rushes to her side and takes a knee beside her, puts his head on her belly and envelopes her around the waist with his arms. "Honey, what's wrong?" he whispers.

She sniffs. "You'll never marry me," she says it like a flat-out observation. Matt sighs but says nothing and the seconds pass. "See?" Janet says. "You won't even contradict me." Matt straightens up but does not look at Janet. He looks hurt and confused. As much as she.

"I have to ask you something," she says quietly, gently pushing Matt away to collect a few tissues with which she dabs at her eyes. Matt sits cross-legged on the floor, looking up at her. She studies his face. "What do you want from my sister?"

"I don't want *anything* from your sister," Matt says without hesitation.

"I don't believe you," Janet says.

"You think I'm ly-"

"I see how you look at her! You treat her like a princess. Like you treat *me,* without the sex." He starts to object, and she raises a palm. "I'm not *accusing* you of anything. Understand that. I swear I'm not. But I need you to honestly tell me, how do you see you and I working out?"

Matt looks away, his expression betraying the fact that he has never quite considered the definitive answer to this obvious question.

Janet chuckles in spite of herself. "I guess this is a men-versus-women thing."

"What do you mean?"

"Well, a woman would never stop thinking about a situation like this, but a man could just let something like this go on and on, never thinking about it as long as nobody made a big *deal* about anything."

"We'll…" Matt looks a little bitter, "that time is over."

"It's been a *long* time, Matt," she notes sadly. "Almost two years. And I've kept it all… bottled up." Starting to cry again. Matt is looking thoughtfully at the floor in front of him.

She braces herself for the answer to the million dollar question. "Are you in love with my sister?"

Matt rubs his forehead and sighs loudly. "Of course, I love your sister."

"Are you *in love* with my sister?"

"Have you talked to *her* about this?"

"I wish you would answer me!" she says hotly and quickly recovers. "But, yes. We talk about it." (They have *never* talked about it.) "She's concerned. As long as the construction was going on, all the confusion, and the baby – she was happy as a clam. And I was okay, too. The job and everything. But now she's anxious. We're both anxious."

Matt gets defensive. "I've never acted in any way-"

"Honey, I *know*. Okay?"

Matt groans and lies back on the floor, petitioning the ceiling. "Why the hell can't things just…"

"Because Emma and I need to know what's going on with you!" A little anger now. "This is just starting to seem… *unnatural.*"

Matt sits up, gets to his feet and looks resolved. "Go get Emma, please."

"What?" Janet is not prepared for this.

"Please. Bring Emma up. Actually, let's meet in the big room. We need to talk."

Janet stands, defiant. "Absolutely *not!*" she says.

"I thought you wanted to get this thing-"

"This *thing,* as you call it, needs to be worked out between *me and you!*"

Matt considers for a moment, then motions to Janet to sit back down at her dressing table, facing him sitting on the bed. They will have the talk.

"What do you want to know?" Matt asks, resigned.

"Are you in love with Emma?"

"I don't know what that means."

"Are you attracted to her?"

Matt is wary. "I'm a *man*. She's beautiful and young. But I've nev-"

"Younger than me. I *know* that. Do you fantasize making love to her?"

"Jesus Christ, Janet!" The civil mask is slipping. "There isn't a man alive who *wouldn't!*"

"So, if I wasn't *in the way* you'd be having sex with her."

"Why do you have to spin it that way?"

"She could give you babies, you know. Have you thought about that? How could you *not* be thinking about that?!"

Matt hangs his head and is silent. Long moments pass. He looks at her. "I suppose," he begins carefully, "that I love Emma like I love you. And I love Jofi and he needs a father. And being here with all of you enriches my life *so much,* keeps me busy, and makes me feel like I'm doing what I need to be doing."

"While fantasizing about my sister," she says with bitterness. Matt makes a dismissive, impatient noise. "I think *I'm* the third wheel here, Matt. Not my sister."

"There are no 'third wheels' *in this house!*" Matt snaps hotly.

"You just said that you feel like you're finally doing what you need to be doing. The difference is, that apparently you *didn't* feel that way when it was just *me*. Matt – do you know how that makes me feel?"

"I think you're looking at this, and spinning it, in the worst possible ways! I'm fine like things are!"

"Yes, well, I'm not. And either is Emma, though Miss Sugar-Wouldn't-Melt-In-Her-Mouth won't come right out and say it."

"So now you're unloading on Emma? What the hell has she done that-"

"And so you're taking *her* side now."

"*What* side?! She's never said anything about this to me! I don't know *what* she's thinking!"

"Well I do. And I can't discuss this anymore tonight. We'll talk tomorrow."

Matt is dazed. "I gotta see the lawyer tomorrow morning," he mumbles. "You remember."

"So, we'll talk later," she says tersely, with a gloomy finality. "Would you mind sleeping in the guest room tonight? I don't feel like I'll be very good company."

And Matt, terminally puzzled, gets to his feet and trudges out of their bedroom, shaking his head in frustration on his sad way to the doghouse.

Janet waits until Matt is safely banished and opens the bottom drawer of her nightstand. She takes out a bottle of Scotch and a little juice glass, pours herself a stiff one, and shoots it back.

The next afternoon, about one o'clock, Matt pulls into the garage after his endless lawyer meeting, turning off the growly Austin Healy, and notes that Janet's little Lexus is not in its space. He takes the garage entrance into the house and spies Emma in the kitchen, holding little Jofi. She smiles and says hi.

"Emma, hi," Matt says. "Have you seen Janet?"

"Hi Matt!" hails Jofi.

"Hi, buddy," Matt smiles in spite of himself.

"Do you know Sam Morgan?" Jofi asks brightly.

"What?" Matt is jarred at being derailed here. "Sam Morgan… no. Sorry son. Never heard of him."

"O." Little Jofi is lost in thought.

Emma addresses Matt. "I saw Janet early this morning, kind of scurrying about, but she left about an hour ago. Said it was some work thing. She seemed upset, though." Emma darkens.

"What. What's wrong?" Matt asks.

"The sad way she kissed Jofi goodbye this morning…"

"Yeah…" Matt whispers.

"Is everything okay?" Emma asks.

Matt looks at Emma. "I dunno," he says, guardedly. "I'm not sure."

He dashes upstairs to his bedroom and finds an envelope on his pillow with his name on it in red pen. With dread in his heart, he rips into it and extracts the letter.

Dear Matt,

I have to leave. I don't know for how long. Maybe I'm just gone. I'm not sure yet. I've taken what I need with me. I have plenty of my own money and need to find a place in town.

I don't want you snooping and coming after me. This is for the best. If I need to I will get in touch with you. When I need to. Your impulse will be to find me. Please don't. Just let me be. This has been brewing a long time and I'm sure I'm doing the right thing.

Honor my request.

Janet

As if in a trance Matt walks downstairs. He sees Emma and the babe. She looks heartbroken. "She's gone?" she says to Matt. He nods. He's going to cry. With Jofi on her arm, Emma embraces Matt with her other arm. She holds him as he cries. Sad little Jofi leans forward to kiss the back of Matt's head and pat his shoulder with his little hand.

9

Matt is reluctantly honoring Janet's wish. It's been a whole week now. His background and training makes finding her a trivial detail, but he restrains his tendencies per her request. He spends most of his time in his office tweaking the endless details of the estate's transformation (all for naught?), or reading, or sharing mostly silent mealtimes with Emma and Jofi.

Emma feels he is avoiding her. Guilt overwhelms her. *I'm the one who should have left,* she thinks. *If Janet had only spoken to me before leaving I would be gone in her place. They would be married and happy and I would be out of their hair.* But only this moment does it dawn upon her the true reason she hadn't considered leaving before now: because of the joy and meaning that she and her baby are giving to Matt. This is as oddly comforting as it is upsetting.

She needs to talk with Matt but she's afraid to. Matt senses this and mercifully asks if she would mind talking together after she puts Jofi down for the night. She is now relieved and anxious at once. Matt has no idea what he will say; Emma has no idea how she will respond.

After Jofi is put to bed, Emma takes a shower. This is odd for her this time of day. She tries not to think too much about why she is doing this just now. She towel-dries her long brown hair but leaves it uncombed, then puts on her nightie, and then a freshly-laundered nightgown on top of this.

With much apprehension, she joins Matt in the great room in front of the fireplace, in which a fire is burning, the first of the season. Matt, who likes to wear carefully-ironed pajamas (which nude-sleeper Emma secretly finds terribly comical), is sitting in one of the two large leather chairs in front of the fire and motions Emma to sit in the other. Between them is a small table on which sits a newly-opened bottle of old Port, half empty, and two small glasses. Yes, she will please have a glass.

Matt takes another gulp. It's good. Special and old. "I haven't been too… social lately, I know."

"Well," Emma says quietly, "it's no wonder."

"No. I guess not."

They stare into the fire. Mesmerizing.

"There's something I need to tell you, Emma," Matt says.

Emma smiles at Matt and nods, then stops and lowers her head. "Matt, O Matt…" and she promised she wouldn't cry but there goes that vow. "I'm so sorry. All this is so completely my fault, but I didn't have the... the courage... to-"

"Stop." Matt orders. He puts his glass back on the table and leans toward her. "Listen. It was never a matter of courage. I know why you stay."

"O, please, Matt..." begging him to be gentle with her, not knowing what words might come.

He can't look at her. He recites this to the fire. "You stay, not because of the security I give you, or the trappings of well-being, or the burdens I lift. You stay because of the joy and the meaning that you've brought into my own life. You stay... because you *love* me, because you sense that I *need* you to stay."

Emma is weeping, at first trying not to, then giving up and releasing the tears.

"And you stay," Matt continues over her tears, "because you know, clearly and completely – how much I love you. And you felt that love of mine enter into you the very first time I saw you and nearly fainted at the sight of you. You felt that love enter you and it has never left."

Emma looks up and meets Matt's gaze, tries to smile and sniffs. "Yes."

Matt rises and stands in front of Emma's chair and with his hand outstretched bids her rise, too, and when she does he puts his arm under her knees and sweeps her up and off her feet and holds her in his strong arms like a child with his face against hers, sharing the wetness of her cheeks, and sways her gently, a slow dance, not to music but to the crackling of the fire. And there they stay for a long enchanted minute. He pulls his face away and their eyes meet. They kiss their first kiss.

Without putting her down he conveys her upstairs to her bedroom and lays her softly in her bed. He sits next to her and pulls loose the easy knot that binds tight her outer gown.

They will cleave together in love and she will
conceive another child this night. I look hard to
discern who is coming but I cannot perceive this.

The Angel Jophiel

Therefore, it must be a human soul, not one such as I. I bless this conception, and this soul newly incarnate, and know it must be a remarkable person to come through my mother's gate, unforeseen, to be my brother in this mission. Yes! That's it! It is a brother I shall have! I feel him close. He is anxious to go between and enter in.

— from *Chronicles of Jophiel, Vol.*

10

The thermometer across the street at the bank says 98-degrees. *If I didn't have this goddam sandwich-sign on maybe some air would circulate and I wouldn't be sweating like a fucking pig. I think my balls are growing mushrooms.*

The straps that hold the sign up are likewise adding immensely to his discomfort. Also he's thirsty and by now severely dehydrated, but if he leaves his post again to get water and gets caught they will be pissed. Maybe dock him. He looks at his watch, which he usually tries not to do. It seems as though at least two hours *must* have gone by, but it's only been 45 minutes. So that means lunch isn't for two hours and 15 minutes. *I'll never make it.*

For the last month, since he got this 'job,' he could space out and work on the string symphony he's writing. Work all the parts out in his head, write them down when he gets home. The time would fly by then, but the strategy has had a negative impact on his work habits. Instead of cheerfully beckoning customers to the furniture store in the nearby mall, he would just stand imbecilically still, staring into space, working on his music in his head. This inert coping tactic is not congruent with the forced jollity of his job specification.

But today the music isn't happening for him, for he is feeling every degree of the blistering heat, and every tortured second pass.

His post is the hectic intersection near a busy Ann Arbor mall, in front of a gas station. A woman and her young teen daughter are about to pass on the sidewalk behind the fidgety man with the sign strapped to him, when all of a sudden Bran unleashes a bloody scream at the top of his lungs. *"FUUUUUCK!"*

The two scamper past him in a panic, then the mom stops and turns to him. "Are you okay?" she calls to him.

"Jesus. Ma'am, I'm sorry. I didn't see you coming. I'm okay." And deeply embarrassed.

"Really?" she is concerned.

"Yeah. I'm all right. I just… I just hate my job."

She considers this a moment, looking him over, then nods and smiles, takes her frightened daughter's hand and scurries along.

His name is Bran Englander. He is 19 years-old and not going to college, even though he's terribly bright and his family was glad to foot the bill to the music school at the university. He didn't even have to work, they told him, or live at home. He just had to go to college like a good boy and work on a degree, preferably in something "reasonable," but music would work if that's the only thing that would get him there. Then Mom and Dad would take care of all his needs.

"FUCK THAT!" he yells again to the whizzing traffic, and then again, "FUCK THAT FUCKING FUCK *FUCK!"* then looks around in a panic in case more unseen pedestrians. Nobody.

He notes a car stopped in front of him at the red light. There is a little kid frantically waving at him from his car seat in the back. The kid turns to his mom. "Mama!" he cries in his little voice, "There's Bran!"

"There's who, hon? Who's Bran?"

Little Jofi doesn't answer. He just keeps waving at the unresponsive man wearing the funny sign costume.

"Honey, you can't possibly know that man. And stop waving, please. He seems terribly upset at something." The light turns green.

Huh, Bran thinks, as he watches the car speed away, kid still waving. *That was weird.* His mouth is so dry he knows he can't hold out much longer. *Could this possibly get any worse?*

"Bran!" he hears call. He turns and notes a new Cadillac pulled up in the gas station behind him. "Bran!" He recognizes the voice.

Son of a bitch, he says to himself. It's his supervisor. He ambles over clumsily to meet his boss halfway.

"Say, Bran, meet me in my office at nine tomorrow morning. We'll talk." His boss looks closely at Bran then recoils a bit in revulsion. "You okay there?"

"Well," Bran says, throat so parched he can hardly say the words. "I'm a little dry. And hot."

"Listen – go home early. Go *now*. It's too hot for this."

"But, I could use the-"

"I'll pay you for the day. Okay? Just… just go home."

Bran is so happy he almost starts to cry. With the Cadillac zooming away, he unhooks the straps binding him to the heavy torture device and leans it up against the gas station barrier. 'WALLY'S FURNITURE CLEARANCE' it proclaims in red letters on a white ground.

Son of a bitch could have taken the sign back with him, Bran muses, hefting the sign and heading to the store in the mall, behind the gas station, across the burning asphalt of the parking lot…

Bran has a Cadillac, too. Except his is a rusting 30 year-old boat, but a nice interior, no rips and everything works. It's his Dad's old car, older than Bran, a gift to a 16 year-old with his new license, and an excuse for Dad to buy a new one. He hops in and zips across the lot making for the good overpriced yuppie grocery store in the mall.

He needs a few things, but once inside makes a beeline to the bottled ice-tea. He opens one and drinks it down in a single go, his throat seizing up from the ice-coldness of the drink. He puts the empty on the shelf and grabs another, and repeats the ritual, ignoring the ice cream headache. When he's done he gives a great groaning sigh of relief, then spies a pretty stockgirl on her knees down the aisle who is staring at him in wonder. Or terror. Bran isn't sure which.

"So," he says to her, holding both empty bottles up. "I suppose you expect me to *buy* these now." She laughs (she thinks he's cute but scary) and Bran laughs with her. He tosses the two dead soldiers into the little basket, resuming his shopping. He selects a frozen pizza and (with a wince) a bottle of four-dollar red wine. That pretty much cleans him out right there.

The next morning, at 9 a.m. sharp, Bran is seated in his boss's office waiting for The Man to saunter in. *What the hell could he want? Don't I get paid little enough to be left alone? Or is it the less you make the more you get fucked with?*

He looks around the office. It's the most completely sterile environment Bran has ever seen, sporting a single personal item, the only hint that a human being has ever entered herein: a silver-framed pic of a homely woman and two horse-faced kids. *Jesus… are they boys or girls?* he wonders in horror and looks closer. *I hope they're boys. Oh-oh. Here he comes.*

"Good morning, Bran," the boss pipes and heads to his chair and sits.

"Good morning, Mister-"

"This won't take long, so let's get to it." He looks at his watch and shakes his head worriedly. "Not much time!"

"Okay," Bran says. "So… what can I do for you?" He is thinking, *perhaps a promotion?*

"I'm afraid…" the boss takes off his glasses and grimaces, looking for the right words. "I'm afraid you're not working out in your position here at Wally's."

Bran nods. "Sooooo… that means…"

"I'm afraid your brief career here at Wally's has come to a close."

Bran squeezes his eyes shut, sighs and slumps.

"See," the boss continues, "we think it's an attitude thing." He pauses, generously allowing the important life-lesson to sink in. "Instead of beckoning folks to visit the store in a welcoming sort of way, you just usually… stand there, staring into space, not moving for large parts of an hour."

"Yeah… well, here's the thing about-"

"And sometimes you scream obscenities."

"You got people *watching* me?"

"Once in a while we monitor you out there, yes, but we also get *calls* – complaints from motorists who hear you yelling swears. Also the gas station owner believes you are discouraging business. *That* could turn into a real problem."

"Okay… I get it." His fate is obvious; he's resigned. "So, you're going to replace me with another lucky young man?"

"Well… ignoring your sarcasm," putting his glasses back on, "what we've replaced you with, starting today, is a piece of cardboard we found in the trash."

The Man pauses and watches while Bran lets the full implications sink in. *A Piece. Of Cardboard… From the trash.*

"One of the salesmen found a discarded piece of cardboard that is an oversize human cut-out, holding a large sign, on which one may print or have printed upon it, whatever message one is trying to get out there. We just want to lean it against the telephone pole, near where you used to stand."

Bran whispers, as if to himself, "…a piece of fucking cardboard."

"Frankly, we think it will do a better job than you, and we don't have to pay it a salary! Or even pay *for* it, for that matter. I mean," he chuckles, "it was in the *garbage.*"

Bran stands. He's had enough. The former boss stands, too, and with his hand bids him stay a moment. Seems he's not done.

"One more thing… umm… Don't be discouraged."

"What?" Bran is getting angry. "You just told me that a piece of *cardboard* somebody *threw away* is better at my job than I am. What the frickin' hell am I supposed to think?!"

"Well, just that you're… young, umm… you seem like a smart young man, plenty of doors will open for you, but you just aren't cut out…" and at this his boss smiles and then stifles a laugh. "Sorry. I said, 'cut out,' like the cardboard guy… umm… you're just not… *cut out,* for this type of thing." And then the boss can't hold back anymore and breaks out into loud and sustained laughter over his little joke.

"Yeah… that's fucking *hilarious.*" And Bran turns to go.

"Wait! I need to pay you for the week," The Man says, taking out his wallet and wiping tears of mirth from his eyes.

Bran's had it. "Fuck it. Fuck your money. Fuck *Wally* – whoever the hell he is. And *fuck you."*

And thus ends Bran's completely unpromising career at Wally's Furniture. He has so little money now he doesn't know if he can make it home on the little gas he has in his car.

But while he was cussing out The Man in his office, it did occur to Bran how exactly to begin the third section of his string symphony. That's a load off. He can't wait to get home and write it out.

11

When Janet found out that Emma was pregnant with her former fiancé's child (they had no idea how Janet could have known this), Janet sent along an email to Matt congratulating him on becoming a father, along with her regards to Emma and Jofi, and though the tone was not accusatory it smacked of hurt and insincerity. The email also had a list of things she had not taken with her when she left, that she wanted back now. It was quite a list. She hired two men and a truck to do the dirty work.

There was no contact information in the email, and the movers were put on their guard in case Matt or Emma in-quired after her. Matt knew he could trace her down in minutes, and Emma asked him to do this so she could at least try to reconcile, but he refused, insisting upon honoring Janet's request, at least for the present. Emma was heartsick that she had lost her sister, her only family, to the blind ravages of Love, eternally indifferent to consequences.

Matt and Emma wed. The ceremony was small – a few of Matt's friends and a few of Emma's – and they declined the honeymoon.

They live on one side of the house – most of Matt and Janet's former section has been closed off, even unheated in the winter months (except for Matt's office, where he retreats when the noise of the family gets annoying), but there is still far more than enough living space for three times the three of them. He bitterly regrets most of the work he put into the place.

Jofi is three now, getting more talkative. His precociousness is obvious, and a little disconcerting. "Scary" is the word Matt uses, but as an endearment. Jofi reads and writes but was not taught to do so. When asked about this Jofi says, "I just remember." He is articulate in speech and his parents note with a bit of a shiver how he laughs at overheard jokes and stories that only an adult should pick up on.

Matt has resumed his consulting work, and both spend a few hours each week at the health club, where Matt also teaches martial arts. They both read a lot and Emma is getting quite good at her piano studies. She now has a teacher, a piano professor from the music school, to whom they pay a king's ransom. Add her duties as mom and she is as busy as she is happy. She has never *been* so happy.

They even socialize! This is something she never did when living with Angus, for he kept his old life and friends separate from her. Both Matt and Emma have a couple of friends, and the chemistry when all together is happy and strong.

They dance! Emma is settling in nicely as both a woman of her own as well as the lovely wife of a wealthy and vibrant man. And though neither is the 'society' type, Matt's wealth and status see him often approached by foundations and charities with attendant events that enhance their social calendar and visibility in the community.

It's safe to say that someone who knew Emma three years ago would not recognize her now. She puts on no airs – she wouldn't know how – but her knack for flattering dress and her princess bearing were never even hinted at in her role as the 19 year-old mom struggling to get by in the shabby hovel of the outlaw drunkard who knocked her up.

Emma's last name is now Fischer. She is 22 years of age. She just clips 5'4", and she has long curly brown hair. Her eyes are blue, and her skin is pale. She has a lovely Celtic face of northern French ancestry which blushes at the drop of a hat. She was skinny as a girl, and after two babies she hits the scales (the obsessively-scrutinized scales) at a normal weight now for her height. Because her body is unexaggerated in bosom and bottom, she buys clothes off-the-rack (but in nice places) that look custom made. She gets manicures and pedicures every month. She had never had one before she married Matt.

Matt Fisher is a six-foot whippet-thin athlete. He likes to be comfortable, and he lets Emma dress him when he needs dressing up. She has a knack he sorely lacks in this regard.

Jofi is, if possible, even more beautiful as a child than he was as a baby. But his precocity is becoming alarming.

12

Emma doesn't like to play Bach. She plays it at sight, and at the proper speed, but her teacher sees through her false facility.

"You may as well be typing," the irksome old greybeard notes (somewhat insultingly, Emma thinks). She stops and glares at him. He's not done criticizing. "These lines are long, independent melodies that knit around one another, and you are simply playing one block of notes after another. You see the notes vertically, but not the horizontal lines. That's sight-reading. It *sounds* like sight-reading. We *talked* about this."

He removes the *French Suites* from the stand and replaces them with the *Two-Part Inventions*. Emma sighs.

"That's quite a demotion," she says, discouraged.

"Wrong. Bach is Bach. Always perfect. Now, each of these 15 pieces has only two lines of music, one for each hand. When you can play these and make the two lines sing independently of one another, we'll move on to the suites."

The lesson concludes with a Clementi sonatina, much more allied to Emma's light and cheerful temperament – broken chords with the left hand and melody on the right. The teacher nods sagely. The maestro is pleased.

When the professor is safely out the door, Emma closes it and hisses, *"Bastard."*

Jofi laughs, sitting on a chair nearby, stuffing his little face with the three allotted Fig Newtons.

Mom is amused and annoyed in equal measure. "Why are you laughing at me?"

"Because the professor was right about how you play Bach."

Emma glares at him with narrowed eyes. She is used to the brilliant child routine, but this is a bit much. She studies the three year-old. "And how would you know that?"

Jofi pops up from the chair and pads to the piano, climbs up onto the bench. Emma is astonished but housewife enough to cry out, "Wait! Jofi don't you *dare* touch my piano!" and she flees to the kitchen and returns straightaway with a damp towel to rub the cookie remains from giggling Jofi's little hands and mouth. When she's satisfied she says, "Okay, now just what do you think you're doing?"

"Mama," he says. "Here's how *you* play Bach." And he pounds out just the opening of the first of the assigned two-part inventions, much as a sausage-fingered zombie might render the music. They both know he's exaggerating. Emma laughs in spite of herself.

"Now." He wiggles his little butt into a more comfortable position. "This is how the *professor* wants you to play it." And the atmosphere of the whole room is changed in an instant.

The music is by turns light and sparkling, then savage and deep as his little hands are pushed to the limits of the flesh to keep up with Bach's simple elegance. The eye could tell how difficult this was for those tiny hands, but the ear betrays only refined skill and beauty that want for nothing. The two parts soar and flutter like birds in synchronized celebration of their own individuality – exactly the lesson the professor was trying to drive home.

He plays the entire piece (from memory? the score is not open), and when he finishes he finds that Emma wears a look of horror on her face. "I'm sorry mama, my hands are still so small-"

Emma bursts into tears and runs from the house out into the front yard. Jofi is very upset. "You play Clementi nice, mama!" he yells pathetically, believing that he hurt her feelings. He wiggles down from his perch and scampers after her.

She's in the front yard leaning against the big tree. Jofi runs to her and hugs her leg as if *it* were a tree. "You play Clementi nice, mama," he mutters apologetically. "I'm sorry…"

"Honey," she sniffs. "How can you do these things? These things you can do and you're so little." She's crying again and Jofi hugs her leg ever tighter, hoping that this will somehow throttle the flow of tears. She squats down and hugs Jofi, who hugs her back around her neck. "You weren't even reading the music, you were just playing it. How?"

"Sometimes I read your stack of music. And sometimes I just…"

"You just what, honey."

"Sometimes I just… remember."

Emma stands up and regards her son. "But that's what you *always* say when we ask how you do the things you do." She picks her little one up and holds him in her arms. "I've been playing the piano for more than ten years. Practicing every day when I took lessons, like I do now. And my three year-old just sat at the piano for the first time ever, and played Bach better than I *ever* will, like an old master might, without even needing the music. Do you see why that can be upsetting?"

"Yes… I'm sorry, mama."

She hugs him tight. "Don't be sorry, sweetheart. I should be happy and proud. And I will be. I promise."

And she carries him back into the house, hugging her precious cargo tight along the way. Emma is off to her bedroom to think, and Jofi, fully recovered, heads quickly to the couch for the precious last of the Fig Newtons.

Matt just stares into space with this vacant expression after Emma fills him in on the events of the day. "Honey," she asks him, "are you even listening to me? This is important."

Snapping out of it, he says, "Yeah… I heard you. I'm just wondering."

"About what?"

"About what else?"

"What do you mean?"

"I mean, what *else* can this kid do? I mean… reading, writing, piano – what else do we not see yet?"

They stare at one another in discomfort. Matt has an idea. "Where's Jofi?"

"In his room. He's reading my new edition of Bach's *Well-Tempered Clavier* after complaining that the old edition I had was poorly edited. You know – the usual problems that three year-olds have with editions of their mother's piano repertory." Serious or not, they had to crack up at that one.

Jofi is retrieved and happily parks himself on the couch between Mom and Dad. "So, what do you want?" he chirps.

"Jofi," Matt begins, "you know how… ah… me and Bruce play chess here on Tuesday nights?" Jofi nods and points at the two leather chairs in front of the fireplace with the little table between them. "Sometimes he brings Bobby along and you two play or watch movies. And if Bobby doesn't come with his dad, you like to sit here," Matt says, "right where you are now, and watch us play, don't you?"

"Yes. But the movies are pretty boring."

"Yeah, well, they're for *kids*," Matt says sarcastically. "Anyway, what do you think of when we play?"

Jofi grins. "What I think about the most is, that you two always make the same three opening moves, even though there are," and he doesn't even pause here, "5362 possible positions after three moves, you guys always have the same one!" And Jofi laughs and laughs.

Matt nods and considers. "Jofi, do you know how many possible chess games there are?"

The little lad freezes into a stare for a few seconds. "Any game which allows repetition has infinite possible games," he says quietly.

Matt smiled. "Huh… I never thought of that." He looks at Emma and leans back in his seat, scratching his head. "I actually thought I knew the answer to that. Looked it up once."

Jofi just smiles and nods.

"I read that there are more possible games than there are atoms in the universe," Matt says.

"In your *observable* universe," Jofi corrects. "But even disallowing repetitive moves, the possible number of chess games is so huge that it's not possible yet for anyone to calculate the exact number."

"Really?" Matt is astonished.

"Jofi," Emma asks. Jofi squirms, as if he knows what's coming. "Do *you* know how many possible chess games there are? Not counting repetition moves?"

Jofi hangs his head and pouts.

"Jofi, honey?" Emma asks with infinite gentleness. "Do you know the answer?"

He looks at his mom with a tortured little face, then turns to Matt. "Yes. I know."

Matt asks, "How many, son?"

"I can't… I can't tell you," he says in his small voice.

"Why not?"

"I'm not allowed."

Matt and Emma exchange worried looks and Jofi stares straight ahead, uncomfortable but co-operative.

"Who won't allow you, honey?" Emma asks.

Jofi climbs down from the couch and stands in front of them, looking from one to the other. "I want you to know that I'll never tell you lies. Ever."

"But-" Matt starts to speak but Emma shuts him off with a firm but gentle hand to his thigh. Matt looks at Emma.

"That's enough, now," she says to Matt. Matt considers and nods to her, accepting her wisdom.

"I have to ask you both a question," Jofi says.

"Of course, honey," Emma replies. "What do you want to know?"

"Do you know Sam Morgan or Alma Pierce?"

Matt and Emma look at one another, puzzled. "I've never heard of either one of them," Emma says.

"Doesn't ring any bells," Matt agrees. "Why, Jofi. Who are these people?"

"Do you know Bran Englander?" Jofi asks.

"Another one?" Matt says. "No." He looks at Emma. She looks at Jofi and shakes her head in the negative.

Jofi looks away, distracted. "I saw him when I was in the car. I think he lives around here." Jofi looks away, struggling with dark thoughts. "I have to find these people…"

Emma frowns and looks at Matt. He gives her the 'who the hell knows?' look. Matt turns to Jofi. "Listen, son. What were you doing in your room before you joined us here?"

Jofi brightens at the change of subject. "Reading Bach. And before that I was drawing a picture!"

Cute, thinks Mom and Dad.

Emma asks, "A picture of what, hon?"

The smile gets bigger. "A picture of you!"

"How sweet!" she says. "Can we see?"

And Jofi zooms off like a little rocket to his room, returning directly with a piece of white printer paper. A little bashful, he hands the paper to his mom. "I used the pencil," he tells her.

What Emma sees is a high-resolution laser printout of a photo of her face, a simple portrait, sent to the printer from her PC, which the little lad is always fiddling with. She gives Matt a peek, then looks back at Jofi. "Honey, this is a printout from the pictures on the PC." Matt nods, confirming the obvious.

Jofi looks confused. "There's no picture of you like that on the PC, mama. Those are all color photographs. I did this with the pencil while thinking about your face."

Matt gently takes the drawing and gives it a critical eye, wondering why Jofi is lying about this. He flips it over to examine the back of it. With a chill he notes the indentations of the pencil on the darker parts of the sketch. He flips it back topside and rubs his finger on the drawing, then examines the graphite residue on his finger. "Jesus," Matt sighs. "It looks like a photograph but it's a pencil sketch."

"O my god…" Emma whispers.

"From memory," Matt concludes, and the pair stare in wonder at their little boy.

Jofi darkens to sadness. "Don't you like it, mama?"

"Honey, I *love* it!" she says quickly to erase his hurt. She studies the picture and shakes her head in disbelief, and whispers, "But I'm not this beautiful."

"Yes, you are!" Matt and Jofi cry in unison. They look at each other and laugh heartily.

Matt takes Emma's hand. "Of all the pictures we have of you, I don't think I ever saw one I really loved until this thing here. This drawing *gets* you." They look at their strange little boy, both smiling. "I'll get it framed."

"No!" Jofi jumps up and down, chanting in merry rhythm, *"Put it on the fridge, put it on the fridge, put it on the fridge!"*

Matt laughs uproariously while Emma asks, "Why the refrigerator, honey?"

"Bobby says that's where pictures always go when moms and dads like them! So, okay?"

Matt and Emma nod affirmatively. "Absolutely okay," Matt says. "I'll buy a whole box of them tiny magnets and you can draw your little butt off."

"Okay!" Jofi cries and bolts from the room, flying up the staircase, presumably to get back to having fun with "the pencil."

"Maybe get him some good colored pencils, too?" glad Emma says to Matt.

Matt's smile disappears. "Emma – *what is Jofi?* And I don't mean *who* is Jofi. I mean *what* is he? The only baby ever born without a sex, the most precocious child, maybe, ever? I mean what the-"

Emma flares with anger. "Jofi is our *child*. He's a *child!*"

"No. Sorry. He's not *just* a child. He was even born with a name that nobody gave him. And we can add chess and drawing and music to the list, *but what else is on it?* What else that we don't know?"

Emma wants to think that there is a good, disarming answer to this she can fling back at Matt – but there isn't, and she slumps back into the couch looking defeated.

Matt is troubled and does not want to fight. "We have to protect him. If the eggheads get his hands on him…"

"What do you mean?"

"They'll never stop badgering him. Or us. Everyone will know about him."

Emma leans onto Matt, who caresses her and kisses the top of her head. "One day at a time…" she whispers to him.

"Well… one thing for sure," Matt says.

"What's that?"

"I sure as hell ain't playing chess with him."

They had some idea now, so what was to come would be less of a shock to them. The frustration I was having with my tiny body, my miniature fingers, the smallness of my stature, the immaturity of my vocal apparatus – these things were my greatest obstacles, but they reminded me that I was still 'a child,' and I needed the reminders. *Adding to these impediments would soon come my loving guardians' attempt to socialize me with others. There are none here like me, but I knew I must strive to be a good friend to all who share my path, and somehow even a boon to those who merely cross it. For this is the way the task shall be fulfilled. But above all, I must find Sam Morgan and Alma Pierce. Bran Englander lives nearby. I saw him, and I can feel his presence.*

— from Chronicles of Jophiel, Vol. I

Part II

I t has been entirely due to Matt's intelligence, wealth, and ferocious protective instincts that Jofi has remained out of the clutches of the medicos and media hounds as this, his 14th birthday, approaches. From the very beginning it had not been easy.

At the start Matt had to use lawyers to fight the University hospital about follow-up examinations and research entanglements, the authorities threatening intervention on grounds of child endangerment and finally playing the 'public good' card in their attempt to access Jofi, or at least his medical records, of which there are none except for his birth ordeal. His health is perfect, but when the parents declined all his vaccinations, the campaign against the privacy of Jofi and the family was renewed. Again, the family's lawyers won the day, as well as about $100,000 in total legal fees by the time these particular salvos burned themselves out. If they were a normal family on a standard income, they never could have withstood the onslaught. Justice has always been for the wealthy.

When Jofi did not register to attend the first grade, Child Services was dispatched to make sure his 'homeschooling' was not a fraud being committed on an abused boy by his uncaring parents. Jofi was briefed by Mom and Dad on the nature of the bureaucrats' home visit, and he played the role of the (not-too) precocious, well-behaved child so well that the family had a laugh-filled celebration when the visit was over.

Early in the game, it was the hospital that unleashed the dogs of media by leaking a story to them about Jofi's odd anatomy but did not mention him by name. Threats against the University for unauthorized release of medical records slammed the lid on that indiscretion, but it was too late, as the media had by then smelled the fresh meat, but Matt's law team had long proved their mettle, and as the overly-curious began to fathom just how good the legal team was, and how aggressive Matt – a well-known and respected pillar of the community – could be to his enemies, the threat gradually evaporated. The invading forces were never sure of the exact nature of Matt and Emma odd child, they just suspected something sensational, but were not prepared to be sued out of business by printing a story later judged libelous.

Matt actually enjoys this. He revels in his role as family protector and he loves Jofi, who now has a little brother, Eric. He is 10 to Jofi's 14. Unlike Jofi, he is in no special way precocious. He is as average a boy as could be, with Emma's eyes and Matt's strong chin. Unlike Jofi, Eric goes to school and he likes it. He has many pals who are always welcome at the Fischer home, and they all love Eric's big brother Jofi. Jofi watches over them in ways they could never imagine. He has been infinitely tolerant of his little brother's normal childishness (a trait that Emma cherishes since Jofi was never really a child).

Matt, at Emma's request, at last agreed to locate her estranged sister, Janet, whom she has not seen in ten years. Matt found her: she is married to a wealthy architect and lives in London. Emma is glad she's wed and seemingly secure, but sad in her heart she may never see Janet again.

Nearly 14, Jofi is still the most beautiful of children. Dressed properly, one could believe he was either male or female. Puberty has not come. Nor shall it. There shall be no budding breast on Jofi's forever hairless chest, so the notion of rearing him as a boy seems to have been the easy way to go.

Jofi has no friends. He is not lonely, and he is not seeking that sort of companionship. Mom and Dad know Jofi well enough to believe him when he says that he is fine with no companions. Jofi reads, play music, and meditates, sitting sometimes for long hours undisturbed in his room.

He has no friends, but he does get out a lot. He takes long walks on this side of the river, as well as across the river into downtown Ann Arbor. He likes being around people almost as much as he likes being alone.

He also plays the harpsichord. Since Jofi was so young when he started playing, his little legs would not reach down to the piano's pedals. Except for organ, early keyboard instruments did not have pedals. So Jofi began to play the harpsichord repertory, a huge and varied body of work, from the 16th century through Bach (who wrote for harpsichord as the piano was not yet in use).

Matt purchased a vintage William Dowd double-keyboard harpsichord for the study. Jofi plays every day, sometimes for hours, never with the music in front of him. He reads, then plays; once read, the written score is of no more use to him. In eight years, he has mastered the entire core repertory of the harpsichord literature and can play any of it from memory at competition level.

Mom and Dad have wisely kept the lid on this activity. They know that one day he will be 'discovered,' if indeed music is how Jofi wishes that to happen, but a teenage prodigy is a much more digestible phenomenon than a six year-old who can play all of Bach from memory and play it as well as anyone who ever lived. That's not a 'prodigy.' That's something else.

The jig was almost up one day when Emma's ancient piano teacher heard harpsichord music on the way out of the house after giving Emma her lesson. Emma told him (a bald-faced lie) that it was the stereo, but the nosey old bird pushed past her and cracked open the door of the study to witness her four year-old playing from Bach's *Goldberg Variations*, from memory, natch. He turned white as a ghost as he listened and watched, then glared at Emma all bug-eyed, and walked out of the house as if in a trance. He never mentioned the incident.

But now Jofi is a big boy, his feet can reach pedals very nicely, and he is excited as he waits for his 14th birthday present – and the truck has just arrived! The cargo is a nine-foot

Mason & Hamlin CC, a concert grand from the 1920s in perfect restoration. Jofi likes them better than Steinways, but they are hard to find. Funny how enough money seems to find just about anything.

When the piano was finally set up in Jofi's music room, Mom and Dad asked if he would tickle the ivories for them a little, take it for a test drive. Jofi looked at them as if they were space aliens and told them that the piano had to sit and acclimate for two weeks, and then be tuned and regulated, and only *then* would he be happy to play. After issuing his little edict, smiling Jofi caressed the real ivory keyboard of his new friend like your average little girl might stroke her new puppy, smiled and thanked his parents, and then was off to the study to play the harpsichord – well-acclimated and in perfect tune and regulation. Jofi sees to these things himself.

14

After dinner that night (a special birthday dinner for Jofi, for Emma has long resigned herself to becoming a capable vegetarian cook) all four of them sit in front of the fire in the great room.

"I'll be having dinner in town tomorrow night, if that's okay," Jofi announces. This is uniquely peculiar. Emma catches Matt's eye and then turns to Jofi.

"Well, that's interesting," she says. "Anyone we know?"

"Not yet, but you will. I think he'll become a good friend."

Matt is curious. "Who is this person?"

"He's a composer. He lives in town."

"Does he go to the Music School?" Emma asks.

Jofi laughs. "Nooooo." He sees that his parents are a little unsettled, so he clarifies quickly. "He's just a composer. And he's very good."

"How do you know him?" Matt asks, hopping up to visit the bar in the corner and about to pour a Scotch.

"I know his work," Jofi says.

"Yeah, but how do you *know* him?" Matt presses.

Jofi realizes there is no way out for him here. Nothing graceful. He takes a deep breath. "He's going to get in a bar fight tomorrow at 4:30 downtown, fly out the door into a lamppost, and fall on the sidewalk with a concussion. I need to call an ambulance and be with him in the emergency room. After that we'll get hamburgers. Well… Bran will get a hamburger; I'll get a… piece of pie or something."

Matt and Emma are dumbfounded. Eric looks up at his big brother and grins. "Jofi… that's reeeeealy weird!" And then he laughs, and Jofi looks at Eric and can't help laughing back at him. This makes Emma giggle.

"Not funny," Matt says, as he resumes his seat on the couch next to Emma. The laughter stops. "Me and your mom know that you are mature beyond your years and all that, but you're *14*. You *look* 14. And we don't want you clomping around Ann Arbor at all hours of the night by yourself!"

"I have a phone," Jofi offers timidly.

"Don't care," Matt says. "Not the issue. Plus – how do you know all this is going to happen to this guy? What's his name again?"

"Bran."

"This Bran. This is that Bran Englander guy you've mentioned before? How the hell did you-"

Emma shakes her head and takes Matt's hand across the couch. "Honey…"

"All right," Matt says. "Nevermind about that part of it. But this is just too… too… Listen, this guy goes to bars in the afternoon and gets into fights. You're 14. Now. Tell me again why I should want you to be his pal?"

"He's a good man and has a good heart. He's going through hard times."

Matt closes his eyes and rubs his forehead. "So am I at the moment."

Emma leans against Matt's shoulder. He kisses her head.

"You can watch me from your car," Jofi says. "Plus, I won't be late. Plus, you can drive me there. And you can watch."

Matt gives Jofi a critical look. Big sigh. "You say you *have* to do this?"

"I absolutely must."

"If this goes down like you say," Matt says, "I could drive him to the hospital in *my* car."

"No, please, Matt. You *must* stay out of the workings of all this. Please."

Matt considers. He looks at Emma. She betrays nothing. "What time will you be home? No… wait. You call me from your burger joint and I'll pick you up. Or else… okay… here's the deal," Matt has it at last. "I'll drive you there. If this composer fellow Bran falls out of this bar at 4:30, and I watch you two get into an ambulance… Then I'll go home and wait for your call at… at what time will all this be done?"

"About eight o'clock. No later," Jofi says.

"And then I'll pick you up at the burger joint. That work for you?"

Jofi smiles and nods a big yes. But he sees Matt isn't quite finished.

After the long pause, Matt asks, "Which burger joint?"

"The McDonalds on Maple. That's near his house. We'll take a cab from the hospital."

"Hmm… high class."

"He's broke," Jofi says.

"I need his home address before we go."

"Okay." Jofi wonders if the inquisition has ended.

"All right. Listen. Jofi, you've never screwed anything up as long as you've been with us. But son… don't screw this up. Okay?"

"I won't Matt," Jofi says. "You'll see."

Eric stands up and looks at Jofi. "Or else," Eric mimes a knife slowly slashing its way across his white throat, *"agggg-graragegeggegchchchggh!"*

Jofi and Emma laugh, and Matt tries not to. He fails miserably. "Go to bed, you!"

15

"O Bran, honey, you are ten times the man Clint could ever be. So hot! Don't stop, don't stop, don't stop… how come you stopped?"

"Um, my gut hurts. It's pretty bad."

"Well now, you just lay there, Bran honey, and let me take over! I know just what to do." And she does! And it is soooooo sweeeeet.

"Yeah… that's good… that feels good…" Bran is feeling better; the ache is subsiding. He's enjoying this immensely, but she stops. "What's the matter, baby? How come you stopped? I was almost there!"

She reaches into her purse and pulls out a small stick of… what the hell is that? Dynamite? Like from a cartoon. And she lights the fuse with her Bic lighter.

"Baby, what the hell are you doin'?"

And she takes the lit stick and rams it between Bran's butt cheeks.

"WHY ARE YOU DOING THIS?!" he screams, groping frantically at the device.

"Do you really want to work here, Bran?" she coos. "I mean, really?" And the dynamite detonates.

With a guttural yawp, Bran's pelvis slams up from his chair into the long table at which he is sitting, and back down. He opens his eyes in shock and looks around at the seven well-dressed men and women, jaws open and eyes agape, staring back at him from around the big table. And it dawns upon him: he's at work; it's the Monday meeting. He feels hot liquid dripping onto his pant leg. It is Marian's coffee; the force of his body against the table has spilled it.

The horror dawns upon him along with the odor: he fell asleep and woke himself by farting so hard he almost jetted out of his chair.

Marian rights her cup, makes a face and says "Ewwww!" stands, *"Gross, Bran!"* and rushes from the room.

Alan, sitting on his other side looks at Bran and shakes his head. "Dude. What the hell?" he says, then leans and whispers. "That was like the loudest fart in human history."

Joel is at the lectern wearing a forced smile. "Why don't we adjourn for ten minutes, huh?" All mumble agreement and file nimbly and swiftly from the room as if from a vessel in distress.

Bran rises. "You *sit*," orders Joel, who goes to the open door and closes it, then joins reseated Bran at the table. Bran's *déjà vu* is upon him; he knows what's coming.

"Bran, may I ask what you did last night?" Joel inquires with exaggerated civility.

Drank, smoked reefer, got the munchies so bad I ate an entire pizza on the way home from picking it up. Don't remember doing it. Box still in the car. Drank more. Woke up on the kitchen floor. "Nothing too terribly out of the ordinary, actually," Bran responds with an air of forced dignity.

"You're hungover," Joel observes. "I can *smell* it on you. I mean, *in addition* to the fart you just entertained us all with."

"I am very embarrassed and sorry about that."

"Did you see who was at the table this morning?"

"It looked like there was an extra person, but I… don't know…"

"That was our regional director from NPR in Washington, whom I introduced at the commencement of our meeting."

"Oh."

"Bran, you got the deepest musical knowledge of anybody and the most airtime here, you treat the music like gold, you have the most specialty programs…"

The nausea was returning.

"But this!" Joel was getting agitated. "There's more to a radio job than just playing and talking on the radio! There's the *job* part, and you ignore almost all of it, and it's been getting much worse! And it's not like you haven't been warned. Anybody else would have been cut from here long ago. But this isn't just the straw that broke the camel's back, this is an entire goddamn *tree!* And the *camel*, just in case you haven't

62

noticed in the past three or four years, *isn't too spry to begin with!"*

Joel tries to calm himself, takes a deep breath. "This morning, I thought I would show off my brilliant staff to the regional director before we meet later, so I could kiss his ass and *beg* him to extend the old terms into our new contract!"

"Sorry."

"Sorry!?"

That really was not an adequate response, Bran thinks hard but nothing else comes. He closes his eyes and drops his chin to his chest, waiting for the inevitable.

"You need to pack up your things and go home," Joel says sadly, looking away. They always got along okay. "Personnel will call you."

Bran stands up, nods at Joel, lumbers sadly to his desk to grab a few things and leaves the building, after almost a decade of work, never to return.

16

The Old Town Bar is right on the edge of downtown. It's 4:15 on a nice sunny day and Jofi hops out of Dad's Austin Healy right in front of the bar.

"You go somewhere and watch now, okay Matt? Don't let us see you, though. You can do that, right? You're good at just that kinda thing, right?" Jofi has a laugh in his voice.

"Yeah, smartass, I'm pretty good at that," Matt quips over the gurgling motor of his little car. "And Jofi – don't screw this up. Remember what your brother said would happen if you did?"

Jofi laughs. "Yes! I fear the consequences!"

"You better," Matt doesn't smile, and roars off.

Jofi looks at his phone and sees that he still has ten minutes before the festivities begin. He decides to just pace along in front of the bar. Two frat boys stroll by and one remarks, "Whoa, she is *hot!"* The other gives Jofi the once-over without stopping and adds, "Nah – no titties!" And they laugh their mindless sophomore laugh and pass by.

Jofi ignores them; he is used to this. He tries to look like a male – it's the easiest way to get along – but he's just too beautiful.

With but two minutes left on the clock a young woman not much older than Jofi saunters by, gives Jofi a big smile and stops. "Hi!" she chirps.

"Hello," says friendly Jofi.

"You are *amazing*. Are you, like, an actor or something?"

Jofi considers this and chuckles. "Yeah… I suppose I am. Or something."

She opens her purse and scribbles her phone number on a scrap of paper and hands it to him. "Call me," she says.

"Umm… thanks."

"Don't forget," she adds as she departs, blowing him a kiss. "Day or night!"

Jofi is almost six-feet tall now, blazing big blue eyes and wavy long brown hair. His body is, like his mom's, perfectly proportioned without exaggeration. Picture the *David* by Michelangelo, in jeans and a white tee-shirt, but softer and more feminine in the facial structure, the hands and feet. Young men think Jofi is a hot girl without the curves, and women just think Jofi is so beautiful they can't take their eyes off him.

He watches the girl stroll away, doing the exaggerated butt-swing that the TV taught her to do, when the bar door slams open and a man flies out headlong into the lamppost, hard, then collapses onto the sidewalk. Jofi looks down at him and notes that he is unconscious. He calls 911.

A gaggle of gawkers gathers, natch, and a squad car arrives in minutes, just ahead of the meat wagon. Jofi claims to be the injured Bran's brother (for is he not?) and the cop notes this, and steps inside to talk to the bar people. He'll see Bran later at the hospital to ask if he wants to press charges against his assailant. The medical guys rouse the injured man brusquely and conclude that his injuries – a bleeding forehead gash from the lamppost and a sore arm and back – need to be evaluated and they whisk him away, with brother Jofi as passenger.

After dropping Jofi off, Matt had parked his car out of sight and took an elevator to the 4th floor of a near office building in sight of the bar, went to the corner window, whipped out his portable binoculars, and witnessed the entire scene. *Son of a bitch…* he mused as he watched the ambulance pull away. *Exactly like he said.*

Bran has finally come fully awake in the ambulance on the way to the hospital – a short drive. He is still drunk and in pain. He turns his sore head to the right and sees Jofi sitting on the jump seat, smiling at him.

"Wow…" Bran mutters. "Am I dead and gone to heaven or something? You are really amazing. Who are you and… and where the fuck am I?"

"My name is Jofi and you're in an ambulance because you got in a barfight and got thrown out by someone you must have offended."

Bran just stares drunkenly at Jofi. "Baby, you are amazing! Why are *you* here?"

"Well, first of all, I'm not a girl."

"*Dude!* You gotta be kidding me!"

"Nope," Jofi says.

"Well. That's embarrassing," Bran moans. He suddenly perks up. "Listen, dude, I'm not gay, okay? You just look like a chick. And why did you say how come you're here?"

"I watched you hit the lamppost and fall down, then I called 911, and I wanted to make sure you got to the emergency room okay." Then Jofi leans forward and whispers to Bran. "I told them I was your brother, so don't blow my cover."

Bran gives Jofi an exaggerated wink, nods, and passes out.

Massive drunkenness, a mild concussion, and three head stitches declare the sawbones, and they want to keep Bran overnight to observe him, but he declines this sage medical advice and takes his leave against their wishes. He will not press charges against the man who flung him out the door of the bar because, as Bran shamefully recalls the scene to Jofi, "I would have done the same thing if I were that guy."

They sit together now at the Burger King on Maple Road – not the McDonalds across the street that Jofi foresaw. This disturbs him. It's a little thing, but what else is he getting wrong?

They are enjoying their food and conversation. Jofi had tried not to laugh at Bran's tales of the day but just could not help himself.

"That must have been quite a fart!" Jofi says, wiping tears of laughter from his eyes.

"Well, I didn't hear it, but that's what I was told," Bran mumbles, his mouth full as he is pounding down Whopper number two.

"I'm sorry for laughing but that has to be the most embarrassing job termination story ever."

"Well now, you'd think so, wouldn't you? I wish!" Bran says, not willing to go into details. He takes a long gulp of his giant Coke, belches politely and considers Jofi with a stare. "You're all right, little Jofi, the dude who looks like a chick. Sorry, but you do. How's that working out for you?"

"I don't mind too much."

"Thanks for keeping me company on my day of shame," Bran says, head down, obviously disgusted at himself.

"What will you do now?" Jofi asks.

"Ahh… the university will give me some kind of severance. Plus, I can keep my insurance for a year or so. They're pretty generous. I gotta talk to them." He pats his belly. "I haven't had two Whoppers in a while. Damn, they were good! Listen, can I drive you home?"

"No thanks, but I'd like to show you something."

"Sure." Bran sits back. "Go ahead."

Jofi smiles. "Not here. Back at your house."

"What the fuck?" and he gives Jofi a suspicious look. "Is this some weird kinda…" he flutters his fingers at Jofi.

"O! No. All I can say is that it will be clear to you when we go to your house. Just for a few minutes. My Dad'll pick me up at that McDonalds across the street. I'll walk from your house."

Bran strokes his beard stubble and regards Jofi darkly.

"Trust me," Jofi says.

Bran lightens up at this. He nods. "Okay, pal. Reckon I owe you, anyway. Let's boogie."

They climb into the old Cadillac, windshield still festooned with the parking tickets of the day and drive the three blocks to Bran's rented home.

Bran opens the door to an almost empty, but clean, living room: a small old Yamaha studio piano, a chair in front of a big TV, two enormous loudspeakers, a stereo setup, couch and a couple lamps – all the necessaries.

"Home sweet home," Bran says as he closes the door and turns to his young guest. "Have a seat."

Jofi looks around and chooses the piano bench, facing away from the keyboard and directly at Bran, who takes a seat on the couch.

"So, what do you want to show me?"

Jofi considers how to proceed. "Name a keyboard work by Bach," he says.

"What? Why? Heh-heh… you pronounced his name right – that's unusual."

"Please. Humor me. Any keyboard piece by Bach. Name one."

Bran considers this. "Umm… the *Chromatic Fantasy*. Why?"

Jofi nods and turns on the bench to face the keyboard. He begins the fantasy, delighted at the fine tuning and regulation of the little Yamaha that will allow him to play with good expression and as fast as he wishes. It's a seven minute-long, difficult piece with tons of flash. Jofi plays, not just note-perfectly, but a blistering emotional roller coaster of cascading sound. When he finishes he turns to Bran.

"Shall I play the fugue?"

Bran is pale in the face. His mouth is open. He blinks and finally speaks. "Who. The fuck. *Are* you?"

"I'm… I'm Jofi Fischer. Like I said."

Bran just stared. "It didn't matter what work of Bach's I picked. Did it."

Jofi shakes his head. "No. It wouldn't have mattered."

"Not just Bach, either, I suspect."

"No."

Bran shakes his head in wonder. "How old are you, Jofi?" Bran whispers.

"I turned 14 yesterday."

Bran looks away and tries to assimilate. Almost half a minute goes by, Jofi waiting patiently. Bran looks at Jofi. "Why are you here? What do you *want?*"

Jofi leaves the bench to sit next to Bran on the couch. He folds his hands in his lap and looks into Bran's eyes. "I'm a messenger, and I have a message for you," he says.

Bran pulls back and regards Jofi. "What message? From who?"

"Finish the *Anticanon*," he says.

Bran hops up in a shock. "How the fuck do you know about the *Anticanon?!*"

"There's more. Don't look for another job. Stop worrying about money. You won't need to. Remember who you are. Finish the *Anticanon* before it's too late."

Bran is appalled. His fists are bunched at his side. "Who told you to tell me that? How do you know what I'm doing?"

"I can't tell you right now."

"What the fuck do you mean you can't tell me?" And Bran grabs his head with both hands and slumps to the couch with a grunt. "Ohhhhhhhhhh… fuuuuuuuuuuuck…"

"Bran," Jofi says, "your concussion. You need to go back to the hospital. I can't drive you."

Jofi dials 911. He looks at the clock and sees that it's almost 8 p.m. He calls his dad and tells him that Bran has to go back to the hospital. Matt should pick him, Jofi, up at the emergency room in one hour. Jofi considers all this with discomfort. His perceptions of how the situation would unfold are off. Can he not rely upon his intuitions? The ambulance arrives within minutes and they're on their way.

Bran is back in x-ray and Jofi waits in the hallway, but it is now almost 8:30 and he might have to abandon Bran rather than push things with his dad.

Ten minutes pass and Jofi is getting antsy. The door to x-ray opens and here comes a cart with a patient… but it isn't Bran. On it lies a small old woman, ashen in hair and face, with little sign of life. They wait for the elevator. The old lady's eyelids flutter and she opens her eyes and looks right at Jofi.

She sits up in the cart with a start. Her eyes wide as saucers. *"Which one are you?!"* she rasps loudly. *"Which one?"* The aide puts a hand on her shoulder to calm her, but she shrugs it off.

Jofi knows exactly what she means but pretends he does not. "Are you speaking to me, ma'am?" he says.

"O please don't do that. I'm old and dying and can't play games now. *Which one are you?"*

The elevator door opens. Jofi smiles at the old woman but will not answer her.

"She's a little delirious, I'm afraid," says the aide as she pushes the cart into the lift.

"O, be quiet you!" the old lady snaps and turns back to Jofi. "I'm in 535. Room 535. Will you come see me? I'm dying. I'll be dead soon. Will you come?"

Jofi must do this. Yet another unforeseen event. He simply nods at the old woman. She smiles and falls back to the bed as the elevator door closes.

The same instant the radiology doors open again and here comes Bran on his gurney. He looks better. Wide awake.

"Bran," Jofi greets him, "My Dad will be here in a few minutes and I'll get in trouble if I don't go now. Can I get in touch with you tomorrow?"

Bran looks suspiciously but not unsmilingly at Jofi. "Dude, you *better* stay in touch. You got some 'splainin' to do. Got it?"

Jofi grins. "I got it. See you soon." And off he goes, down to the emergency ward and outside to look for the little green roadster with Dad in it.

> *I was troubled by these unforeseen events. When my world was my home and family, all was as expected; here, with my first steps out into the world, some of my presumptions are mistaken. There is no other word for it. It is strange to be so out of touch. Why is it that the events and circumstances that I foresaw so clearly have taken strange turns, and occasions which I have not foreseen, important ones, have thrust themselves upon me? There is an element at work that was not accounted for in my mission. What seemed to be a predictable and even cozy path now appears as a minefield.*
>
> *— from Chronicles of Jophiel, Vol. II*

17

Not much was said that evening at the Fischer home about the day's events, but the next morning, at breakfast, Matt voiced some of his concerns to Jofi. Emma, as she often did in these encounters, simply observed.

"Things go okay last night?" Matt asks.

"Sort of," Jofi replies. "Not completely."

"You didn't see his relapse coming, eh?" Matt pours himself more coffee.

"No. No, I didn't. Not just that. There were a couple other things…"

"That trouble you?"

Jofi looks uncomfortable. This is rare. "Hugely," he admits to Matt.

"You learned an easy lesson, son," Matt says earnestly.

"How's that?"

"It would be a shame, for all your gifts, gifts which we don't understand, me and your mom, if you let hubris bring you down."

"Hubris?"

"Excessive pride or self-confidence," Matt defines it for him. Eric reaches for a piece of jammy toast and upsets his glass of milk. Emma gets a towel to wipe it up.

Matt gives Eric an annoyed look. "I didn't *mean* it!" pouty Eric says in his defense.

Matt continues to Jofi. "In my old job… my old company… that was the hardest thing for us to get our clients to understand, and to guard against. And when there were casualties, rarely, it was almost always attributable to people thinking they knew more than they really did about other people, or else circumstances that they were overconfident about. And when they found out the hard way, they were unable to adapt to the changed situation quickly and effectively enough to survive. See what I mean?"

Jofi considers this at length. "I did get off easy," he whispers, as if to himself. "The stakes could have been much higher."

"That's right. Nobody *really* knows what's going to happen. Not even you, for all your gifts. And the more sure you are that you do, the more danger you're in." Matt drains his cup and wipes his mouth with his napkin. "Hubris kills. Let it sink in, son." He rises to leave the table.

"Thanks, Matt." *I will,* he thinks to himself. *I must.*

Jofi hitched a ride to the hospital with Matt, his intention being to visit the injured Bran and perhaps continue their conversation. Since he was listed as Bran's brother he had no problem being briefed as to Bran's condition. He was stable, they told him, but he has requested no visitors for the day. Also, he was told that Bran would stay another night and "may or may not go home tomorrow."

This is a little distressing to Jofi. Had Bran shut him out? But at least it's not just Jofi – Bran requested no visitations from *anyone*.

Maybe he needs to think, Jofi considers. *This past couple of days must have truly rocked his world.*

He considers walking home; or going for a walk in the Arboretum; or getting lunch somewhere. Finally, he admits to himself that what he is actually going to do, whether he wants to or not, is find room 535 and conclude his business with a very sick, very old woman, who actually has her wits about her in a very strange way: *she pretty much knows who he is.*

Her door is partially closed, and he inches it open slowly. It's a semi-private room, completely private in this case, as the bed nearest the door is empty and made up.

She spies him looking. "That was Gertie's bed. She's dead. She beat me!" she says with a giggle. Then gets serious. "Or did you know that already?"

Her candor surprises him. "No… no, I didn't know that."

They consider one another for a few seconds and then she beckons him come hither with her finger. He goes to her bedside and stands next to her and regards her in a deliberately neutral way. He's just not sure how to act here.

"*My* name is Eleanor." She waits, but no response from her guest. She gives him her annoyed face, then continues.

"I got the pancreas cancer," she says. "I've already lived longer than I was supposed to. So… no more tests. No more anything except pain drugs. I hate 'em." She starts to cry, softly, almost embarrassed that she lets this slip. "But the pain is worse than my will to hold the drugs off," she blubbers pathetically and looks at Jofi imploringly. "Will you help me?"

"Help you to what?" Jofi asks lamely.

"O Jesus!" she cries. "You're still going to play this stupid game?"

Jofi puts his hand on her forehead, and she gets calm. She closes her eyes and sighs one big sigh after another, then opens her eyes afresh.

"So," she says. "Which one are you?"

He draws himself up to full stature and gives her a smile. "Jophiel," he says. "I am Jophiel."

The old woman's eyes get big and her mouth pops open. She is so delighted! "I knew it I knew it I *knew* it! I just didn't know which one! Jophiel!" she repeats. *"The Angel of the Beauty of God!"* she cries out.

Jofi laughs, sharing in the joy at his first revealing. But he has a concern. "What is this 'god' that you refer to?" he asks.

Eleanor frowns. "Is that a joke?" she asks. "You could get in *trouble!*"

"Well… I suppose I just want to know what *you* mean by that word."

"But… but everyone knows who God is."

Jofi looks serious now. "No," he says. "Everyone who believes they believe in things like this 'god' of yours *thinks* they know what God is, but everyone is thinking a different thing. The god of *your* specifications does not exist."

Eleanor looks like she's just been slapped. "What… what do you…"

"Don't worry," Jophiel says. "The real deal is even better than what you imagine." Eleanor looks skeptical. Jofi is amused. "Incidentally – how did you know who *I* am?"

She lightens and laughs. "I've always been a little odd that way. I always *knew* I would see an Angel one day. Totally damn sure of it. Studied up on all of you! I had the best Angelology site on the internet! Before the cancer. None of that new-age gobbledygook, either. Pure scholarship!" she boasts. Jofi is bemused. "And here I am an inch from death and there you are!" Suddenly she frowns. "But why don't you look more like an Angel ought to?"

Jofi studies her for a moment and says, "You mean like this?" And they are no longer in the hospital room. There are no walls in *this* place. There is light everywhere, of every color of the spectrum, it seems, flowing into every other color. Everything is made of this light, in golds and pastels and the rich colors like only butterfly wings seem to have, but so bright she has to squint. And Jophiel has graceful wings folded back tightly. Now, in his white robes made of light, he stretches out these wings into that pose that is the archetype of the bright shining Angel. His face is radiant and his blond curls glowing golden as the thick sash about his waist, which is scribbled with strange occult writing.

Eleanor looks as though she cannot bear such majesty, but in her pain there is open ecstasy. She hears strange, unearthly music. It is a full minute before she can speak.

"It's like I always imagined… except… even more beautiful!"

"So, why do I look like this, exactly?" Jophiel asks, confusing Eleanor. "I mean, do I remind you of something you've seen before?"

"Well, yes! Now that I think about it I suppose you look like that old painting of Michael that I used to have on my wall when I was a little girl!" She frowns and ponders. "Or was it Gabriel."

"Ah… okay… here we go!" Jophiel says. "Michael this, Gabriel that, blah blah blah!"

Eleanor is shocked and puts her hand over her mouth. "O my God! You sound, what… *jealous?*"

Jophiel laughs. "Just kidding. We're all used to it, actually. We joke about it. It's a temporary thing."

"But why are you even asking me?" she says. "Don't you know what you look like?"

Jophiel shakes his head in mock annoyance. "I'm an *Angel*. I don't look like *anything!* I don't have a physical *body!*"

"Then… why…"

"Because this is what you *want* me to look like!" Jophiel says.

"But… you have a body… the… the other body that I just saw in my room."

"Yeah… well, that's a special thing. Most unusual. Got a job to do. You know, sometimes an Angel's presence is required in China. Or Africa. Or India. Angels are imagined a lot differently there. My job here deals with a bunch of Americans. Mostly white ones. Like you. So, I look like this."

Eleanor is trying to assimilate all this but falls short. "O dear… what a day!"

"I think you're doing pretty well. Considering. All this is most untypical."

She looks sad now. "But soon you go, and I lay in this damn bed and wait for more pain pills," she whispers bitterly.

Jophiel shakes his head. "Eleanor, you left that life and that bed behind ten minutes ago."

Suddenly, she finds herself standing toe-to-toe in front of Jophiel, her pain gone. He wraps her, first in his Angel arms, then in his magnificent wings.

"The feathers are tickling my nose!" she exclaims.

"Feathers, huh?" Jophiel giggles.

But now Jophiel can sense a growing panic in Eleanor. She's shivering. It's dawning on her that she has, indeed, *died*. In a start, she clutches at him. "Jophiel! What's to become of me? I've been such a bad person. Save me from hell!"

"Sorry."

"You won't!?"

"No. I couldn't if I tried. But you just haven't been that *bad*, really."

"No?"

"Nope. Sorry. And your idea of hell exists for no one with a shred of humanity in them."

"O – well, that's a relief! So… what then, Jophiel? What *is* to become of me?"

"Well, you've got a couple bad habits that depend on your body to satisfy. Usual stuff. Nothing terribly drastic. So, you need to get rid of those. Soon you'll realize that the body you have now, well, you really don't have it anymore. But the urges – you still got those."

"Oh."

"And all the desires and concepts that tie you to your old life in selfish ways – they need to go, too. It's the time of purification."

She considers these wonders. "Will that take a long time? Will it hurt?"

"Time isn't what it used to be. And I won't lie to you – I *can't* lie to you – it can be uncomfortable. But I guarantee that it's nothing you can't handle. It doesn't miss a thing but there's a strange benevolence about it all."

"Then what?"

"Then you, umm... how to put this to you... you go to your reward. Yes. Let's just put it that way. You live then as a spirit among spirits."

"Forever?"

"Not in your case, no. There are the few who go no more out, but most – no."

"What then?"

"You have a new life."

"Where?"

"Here, probably. Earth. Part of the time that you commune with spirits as a spirit yourself is spent in preparation for your new life. Who your parents will be, where you'll live, your sex – possibly male next time – your goals in that life, the good and imperfect traits that your new body will have, your talents and weaknesses. That sort of thing. Things will be a lot different when you return."

"Why will I have imperfections and weaknesses?"

"You'll have different lessons you need to learn. New challenges."

"Sir!"

"Yikes," Jophiel says.

"What's wrong?" Eleanor can't hear that.

"I'll have to go…"

"O stay, Angel," and she hugs him tight, "… stay."

76

"SIR!"

"Ahh…" Jophiel whispers into Eleanor's ear. "Listen now, you'll be okay, just roll with it. I got part of me back where you just came from, see, and I-"

"Thank you, Jophiel," she whispers lovingly in his ear. "Thank you, thank you, thank you…"

"SIR! What is wrong with you?"

Jofi opens his eyes and looks down upon a very short nurse with a very stern look.

"Sir, what is the *matter?* Are you all right?"

Jofi nods.

"Eleanor has passed, sir. I'm sorry you seem a little overcome, but you are not listed as family and you *must* leave her room! I'm sorry. These are hospital rules!"

Jofi sighs and nods. "Of course. Sorry. I'll go."

"I'm sorry for your loss, but…"

"No problem. I'm off!"

18

The Senator takes off his headphones and rubs his ears. "That was amazing!" he says to no one. He touches his intercom. "Jenny? I'm back from lunch. Any calls?... Okay. Send Phil in please."

Phil arrives within the minute and smiles at the Senator. "I can tell you've been listening to music."

"How so?"

"Headphone-hair."

They laugh and the Senator motions for Phil to take the chair on the other side of the desk.

"What was it this time," Phil asks. He doesn't care in the slightest, but it's good that the Senator thinks he does.

"What was I listening to? Oh. Umm… Charles Ives. One of his symphonies. Quite a workout, actually. It's what I do at lunch instead of jogging," the Senator jokes, leans back and folds his hands across his belly. Bigger than ever? "I probably ought to jog…" he mumbles with a frown.

"Well, it's good to have a hobby, sir."

The Senator considers this. "You know… to me, it's more than just a hobby. It's… it's more like…"

Phil can't stand it anymore and interrupts. "You did want to see me, sir?"

"What? Oh. Yeah. Ahh… Re-election."

"Sir?"

"We have to be more clearly 'about something.' Since we live in a nation that seems to be falling apart at the seams, with leadership that is getting a 'do nothing' reputation, I've decided that we ought to be more proactive."

"In what way, sir?"

"In a law-and-order sort of way."

These, to Phil, are the Magic Words he's been waiting for his entire political career to hear. *"Excellent,* sir. I'm glad to hear you say this. I've been working on a plan, it's-"

"Yes, I know you have. We've talked about it. And I've been considering some of your ideas. Things are taking a nasty turn in America. Things are *boiling over,* is what they're doing. People are scared. We need to achieve some level of control-"

"Yes, sir! Control. That's the idea, sir. We are, after all – the Government."

"Yes. So, we need to set up some talk time. Me. You. Who else? Let's keep it small for now. How about Doug?"

"All due respect, sir – Doug is a bleeding-heart. Just the type we need to avoid at this stage."

"Maybe, but I want Doug. Anyone else?"

Phil is disappointed. It was all going so well. "No, sir. That's a… a good start." He waits. "Anything else, sir?"

"Yeah… there was something… Oh yeah! Season tickets for the National Orchestra. Get me that box I had two years ago if you can. Two tickets. Every show."

19

"So, he played some Bach for you. Big deal. Another prodigy. Another flash-in-the-pan." Bran's oldest friend Li Ming takes a long toke of the joint and passes it Bran's way. Bran shakes his head.

"No, bro'. None of that till the headaches go away," Bran says. "Listen. It's not that he 'played some Bach for me,' all right? There *may* be another 14 year-old alive who could have played that fantasy. But *I* chose the work, not him. And the main thing was, he played it perfectly. Not just note-perfect, he played like… like… a master. Huge ocean *waves* of sound." He points. "From that dinky-ass Yamaha! That's not possible! It's like going 150 miles an hour in a Volkswagen Beetle. Just not possible."

"Huh," Li grunts as he places the roach in the ashtray. "It'll be interesting to meet him." Li looks at his watch. "Soon, right? I can't stay long."

"How come?"

"The U has this thing tonight."

"Oh, no – you're not going to that stupid thing, are you? What is it again? *'Avoiding'-*"

"*'Avoiding Consonance.'* Yeah. Big multi media thing."

Bran picks up his tablet and begins to read a summary of the concert by the local rag.

"A multimedia extravaganza celebrating contemporary political artists who deliberately destroy or avoid beauty in their productions as a sort of artistic–political statement that Beauty has been one of the most important of art's institutional discourses, which is obsessed with power and exclusion. 'Beauty,' director Hughes explains, 'has to be avoided in contemporary art because its traces would redirect viewer's attention from social injustice.'"

Bran puts the tablet down and snorts at his pal. "Why the hell are you-"

"'Cuz I got *friends* in it. You know how it goes. Gotta support your friends. Even if it sucks."

Bran nods in resignation and points out the window. "It's three o'clock on the dot and there's his dad's car pulling up. Punctual. *Damn*, that's a nice ride," Bran says, craning his neck to get a look. Li, who, like Bran, would be a total 'car guy' if only he had the money, is likewise dazzled by the green roadster.

"Who's the chick?" Li asks.

"Good. It ain't just me," Bran laughs.

"What do you mean?"

"I thought he was a chick, too," Bran says, watching Jofi mosey toward the house. "He's a dude."

"Really. Amazing," Li whispers. "Hey. Should we hide the weed?"

Bran snorts. "Hell no. My house," he replies, hops up, yanks the doorknob and beckons Jofi to enter.

Introduction all made, Jofi sits back on the piano bench and the other two share the big couch. Jofi has a Coke, the older fellows each a beer.

"So, you're the piano whiz," Li says with a smile.

"I play," Jofi says.

"How'd you learn?" Li asks.

"Yeah," Bran adds, "How the hell *did* you learn to play like that?"

"I study and play a lot."

"Teacher?" Li asks.

"No," Jofi answers with a smile of his own.

Li studies him for a moment. "Bran tells me you played him the *Chromatic Fantasy*."

"A great piece," Jofi says.

"He also said you bragged you could play any Bach work."

"Not bragged," Jofi is a little on guard here.

Bran says to Li, "Dude, it ain't braggin' if you can do it. Richter pretty much taught himself, and he could play almost anything."

Li gives him the 'are you crazy' look. "At 14? Maybe you just guessed lucky with the fantasy request," Li says. He turns to Jofi. "Play me one of the canons from *The Art of Fugue.*"

Jofi stays still, unsmiling.

"Dude," Bran says, "He's not your piano nigger. Seems he doesn't like to be ordered what to play. Imagine that."

Li nods. "Sorry, Jofi," he says, sounding genuine, "that was stupid and rude of me. Would you please play us one of the canons from *The Art of Fugue?* If what Bran tells me is true, it would be thrilling to hear that. A privilege."

Jofi looks from one to the other, seemingly having some internal conflict about all this. After a long moment, he turns around on the bench and begins to play.

He favors them with the shortest canon of the set. It's perfect, wise, and revelatory. The room is silent when he finishes. No smartassed comments, no nothing.

Li has been stooped forward, elbows on knees, looking at the floor throughout the recital. He doesn't move. He just states flatly, "I've never heard it played better than that. By anybody. Live or recorded. I heard things I never heard before."

Jofi turns on his bench. "Thank you, Li."

"That was memorable," Bran mumbles.

"Jofi," Li ventures, "one more little thing. If you will. I wonder if you know *Mysterious Barricades* by-."

"Couperin! O, I *love* that little piece!" Jofi says.

"Me, too," Bran says, "but what's with the title?"

"Couperin's titles are often pretty crazy," Li adds, "but, yeah, nobody really knows why he called it that."

"It's a double entendre," Jofi says.

The other two glance at one another and grin.

"In, umm… in what way, Jofi?" Bran asks.

"Near the end, at measure 47, when the low D comes in, the music tries to resolve, to go home to B-flat, but the return isn't as easy as it ought to be. There are harmonic obstructions, playful but disruptive, that delay the resolution."

"Uh huh," Li says, "but how is it a double entendre?"

"It also refers to breaking through a virgin's defenses in order to have sex with her. Those mysterious barricades that she puts up are her playful objections to the perceived overconfident seduction efforts of her suitor. But the situation does ah… resolve gracefully." Jofi smiles and drifts away. "Once, in Paris, he told me-" and he stops short, mortified at his blunder.

"What?" Bran asks. *"What did you just say?"*

Jofi's eyes get big. "Nothing. Just remembering from a book I read."

And he spins away on his bench and plays as requested. A few blissful minutes pass and when he is finished, he whips back around with a big grin on his face. The others are not grinning. Jofi's grin disappears. "What's wrong?" he asks.

Now they act like he's not there. Li says to Bran, "Bran, that's not Bach."

"He said he played other stuff. How did you know to ask him to play that?"

"The way he played the Bach piece – as if he were at a harpsichord. I should have asked him for something more obscure in that literature…"

"Hey!" Jofi yells out. "I'm right here!" They stop and look at Jofi. He smiles because they look a little rattled. He decides to come clean with them. "I started playing when I was too young to reach the pedals, so my dad bought me a harpsichord. I know the core repertory."

Li asks, "Will you consider just one more request? Respectfully."

Bran nods assent.

"The final movement of Beethoven's Opus 111."

Jofi looks down and smiles. "Not without playing the first movement also. In the case of that sonata, it would be disrespectful."

"So how do we know you're just saying that because you can't play it?"

Jofi considers this, smiling. "You don't."

"Can you play all 32 sonatas from memory?"

"Yes."

"Why should we believe you?"

"Because whether you believe me or not is of no consequence to me."

Li and Bran just stare at one another for a long moment. Bran sighs and mumbles to Li, "Good answers." Li nods in agreement.

After a few moments Li rises and goes to Jofi. He holds out his hand for a shake, and Jofi takes it. "I have to go, Jofi." He stands and thinks, still holding Jofi's hand. "I don't know what's going on here. I don't believe in miracles. But this… you…" He pumps Jofi's hand and tries to smile. "Till we meet again."

Jofi smiles as Li releases him and heads toward the door, then turns. "Oh… *thanks*. Thanks for the music. It was…" and Li turns and is gone.

"Wow," Jofi says as the door closes, and he turns to Bran. "I never even got to ask him about himself. What does he do?"

"He plays the cello. He a full professor at the music school and makes recordings. He's first rate. You want another Coke?"

"No. I'm good."

"Listen, you'll see Li again. Let's talk about who sent you my way with that message for me. You mind?"

"I can't tell you who sent me," Jofi says.

"Fuck!" Bran barks and recovers himself. "So, then what's this about the *Anticanon?*"

"Finish it."

"How the fuck do you know I'm even *writing* the goddam thing?"

"I'm sorry. I can't tell you that."

Bran squeezes his eyes shut and growls. *"Why* should I finish it?"

"It's beautiful."

"How can *you* know that? It doesn't even exist yet!"

"It's always existed. Our notions of Time are not the same."

"Goddamn it! Who *cares* if it's beautiful?"

"Many will care."

"Why."

"Because beauty is vanishing from the world."

Bran looks like he's been slapped. He slumps back in his seat. "It *is*. Isn't it," he whispers. He stares at the wall. "It's like beauty has become… an embarrassment."

"You haven't touched it for six months," Jofi says, carefully.

"How the fuck do you…" Bran sighs then laughs bitterly, anticipating Jofi's useless reply. "I've barely begun it."

"How come?"

"It's too difficult. Not worth it."

"How so?"

"I have to write 100 separate pieces of music for 100 instruments that have no harmonic connection. All melodies. And in different keys, different meters – I have to compose a hundred solo pieces for every instrument in the orchestra." He sighs again. "Breaking the last taboo with an overdose of beauty. And I think, why bother? All that work. For what? No one plays my music. No one even *looks* at my music. I'm not a member of the club. I haven't paid my dues. I have never ingratiated. I don't know how! I don't *want* to know how!"

Bran pauses here, gathering his wits. Jofi senses a pending oration and gets comfortable. He figures he's about to get 'schooled.'

Bran continues. "Listen… when you go to a concert and hear the rare contemporary piece that somehow snuck onto the bill, do you think it gets programmed because it has any actual value?"

Jofi laughs quietly. "No."

"No is right, dude. You *pay-to-play*. And I don't mean money. Well, yeah, *sometimes* it's money. Rarely. A composer with money or backing can get anything played or recorded by anybody, anywhere. And a critic to say how goddam wonderful it is. It's a business. Art is a fucking business."

"It's always been a business," Jofi adds.

"Yeah, but not like today. Even if you take money out of the picture, it's still pay-to-play." Bran clears his throat. "You go to college, get good grades, kiss all the right asses, wash their cars, babysit their kids, work up to grad student so you can do the professor's work for him while he's out fucking pretty chicks – who use their bodies to get ahead. That's *their* strategy. Then, if you're a good boy who knows how to walk the line, you get introduced to other, more important, composers and conductors in the loop, and you pretend to like all the unlistenable *shit* they write and play for one another to fawn over – *which I can't do.*"

Bran is on a roll. "Oh, and it helps if you're gay. Or can *pretend* to be, so when an early opportunity opens up but that hot, new conductor wants a blowjob to seal the deal, you turn him down at your peril. But you better do it, 'cause you're *almost there!*

"And *finally*, if you've played the game *perfectly* – you can get your music played. You're a member of the club! As long as what you write stays inside the lines, of course. Now you can get a teaching position of your own, because *what the fuck else are you good for?* Now you can teach other untalented jerkoffs how to be as useless as *your* teachers were. But you get played now! You're a success! But does the audience *like* the music you write? *Hell* no. So what? They clap because they're too stupid and cowardly to throw tomatoes. Or rocks. But it doesn't matter, *because whether anybody likes it or not has nothing to do with anything.*" Bran shakes his head and looks hateful and tired. "What a crock of shit."

After a respectful interval of silence, Jofi says, "That was quite a soliloquy."

Bran glares at Jofi like he wants to punch him or throw him out, then breaks into a huge smile and they both break into long, loud and honest laughter. Bran pops up from the couch and fetches another beer.

While he's in the kitchen, Jofi asks, "Stipulating that everything you said is true, and not just for music but for all the arts, what does that have to do with finishing the *Anticanon?*"

Bran resumes his seat, takes a slug of beer, puts it down on the coffee table, turns and looks at Jofi as if Jofi had grown another head, which by now wouldn't surprise him. Strange kid. "I just fucking *told* you," Bran explains calmly.

"That *was* an amazing speech," Jofi says. "Almost like you worked it all out beforehand."

Bran smiles. "I've been refining it in my head for years," he admits, not without a little shame peeking through.

Jofi nods. "Every possible excuse not to do your work in one succinct homily. Slick!"

Bran darkens. "Excuse? Every fucking thing I said is true!"

"So what, though?" Jofi counters, rather fearlessly, brooding Bran thinks. "What does that have to do with doing your job?"

"Now what do you mean?"

"You're a composer. Your job is to compose. You've created a hydra-headed monster to prevent you from doing your work."

"I didn't create it!"

"I grant that the monster *exists*, but the only way to defeat it is to ignore it and do your work. It's not your job to get it played. It's your job to *write* it. The monster can't prevent *that.*"

Bran doesn't know whether to smack this young prick upside the head or… or what. "Okay, Jofi. Are you finished?"

"One more thing, if I may?"

"Cut the shit. Just say it."

"You've been cowed, intimidated. You have this formidable, unbeatable front that you put on, but all the things you hate and rail against have *beaten* you." Bran stiffens. Them's fightin' words to the likes of Bran, and Jofi knows this but speaks on through the thinning ice. "You think you know the value of the *Anticanon,* but you don't. You've been born to write it. But instead you're… you're *pussying out.*" That was hard for Jofi to say, but he knows they're the magic words.

Bran stands and looks down on Jofi. "You little prick. Who the fuck do you think…" he hisses. *"I don't pussy out!"*

Jofi serenely holds his ground. He looks up. "Aren't you?"

Bran is an inch from slapping the bejeezus out of his new buddy, actually moves his hand back in preparation to administer payback for this major insult but stops. Instead, he resumes his seat and for a few moments just sits and looks blankly at the wall. Then he starts to cry, head down and shoulders heaving.

Jofi leans over and touches Bran's shoulder. Bran shakes him off. "Jofi," he says quietly. "You should go." And resumes his tears. "Go on now."

Jofi stands, turns and without another word, leaves Bran's home.

> *For the first and, I prayed, the last time in this*
> *strange life, I had hurt, purposely bruised the*
> *heart, of another being with my words. I hurt*
> *then as much as Bran did, and the pain was*
> *profound. I saw no other way. I prayed he would*
> *forgive me. I foresaw that he would,*
> *but by then I knew: I may be mistaken.*
>
> *– from Chronicles of Jophiel, Vol. II*

20

The next morning Jofi is sitting with his dad in his dad's office at home, the only area in use in the north half of the home. Matt finds it peaceful there, no matter how animated Emma and the kids can get. Plus, no clanging of the harpsichord or roar of the piano.

"I have to find a boy… a man, maybe… name of Sam Morgan," Jofi says. "I haven't been able to find him. Also a woman named Alma Pierce."

Matt smiles. "You asked me and your mom about these same two people when you were a baby. Remember?"

"Yes. I wasn't sure if *you* did."

Maybe we're not as dumb as we look," Matt quips, and they both laugh. "So, explain," he says, trying to appear detached, hoping that clever Jofi cannot divine his intense curiosity.

"I know you're intensely curious, so I'll be straight and quick."

"Umm… okay."

"The same guidance that led me to Bran wants me to find these two people. I was born needing to find these people. Especially this Sam Morgan."

"And you have no idea-"

"None. None whatever. I've been online and find nothing."

"Why do you need them? Let's start with her. Why do you need this Alma person?"

Jofi pauses, as if it isn't entirely clear, then says, "I think it's *Bran* who needs her."

"Son – I gotta tell you: Bran sounds like a terrible drunk with more than a few problems. I wish to hell you'd find another friend."

Reluctant Jofi nods in agreement. "I don't know – can one really pick one's friends? I think he's going to be a great man, Matt."

Matt sighs, a little exasperated. "And this other guy. Who's he?"

"He's very important. Not just for the future of Music, but for all of Art. I really have to find him. Finding Bran was important, but this Sam Morgan – he's the lynchpin. And I need to bring him together with Bran."

Matt looks fondly at Jofi and shakes his head slowly. "For the future of Art, eh?" Matt closes his eyes in thought. "Jofi… raising you has been very easy, and very hard." He studies Jofi, who sits with downcast eyes. "Your Mom… she convinced me early on that… that you would tell us what you could of yourself in your own time."

"I know it's been strange to have me with you."

Matt laughs a sincere laugh. "You'll tell us though, right? One day?"

"I promise," Jofi says. "Trust me when the time is right."

"This girl," Matt asks, "you know *anything* about her?"

"Nothing. Sorry."

"And the-"

"Him either. Not a trace."

"How do you know these two are even in town? Or in the country, even?"

"I don't," Jofi says sheepishly.

Matt chews on his reading glasses, trancing out. He recovers and says, "Give me till tomorrow night, eh?"

Later that morning, Bran telephoned Jofi. He was very glad his offended pal called him up.

"No hard feelings, huh dude?" Bran says.

"No!" Jofi says gratefully. "None! Forgotten!"

"No…" Bran corrects. "Not forgotten. You were right. About pussying out. You were right."

"So… does that mean you're going to write the *Anticanon?*"

"Yeah. It does. Of course, it's gonna take me the rest of my fucking *life*, but yeah, I'm writing it. Say, you wanna come by for dinner tomorrow night? Six o'clock?"

"Really? Do you cook?!" Jofi wonders.

"Cook? Me?" Bran guffaws crudely. *"Hell* no. We'll order a pizza or Chinese or something. That okay?"

"I won't be late!"

Almost as soon as Bran hangs up the phone, Matt comes into Jofi's study with a big smile and says, "I found the girl."

"Already? How could you possibly-"

"Local, young, no record of her? To me, that meant 'student.' The reason you couldn't find her online is because she's not from around here, she's from Houghton, up in the Upper Peninsula. She just arrived for her post-grad classes at the music school for the semester. It *is* September, you know. I just called admissions and they confirmed it."

Jofi closes his eyes and wears a look of complete relaxation and relief. "That's amazing, Matt. Thanks."

Matt hands him a piece of paper. "Here's her name and contact information, her address, too. She's got an apartment downtown. That new highrise on Huron."

Jofi takes the paper and asks awkwardly, "I don't suppose Sam Morgan just started classes, too?"

"Doesn't look that way, sorry," Matt reports. "I found a couple matching names locally, but one is a dentist the other an old lawyer. Nationally, I found lots more, and we can look the list over together."

"Okay…" Jofi says. "He'll be young, I'm pretty sure of that."

"Jofi, if you can give me anything at *all* to go with this guy, other than 'he'll be young,' it will help immensely to pinpoint him."

"I wish, Matt. If something comes to me, I'll report it. Can we look at your list now?"

"Nope. I have a speech in Detroit. The bigshots are feeling the heat."

"What does that mean?"

"Well, as long as it was just the poor and middle class that were the victims of the urban violence plague, nothing was done. But the elite are starting to feel the heat in their gated communities. They don't feel safe anymore. You used to be able to *buy* that feeling, if you had the means. I have to tell them that you can't realistically do that anymore. Not where *they* want to live."

Jofi sighs. "Good luck, Matt."

Matt wiggles his fingers at Jofi. "Tootles. See you at dinner."

As Matt vanishes out the doorway Jofi thinks about his dinner engagement the *following* evening. "Tomorrow's dinner… for *three!*" he whispers.

21

It's early afternoon and Emma is going shopping. She agrees to drop Jofi off downtown. He gives her a kiss and shuts the door of the little Acura coupe. Jofi checks the street for the building that Matt thinks the girl, Alma, lives in. He could have called first, but he knows the charm he has on people in person and he's not above using this talent when he needs to.

He finds the new highrise, enters and is unimpressed. Pacing toward the elevators he notes the concrete walls devoid of pictures or ornament, the barely adequate lighting – a completely angular, hyper-modern, charmless place. This is brand new student-ghetto housing for rich kids, all too common in Ann Arbor.

The elevator halts at the sixth floor. Jofi steps out, notes that the room is to the right and hunts down the target door. He knocks.

She answers. He smiles and observes: medium height, brown, medium-length hair, trim and fit, Jofi finds her pretty. He says hello. Alma tries to hide her astonishment, but her eyes are wide, and her mouth is open. She recovers and returns his smile.

"Can I… can I help you?"

"I'm looking for Alma Pierce."

"I'm Alma," she announced, pronouncing it as 'Elma.' Her smile widens, and she is suddenly elbowed out of the center of the doorway by another young lady, tall and striking. "Hi! I'm Daisy!" Alma turns and gives her a *why do I put up with you?* look.

Daisy is Ms. Friendly herself. "Come on in!" she beckons Jofi in her lyrical voice.

"Daisy!" Alma is objecting?

"What? He seems nice. Plus, he's looking for you."

Alma takes a breath and turns to Jofi. "Would you like to come in?" she says.

Jofi nods and says, "I would. Thank you." And he steps into the living room of the apartment. The ladies stand on either side of him as they stroll inside peeking across at one another with mischievous looks on their faces, which vanish as Jofi turns to Alma.

"Your place is very nice," Jofi remarks, trying to focus on only the nice things, and the ladies beckon him sit anywhere. The room is full of paintings and drawings, not reproductions, and two new comfortable recliners and a couch. It's all clean and tasteful. Jofi picks one of the recliners and Daisy asks him if he wants something to drink.

"Water would be nice."

"Ice?" Alma asks as she steps toward the kitchen to fulfill the handsome young stranger's request.

"Nope. Just from the tap is good."

Daisy sits across from Jofi on the couch. "So!" Daisy chirps. "Who are you and why are you here?"

"Daisy!" Alma rebukes her directness as she comes in from the kitchen to hand thirsty Jofi his water.

"Sorry, sorry… I know. It's *your* apartment."

"Do you *ever* remember that?" she says, along with the old *why do I put up with you?* look. Jofi bolts his water in a single draught, wipes his lips, smiles and puts the empty glass on a coaster atop the little table next to him.

"So!" Alma says, assuming her righteous duties as hostess. "Umm… so… who are you, and… why are you here?"

"Gee," Daisy says, "that's *much* better."

They all laugh, and Jofi introduces himself.

"So, how old are you?" Daisy asks.

"14."

"I'm only 17, for another month," Alma pipes, pointing to her friend, "Daisy is the old lady."

"Yeah. Ancient. I'm 20."

Jofi looks at Alma. "Aren't you a little young for a grad student?"

"I got put ahead a year in high school, and my skills have brought me to the attention of some amazing teachers."

"Yes," Daisy gushes, artificially. "She's *soooo* smart!"

"Okay, okay," Alma says, and tries to look serious. "So, Jofi – what can I do for you?"

Now, Jofi always relies on spur-of-the-moment inspiration rather than mulling things over, after all, he thinks of himself Earth-side as merely an agent, but the words aren't coming as easily as he thinks they ought. This both frightens and annoys him. More evidence that his foresight is not 20-20.

"Well… let's see… this is going to sound very strange to you, but I swear it's true…"

"Ooo, *interesting!*" Daisy croons, leaves the couch and sits (she knows her yoga-pants becomes her) lotus-style on the floor in front of Jofi, but her charms elude him. Alma gives Daisy a cross look, but she protests innocently over her shoulder. "*What?*"

Alma looks back at Jofi and smiles. "Just take your time and tell us."

Jofi nods and begins. "I had a… a dream," he begins. The girls look at one another with raised eyebrows, hanging on every word. Daisy makes the impatient *go-on-go-on* motion with her hand.

Jofi coughs. And continues "In the dream, I was… directed… to find you, so you could meet my friend Bran." Jofi nods his head, like – *there, I said it.*

"Who's Bran," both girls say at once.

"O… he's my composer friend." Smile and more nods.

"How did you *find* me?" Alma asks, concern for the situation shading her voice.

Jofi doesn't want Matt mentioned here. He feels a little, what… panicked? He inhales deeply. "Well, you aren't local, so it seemed like you might have come here for school."

Daisy asks carefully, "Do you often have dreams like this? You know – telling you what to do?"

"No… it's somewhat unusual. I thought it was a little strange."

"D'ya *think?*" Daisy laughs.

"Jofi," Alma asks, "Is Bran 14, too?"

"O, no!" He laughs. "He's 29."

The girls look horrified. "How is he friends with you?" Alma says. "Sorry, Jofi, but that's really terribly odd!"

"O, we're musicians. Sometimes I play for him."

"Play what," asks Daisy.

"His piano."

"What do you play for him?"

"Bach," Jofi replies. "Bach and Couperin. So far."

The ladies look at one another. Daisy hops up, Alma stands, and they start to walk out of the living room into one of the bedrooms, Alma calling over her shoulder, "Come with us, Jofi."

He follows them into the bedroom that is not a bedroom. There is a music stand, two violin cases, and a newish Steinway 1098 upright. Also, a couple chairs and a bench.

Jofi nods. "Nice."

Alma looks stern. "What we're hearing from you tonight is very strange, Jofi. You need to play Bach for us. And if you can't, then you'll have to leave." Daisy crosses her arms and tries to look like a gangster.

Big smile from Jofi, though. He knows it will be clear sailing now. He looks to Alma. "You must be the violinist because Daisy is the singer."

"How the hell did you know that?" Daisy asks, the gangster façade crumbling.

"You can't even keep it out of your *speaking* voice. You sound more like a singer when you speak than most people do when they sing," Jofi laughs.

"Well," Daisy says, "You're right about me singing. But we need to see you play Bach." The ladies were quite serious.

Jofi has an idea. He turns to Alma. "Do you play any of the Bach sonatas with keyboard accompaniment?"

"Umm. The one in G. I play that. Why?"

"Let's play together."

The young women smile slyly at the strange but beautiful young man. Alma opens one of the violin cases and carefully extracts her treasure, placing on the instrument stand.

Jofi assesses it instantly. "That's a baroque violin. Gut strings and everything."

"And the bow to match!" Alma says, taking that and plying the tension of the horsehair with her thumb.

"No sheet music for you?" Jofi asks.

"No. I know this one. It's my favorite and I practice it. But I just know the last movement by heart. Let's play that."

Jofi nods and sits at the piano.

Alma quietly strums the strings to check tuning. "No music for you, either? I have the keyboard part on the shelf."

"No thanks. I'm good."

"Want to warm up?" Alma asks.

"I'm good."

Jofi is poised. They lock eyes. Alma raises her bow and comes down hard on the string.

Three-and-a-half minutes later, Jofi rises from his bench and joins Daisy in applauding Alma's performance, which was quite fine. She hands her violin to Daisy and embraces Jofi. He is surprised but laughs and hugs her back. Daisy gently takes Alma's bow from her fist, making the hugging easier. Alma stays like this, squeezing him tight. Daisy notes that Alma has closed her eyes.

When she releases him, she takes a step back and takes a deep breath. "Did you enjoy that as much as me?" she asks.

"I enjoyed your performance," he answers, "and I enjoyed very much playing with you. I never played with anyone before."

She senses something. "But…"

"O. It's nothing really."

"But what?"

"Well… As much as I love the piano, I don't like the sound of piano and a solo string playing together. The timbres are like oil and water. A bad mix to my ears."

"O dear." She sounds disappointed. "I wish we had a harpsichord, but-"

"I have one!" Jofi gushes. "Come over and we'll play!"

The ladies laugh. Daisy shakes her head and gives a cunning smile. "Jofi – it's definitely time you started playing with somebody."

That went right over Jofi's head, but Alma got it. *"Daisy..."* she warns.

"What?" she says coyly.

"Never mind. Now, about dinner." Alma announces suddenly.

Jofi brightens and hopes for the best.

"I won't go," she decrees.

"O no," Jofi says all frowny.

"Alone," she clarifies. "I won't go *alone*. I'll go if Daisy can come too."

"That would even be more fun!" Jofi gushes.

"What time will you pick us up?" Alma asks.

"Hey, genius," Daisy says. "He's 14. And how do you even know I *want* to come?"

Alma gives her the *don't be stupid* look.

"Okay," Daisy laughs. "I'll drive." She looks at Jofi. "That work for you, angel-face?"

Jofi is jarred, but just for a second. "Yeah. It does. He asked me to be there at six. Can you get me at 5:45?"

"Yeah. Write down your address on the pad there."

Jofi does as ordered, then just stands there, grinning at the girls like a jackass.

"Bye now," Daisy says with a wave.

"O!" Jofi recovers himself. "Right! See you tomorrow!" And the ladies usher him out, Alma annoyed at Daisy's brusqueness.

Daisy closes the door behind him and turns to Alma. "We don't want to appear too enchanted," she explains.

The ladies laugh.

22

They aren't laughing in the car the next evening on the way to pick up Jofi; they are arguing.

"He wants you to meet this Bran guy, right? That means Jofi and I can get to know one another a little better while you're otherwise engaged," Daisy antagonistically explains.

"He's *14!*" Alma actually yells at her. "And I don't *know* this Bran guy. And I'm almost Jofi's age and you're… just… OLD! And SLUTTY!"

This is too much for Daisy and she breaks out laughing. "Stop screaming! God. I'm only kidding. I'm not trying to snare little Jofi in my evil web. He's just fun and interesting."

"And beautiful."

"*And* beautiful," Daisy readily admits. "But way too young. So, relax… And I am not *slutty!*"

Alma narrows her eyes and looks daggers at her friend. "You better not be trying to pull a fast one."

Daisy laughs. "I'm not. I promise. But it *is* fun to tease you."

"Stop," Alma warns.

"Okay, okay!"

They ride in silence the rest of the way to Barton Hills, and since the ladies rehearsed the ride out of curiosity the day before, they know exactly how to get to the place they dubbed 'Jofi's Fantasy Palace.'

They pull into the long driveway and finally up on the hill and next to the house. They are right on time.

"Am I, like, supposed to honk? or should we go in, or what?" Daisy worries aloud.

Mercifully, Jofi bolts out the door of the garage and tumbles into the back seat all cheerful. He clips the seatbelt and says, "Of course they wanted to meet you, but I told them 'next time.'"

"Ah!" Daisy says as she makes a U-turn in the spacious driveway. "That works!" And she zooms down toward the road. Jofi gives her rough directions to Bran's house and they're off.

It's mostly a quiet ride. Halfway there, Daisy asks Jofi, "You think it'll be okay that we brought a nice bottle of wine with us?"

Jofi chuckles. "Umm… I'm actually completely sure that Bran will not object to this."

"So, what's he cooking?" Alma asks. "Do you know? Or is it a surprise?"

"Actually, heh-heh, the two of *you* are the surprise."

"What?!" the ladies cry in unison. Alma turns in her seat to face Jofi. "He doesn't know we're coming with you?!"

"Uh, no." Jofi answers sheepishly, but the girls are waiting for some explanation. "Umm… I didn't want him to have a chance to… question my judgment." Then he gives one of those smiles and nods that he thinks shows that he summed things up pretty darn well there.

Daisy shakes her head. "O God…"

"Well, Jofi…" Alma fishes for the words. "Besides not being prepared to receive the two of us, what if he didn't make enough food for four?"

"Ah! Well! Here's the thing about that," Jofi explains. "Ah… Bran doesn't cook. I'm not sure if his kitchen has ever exactly been used for that purpose. I mean… ever." He clears his throat and continues. "He was going to order a pizza or Chinese or something like that."

"O dear," Alma turns back in her seat and stares ahead at the road. "What have we gotten ourselves into?"

Daisy pats Alma's jean-covered thigh. "It's an interesting situation. Let's just relax and go with it."

Typical Daisy, Alma thinks and nods in surrender.

Bran is befuddled. He holds the screen door open, and the three guests step in. He closes both doors and turns. "Well. This *is* a surprise."

"We thought he told you," Daisy says, with an accusing finger-point at Jofi.

Bran nods. He points to the big couch. "Please have a seat."

Alma hands him the wine. Bran takes it and looks at the label. His eyebrows jump, and he smiles broadly. "I'm Bran," he announces.

Jofi makes the introductions, the girls sit, and Bran asks to see Jofi alone for a minute. Everyone understands.

Once in Bran's bedroom, out of earshot, Bran seizes Jofi by the shoulders. "Dude!" he whispers frantically. Jofi braces for the scolding. "Those chicks are so fucking hot I think my eyeballs just melted. *What the fuck!?*"

"Are you happy or sad?" confused Jofi whispers back.

"Well… they're a little youngish… *but that's okay!*"

Jofi nods. "Happy then. Good."

"How did you…" Bran reconsiders his line of interrogation and figures the hell with it. "Nevermind. Let's go back in." They move to go but Bran detains Jofi urgently with a most serious face. "Is one of them chicks yours?"

"No. Neither," Jofi whispers. "Just new friends. I asked them to come with me. And that's okay, right?"

"Well," Bran pumps his eyebrows obscenely and mumbles, "let's go find out!"

It might have been Bran discovering that Alma is still 17 years-old (and therefore legally a minor in the great state of Michigan) that made Daisy the more appealing consort for Bran that evening, and the chemistry was there. As pretty and pert as he notes Alma to be, Daisy, with her long black hair, tall stature, high cheek-bones and killer long legs in a dress just *barely* too short is more to his type. Daisy is an obvious Scandinavian-type while Alma looks like your all-American girl-next-door. And temperamentally? No contest there.

After an hour or so of get-acquainted time, Alma and Jofi are sitting close together on the couch, *trying* to talk, almost touching; Daisy and Bran are dancing their asses off in front of them. "YOU SAY BRAN IS A COMPOSER?" Alma hollers through the loud rock 'n' roll roaring from Bran's huge homemade speakers.

"NOBODY BETTER. TOTALLY REFINED," Jofi yells back.

"IF HE'S SO REFINED THEN WHY ARE WE LISTENING TO A SCRATCHY LED ZEPPELIN RECORD SO LOUD THAT MY EARS ARE STARTING TO HURT?" (Oh yeah – Bran loves him some bitchin' vinyl.)

"YES. IT'S TERRIBLY LOUD," Jofi yells back.

Alma starts to laugh. Jofi inquires with a look. She yells out, "PLUS, MR. REFINEMENT LOOKS LIKE A GIANT MONKEY THAT SOMEONE IS SHOCKING WITH A CATTLE-PROD!"

Okay, she yelled that too loudly. Bran stops dancing and gives Alma a look that says he's been hurt to his very core. The record ending, the silence is now just as deafening.

"O my god *I'm so sorry!*" blushing Alma pleads with her hand to her mouth. "You weren't supposed to hear that!"

Bran's phony hurt look changes into a mad wide-eye grin and then to hysterical laughter, and he now looks like a giant monkey in a fit of lunacy. Bran suddenly recovers and appears for a moment deep in thought, then he exclaims, "Everybody likes Black Sabbath, right?" and he starts to rummage through his record shelf. Jofi notes the look of sheer horror on the ladies faces.

"Wait wait wait…" Jofi says. "Maybe we should talk about dinner. You know? It's almost nine. These ladies are here for *dinner*, Bran. Remember?"

Bran snaps out of it. "Hell yeah! Of course. Let's take a break! Pizza or Chinese?" he declaims grandly as if laying the entire palette of the culinary world at their feet. "The ladies decide! More wine, anybody?"

There is more wine and Jofi has some. He had always abstained but this night he joins in, the giggles being the obvious effect on him. Bran did not bring out the reefer, frightened enough of entertaining a 17 year-old girl in his own home, not to mention 14 year-old Jofi. He can imagine the scene: *I know he's legally a child, but he acts just like an adult… your honor.*

They talk and drink (cheap red from Bran's cupboard) and get acquainted, and the food has just arrived. The ladies decided pizza was the way to go – vegetarian for the two youngsters while Bran and Daisy indulge their omnivore pleasure with a pie full of yummy meat and grease. "For dancing energy," Bran explains earnestly through a full mouth.

After dinner the talk continues. Bran's threat to play more records hovers over them like the Sword of Damocles.

Bran discovers: that Jofi is a bigger mystery than ever, what with his unknown prowess snaring hot chicks! What is up with that boy? Also that Alma is a sweet but wallflowery girl who is a violinist of alleged rare ability with her early post-grad scholarship to the university music school. She looks at Jofi like a puppy adoring her master, but Jofi is aloof. Finally, that Daisy chick is the most amazing woman he has ever been with. She's hot, smart, and a great dancer, and is neither afraid of, nor repulsed by him. *Big* points for that. He, like Jofi, knows Daisy is a singer just by listening to her speak, but she won't sing for him. At least not tonight. Bashful. That's cute.

Daisy discovers: that Bran is hot and manly in a way that is out of style these days. He's fearless and sincere, and good looking under all that hair and beard and those worn-out clothes. His openness is charming. She knows he likes her. She can sense her spell working in him and he knows that she knows and that's all right. He welcomes and delights in her womanliness and she feels it with him as with no other in her past, even on such brief acquaintance. She feels safe with him. She knows Bran's a composer, but he won't show or play her any of his music. At least not tonight. Bashful. That's cute. She likes Jofi a lot. She has never been around such a perfectly beautiful, guileless – and clueless – male. He seems a little confused about how well she and Bran get on and seems a little unsettled at the heat that she and Bran generate in a room. It's as if he's never encountered such a thing. Finally, she wishes Alma would heat up a little to Jofi herself instead of just pining after him so. *She is so not like me,* she thinks. *Put your head on his shoulder. Hold his hand. Do something!*

Alma discovers: She likes Bran. He's friendly, wild, attractive and funny but scary. And Jofi? Omygod she *loves* Jofi. All uppercase italic boldface underlined blood-red 48-point fancy type with hand-colored hearts popping all over LOVES Jofi. She's never known or seen anyone, male or female, more completely beautiful and not just physically. He's brilliant and kind and sweet and omygod when he smiles at her, her heart spills over. She will never love anyone else ever again and *I want him to touch me.* Finally, she thinks Daisy is acting ridiculous and drunk and slutty the way she's just *throwing* herself at this wildman she barely knows.

Jofi discovers: that he likes the wine, and it makes him wonder how far he is sinking into human-ness. He feels that his true nature is becoming obscured the longer he stays earthbound. He makes a silent vow: *no more wine.* There is nothing more 'of the earth' than wine and he must not sink down into matter any further than he can avoid. He is very confused about the women. He was sure that Alma was meant for Bran, to stabilize him, temper him, and fire pride into his abilities, but Alma is like a frightened doe around him, and Bran's attitude toward her is no more than simple friendliness. But this Daisy woman! Bran seems *obsessed.* And she fans his fires, which seems like the opposite of what he needs. *So, I got this wrong, too,* he thinks. *It looks like Daisy is the girl for Bran.* He is consoled by the fact that none of this would be happening if he had not found Alma in the first place. And finally, what *about* Alma? He senses that she wants from him what he can never give her. Jofi feels tenderness and joy when he's around her, and he wonders what role, if any, she has been assigned in his own life. That he knows not the answer to this frustrates him more than anything has. His conundrum is this: *He cannot 'love' her; he will not hurt her.* Those are absolutes. Seemingly irreconcilable.

It's almost 10:30. Bran has a gas fireplace that he has never before used – he deems it a fake and he hates fakes – but the ladies have prevailed upon him to turn it on. That accomplished, he dims the lights. *Four on a couch,* he observes. He notes that Jofi, who sits on the far-left seat of the couch, has Alma snuggled beside him with her head resting on Jofi's shoulder. *Jofi looks a little stiff,* Bran notes, *but not in the good way.* He chuckles to himself. He notes Daisy has left her chair and is now sitting next to Alma, and she pats the remaining couch space next to her in a beckoning way. Bran seems eager to oblige, but he stops mid-stride and turns.

The horror that Bran's three guests feel when he goes to his shelf and starts to riffle through his old LPs turns out to be entirely unnecessary. He fingers an old Sinatra album, *Only the Lonely.* It's clear when the needle drops that this is make-out music plain and simple (as he turns the volume dial down from 11 to 3), but Bran steps to the couch and holds out his hand to Daisy, she rises with a smile and exaggerated grace, and they begin to dance. Real slow… they melt into one another.

Alma looks hopefully at Jofi. He smiles and obliges her, and they join the other pair on the floor, dancing close. Jofi dances well, with an Angel's grace. So does Alma. They 'fit.' Halfway through the song, bold Alma lets go of Jofi's left hand and puts it around his neck to join her other hand, and she presses against him, rocking gracefully to Jofi's lead. Alma is wrapped in bliss and Jofi indulges her courteously. He is not equipped to enjoy this quite the same way as she is enjoying it. He's troubled. *Where does this lead?*

The song over, they retreat to the couch for more quiet talk. Jofi is relieved, but after a few minutes he and Alma note with alarm that Bran and Daisy are 'making out.' Alma, who is (lucky for Jofi) a Good Girl and not prepared to go bolting recklessly down the Road to Hell quite so soon, knocks her knee against Daisy's thigh, hoping that this simple gesture will jar Daisy's brain loose enough to reconsider the course of the evening. It works. Daisy turns her head and looks ascowl at her friend, but she gets the message. She turns back to Bran and the two of them laugh. Daisy reluctantly rises from her very comfortable little snuggle nest.

"It's getting late," she says.

"I guess…" disappointed Bran says.

Jofi and Alma rise, and goodbyes are said, not without contact information shared among those lacking. Bran hugs Alma a nice goodbye; he *kisses* Daisy – that takes a few moments.

Alma has to drive; Daisy is too buzzed.

23

The next morning Daisy meets Alma for coffee at the café. Naturally, there is a single topic slated for discussion. Both ladies had a great time and look forward to more meetings with their new fellas, both hoping that their phones ring soon with more invitations.

Daisy is a little hungover, and Alma has no sympathy, but she mentions nothing about Daisy's 'slutty' behavior. She is too enchanted at her own magical encounter with Jofi. Nothing can touch her buzz that morning. Except, of course, Daisy in a teasing mood.

"You know, you need to encourage Jofi a little bit. He's a little clueless. Lose the jeans for a skirt. Show him a little leg next time," Daisy purrs.

Alma is already on her guard. "I don't need you to critique my love life," she says.

"Why don't I take a shot at him and you can observe how it's properly done?" nasty Daisy presses.

Alma slams her hand down hard on the table. "Daisy Lee Saarinen! If you so much as *touch* Jofi, *I swear to God I will rip your fingernails out with pliers, and then…* AND THEN STAB YOU IN THE EYE WITH A PENCIL!"

Daisy is shocked. Actually, everyone in the café is shocked. Alma, half out of her seat, is red in the face and still glaring at her friend.

Daisy lowers her head and gulps. "Who are you and what have you done with my friend Alma?"

"*Understand?*" Alma seethes.

"I was just teasing! And yes – I understand. Sheesh!"

And the phones *did* ring, bringing delightful, even impatient, proposals to both women, that very same day.

While the ladies were having their morning coffee, Bran had called Jofi early and asked him to stop by. Jofi wondered why Bran might not stop by Jofi's house instead – meet the parents, check out the music room, that sort of thing. Bran promised to do so "next time," but assured Jofi that they must meet that morning to "talk about the chick situation." Jofi agreed and his mom dropped him off on her way to her morning exercise.

Matchmaker Jofi was amused at how taken Bran was with Daisy. They both liked the idea of getting the foursome together again as soon as possible, "before the buzz wears off," as Bran delicately put it. So Jofi pressed the idea of them all going to Jofi's house to have dinner some night the next week, perhaps to "make some music together," though Bran and Jofi might interpret that phrase differently. They would shoot for next Wednesday evening, nine nights hence. They called the womenfolk as soon as they had made up the grand plan, and after confirmation calls back and forth, both ladies agreed that they would all meet at Jofi's house at six next Wednesday.

24

Jofi decided to walk home from Bran's house. This was a nearly ten-mile hike, but Jofi had nothing planned that day and it was a lovely fall morning. He had not gotten far when he encountered what appeared to be a priest on his morning constitutional coming the other way. Jofi nods in greeting.

The priest passes Jofi, stops and turns. "Pardon me. Jofi? Jofi Fischer?"

Jofi turns and sees a thin fellow in a Catholic priest collar under a wool sweater. He wears glasses with large round lenses and sports a mustache above his smile. A pleasant face. A trusting face that inspires trust.

Jofi nods. "Yes. I'm Jofi."

"Father Preston Holt," the man says, offering Jofi his hand. Jofi takes it.

"How do you do. How do you know me?" Jofi asks, releasing his hand.

"Well, it seems that word is getting around about your keyboard skills."

"Really? I always thought that I kept all that pretty much private."

"Well now… you know how people are. Sometimes a light so bright is hard to hide under a bushel."

Jofi thinks, *Bran? The ladies? My Mom or Dad? One of their friends?*

"Actually," the priest continues, "it's most providential that I should run into you this way."

"How so?"

"There is another who would like to meet you and discuss your gifts. It's he who asked me if you might be a member of the parish so that I could make the introductions."

"Another?"

"A very close acquaintance. He's very powerful in his discipline. In fact, he's staying for a time at the rectory with us and is there as we speak. The way he talks about you… it's as if he truly *needs* to see you." He looks at his watch. "You know, we're only a few blocks from the church. Would you indulge me? I know this is all so sudden, but surely you must be a little curious by now!"

Jofi considers all this, but there is something… not quite… right… about all this. "How did you know what I even *look* like?" he asks the priest. "And… and where I would be this morning?"

"Ah! Umm, Ahri – that's his name, Ahri – showed me a picture. You are quite unmistakable, you know!"

"But how did you know-"

"Coincidence. Providence! As I said. I often walk here about this time, but I have never run into you before. This must not be your routine. Correct?"

Jofi nods. "That's true… but I don't know how he could possibly have a *picture* of me."

The priest points. "Let's just pop over right now and find out. Surely your curiosity is piqued! And I may be doing both of you a good turn today, bringing you together."

This priest, Jofi thinks, *could have been a salesman. He missed his calling.* But his curiosity has indeed gotten the better of him and he agrees to visit the parish rectory, despite the feeling that there is something very strange going on. Or maybe *because* of it.

It only takes a few minutes to attain the rectory steps, and as Fr. Holt unlocks the front door he begins to sniffle. He turns to Jofi with tears in his eyes.

"Allergies!" he explains.

It is instead a great sadness that Jofi perceives in the priest's aura, a quick decay from the *bonhomie* that greeted him short minutes ago. Jofi is now on his guard but does not regret this meeting. He knows it will be important.

Fr. Holt strides briskly down the hallway, unlocks his office and ushers Jofi inside, then points him to the padded chair across from the priest's seat at his desk. Jofi sits. Preston Holt remains standing next to Jofi, now wearing a look of inexpressible sadness.

He begins to blubber and weep freely, all the while staring intently at Jofi, and eventually falls to his knees in an agony of exhausted grief. He leans forward and hugs onto both of Jofi's calves in a desperate embrace.

"Jophiel!" he cries out. "O blessèd Jophiel. Angel of the Beauty of God – forgive me, forgive me, forgive me…" His body is wracked by sobs. Jofi leans over, closes his eyes and lays his hand on top of the priest's head. This has an instant calming effect.

"Preston, please rise up and go sit in your chair. Be calm now," he whispers to the priest, who slowly does as Jofi bids him, sitting now and pulling tissues from the box, wiping tears and snot from his face as he attempts to compose himself. He cannot look at Jofi. Instead, he closes his eyes and takes deep breaths, trying to compose himself.

"Preston," Jofi says in a quiet voice. "Where is this Ahri fellow you've been telling me about?"

The priest opens his eyes and looks at Jofi with a pleading face and says, "It's not me. Please know it's not me and that I can't help it."

"Okay… but, where is he?"

The priest blinks and smiles, takes a deep breath and says in a strong, deep voice full of strength and vigor. "Ah. The celebrated Jophiel."

Jofi looks hard at Fr. Holt and pulls his head back in surprise and recognition. He sees the same face, but it could not be more different.

"You…" Jofi whispers.

"But not Jophiel *really*, eh? Actually, it's Jofi! Good old 'Jofi'," the man says and laughs good-naturedly.

"So, who are *you* this time?" Jofi asks. "'Ahri' is it? You're even more encumbered now than I am… so don't get smug."

"Consider! Both of us, on Earth, in time, at the *same* time, in bodies. Just doing our duties."

"You're hurting your host. Needless, stupid suffering you inflict on him. I sense he'll try to kill himself soon."

"You mean Sniveler? He's tried a dozen times already. I won't let him succeed."

"Sniveler?"

"You've met him. Good name, no?"

"Out of morbid curiosity, how did you pick him?"

"He invited me in!" Ahri laughs. "In his seminary days, he and his pals would try to channel spirits. Very 'new age.' Very

bold and audacious! Very 'against the rules.' Those stupid boys had no idea what they were playing with. I had to come in one way or the other, and it's so much nicer, and cleaner, to be *invited.*"

"So, you gave him his wish." Jofi hangs his head in disgust. "What are you doing here? What do you want?"

"The same as you – to control a situation of grave urgency."

"I was thinking this would be more up Lucifer's alley."

Ahri brushes that away. "Those spirits have been eclipsed. They had a long roll of the dice! It's our time now. Of course, we work together, and we both serve the same master, but it's time for humanity to learn what *we* on the other end of the spectrum have to offer."

"He is the tempter; you are the father of lies. At bottom, are you really that different?"

"The Bringer of Light and his crew have brought the opposite of what *we* need to bring to humanity, and what humanity needs us to bring forth. Lucifer's crew was all about hyperactivity and unification, a unified language, perfection in speaking and thinking, the cultivation of fantasy, illusion, superstition, a soaring imagination. They were all about ultimate mental flexibility, the wisdom of the spirit dragging humans away from the Earth and into the cosmos before their time. Not us. We're here to cure all that. Very much so."

Jofi snickers. "And bring what instead? Amoral, atheistic, mechanistic materialism."

"There's more to it than that view," Ahri objects.

"Sure. You like lists. Here's one for you. The deadening of aesthetic, the worship of technology, the deification of science, convincing humans that they're nothing but higher animals, that there's no spiritual nature in man, that we have no responsibility for one another, that the universe is nothing more than a great machine. That men and women should be proving things in research papers instead of experiencing them, sowing conflicts between groups and getting them to attack each other, believing that all they need to provide for themselves are economic and material needs. You're for rabid sectarianism and believing that passing tests is the same as education. You have fostered the creation of a digital-ego, drowning in data, that appears to relate to other human egos, but is, in fact, a complete mirage of one's *true* ego – please… stop me if I'm missing something."

Ahri laughs heartily. "Well now, that *was* quite a litany."

"I could go on," Jofi says. "But mainly your mission is to materialize, densify, darken, silence, and kill the living spirit, and promote the illusion, the *lie*, that matter is the only reality. Society is falling apart at the seams. Playing right into your hands."

Ahri raises his hand. "Now, now. Let us go back to our esteemed colleague and *his* historical influence. Lucifer would say that matter didn't matter! He and his crew are too hot, too flighty, too unstable; he inspires human fanaticism, false mysticism, hot-bloodedness, and the tendency to flee earthly reality for hallucinatory pleasures.

"We are the antidote to all of that! We bring mankind back down to Earth, where they belong, to be more productive. You know as well as I that there awaits an age of tech-nological mastery that we are just now bringing to fruition that will harness powers so great that it will be indistinguish-able from magic. We are what mankind *wants*. Humankind is rolling out the welcome mat and they are *eager*. We will banish ignorance and superstition. The current unrest will worsen. Surely you know this. The solution to the problem is law-and-order! We'll call it, 'Safety through Sacrifice.' Catchy, no?"

"Humanity is a great prize. You want complete power over it. That's pretty much it isn't it? Shorn of all the pretty speech."

Ahri looks annoyed. He studies Jofi. "Let's get down to business, shall we?"

"Agreed."

"You will never find Sam Morgan," Ahri says. Jofi grits his teeth and looks at Ahri as if he wants to kill him where he sits. "And in your heart, you know I'm right." He smiles malignantly. He's enjoying this. "You will fail. You *have* failed."

"I found Bran. And Alma."

"Part of your mission has so far been successful, I admit, but not even half, and Englander's work has not yet come to fruition, and I am here to tell you that it *shall not.*"

"You know he's writing the work."

"I also know that he has barely begun, and there is many a slip between the cup and the lip. Case in point: that new whore of his is quite the distraction! And even allowing for the small chance that he *may* finish it – or *live* to finish it – he would still have to get it performed. And more importantly, noticed. Surely you will admit that the odds are very much in my favor here."

"I admit nothing of the kind."

Ahri stretches and sighs. "But mainly you know that Englander's accomplishment without Sam Morgan is an empty feat. Englander is just a sideshow. Morgan is the main event and you, Jophiel – Angel of the Beauty of the Eternal Presence, were assigned to *personally* bring them together. *And you have failed.* For you know in your heart that you shall never find him. That much of the future is clear to both of us *and you can feel it.*"

"You've already made that point and you're beginning to bore me," Jofi says with a shot of irritation, the sort that comes when someone you don't like tells you something you know is true. "Are we done here or is there something else we should discuss."

Ahri pretends to think a moment. "No. I think we're done here. But we will meet again, as you well know. In our special arena of battle." He smiles the smile of the victor.

Jofi rises. "Oh. Before I go, there *is* one minor issue."

"And? What might that be?"

"I'm taking Sniveler away from you."

Ahri laughs. "You can't. He's mine."

"He'll still be your host. But you'll have to change his name when I'm done with him."

Ahri is suddenly very annoyed. Doesn't even try to hide it. "That is *very* unsporting of you, Jophiel. It took me a long time to train him properly. As a courtesy to a colleague why not let it alone, eh?"

"It will take me scant minutes to undo your work. Why not go away now so I can get started? You must be fatigued. Let him through."

"I will *not.*"

"I'll summon him forth. I'll call him through."

"I'll fight you!"

"You'll lose. You're fatigued. I can feel it. That's one advantage to *having* a body over just renting one, like you do. Imagine the embarrassment when I rip him back through your feeble resistance." Now it's Jofi's turn to smile.

Ahri's face is a mask of rage. "The greater embarrassment is waiting for *you*, Jophiel, when I thwart you and send you back to your master as the pathetic failure you are." At this Ahri closes his angry eyes and seethes. "You on the other side are such *fools*. How can you take joy in winning a war when you lose all the battles?"

When the being on the chair opens his eyes again, seconds later, Ahri is gone and Jofi is again looking at Sniveler, now pathetically trying to get his bearings in his body once again. He seems smaller, and his hair looks greasy, though nothing has actually changed.

Jofi is not gentle with him. "He calls you 'Sniveler.'"

"And he's right," Fr. Holt breathes. He can't look at Jofi. "I lied to you. An Angel of God. I betrayed you. At least Judas was able to hang himself."

"Judas was important. You, Preston Holt, are also important."

Holt looks up, confused.

"The Great Mystery could never have been consummated without Judas," Jofi explains. "Too many of those who call themselves Christians would think to look for Judas in what they call hell, but they would not find him there. He did his job perfectly. I need you to do your job just as well."

The priest starts crying again but Jofi puts a stop to that. "STOP THAT INFERNAL BLUBBERING!" he roars. Holt stops instantly, terrified at Jofi's sudden fierce aspect. "The sure way for you to fail in your role is to keep on with your damn *sniveling. Never again! Do you understand me?*"

Preston can only nod assent, so frozen in fear is he, being blasted so by a furious Angel.

Jofi gets quieter now, leans forward, says almost soothingly, "Listen to me: *you have been chosen for this.* You have lifetimes of offense after offense against your own soul as it tries to align itself to the good and the true while you worked against it, culminating in *this* lifetime when you summoned a demon *into your own tabernacle! You invited it!*"

The suffering priest closes his eyes and whispers, "How many times have I hated myself for that act."

"Stop hating yourself and look forward. This is a hard lifetime of purification for you. If you acquit yourself well, you'll take your place among the righteous; if you fail, then what you experience here will pale compared to what awaits you."

The priest is now calm, looking at Jofi with hope beginning to stir in his eyes and heart, something he has not felt in decades.

"Become an aide to me and save yourself," Jofi says. He rises from his chair and goes around the desk. Holt swivels to face him. Jofi places his hand on top of the priest's head and says softly, "Cease your groveling to that foul spirit that has you in thrall. This is temporary. He can't *really* hurt you. Only *you* can hurt you – by letting yourself be mastered by hopelessness and fear. When your mission is complete you will never again be bothered by such as this. Until then, know your importance; be watchful; carry your cross with dignity, and know that, even through your travails, your soul is safe from harm, and that we are watching you."

Tears fall from Preston's eyes, he wipes them away quickly and hides his face. Jofi laughs softly. "Don't hide. Tears of joy are permitted." Preston turns his face back to the Angel and smiles.

"But one last thing," Jofi warns gravely. "No more suicide attempts. If you find a way to die Ahri will infect another, and we do not want that. Too unpredictable. This is *your* role and you *will* see it through."

Jofi bends forward and Fr. Preston Holt feels an Angel's own kiss on the top of his head. When Jofi unbends the priest rises from his chair. It turns out he is actually taller than Jofi by a couple of inches, but he has not stood up straight in years. His *visage* is now as dissimilar to his old self as it is from his possessed self. There is dignity in his features and a touch of fire in his eyes.

Jofi stands back and takes a good look. He nods. "That's more like it."

Holts says, simply, "Thank you, Jophiel."

Jofi smiles. "When Ahri returns he's going to be very, very angry."

At that, they both break out into the relief of laughter.

25

Young Eric is the first to the front door when the bell rings. He gives the heavy old door a good yank, it opens, and he looks up. "Who are you?" he inquires at the hairy man.

"Hi there. I'm Bran. And you are?"

"You're *Bran?*" Eric says with wide eyes. "You're the drunk guy who gets in barfights! Jofi told us that you-"

"ERIC!" That's Mom, who for some reason never likes Eric to answer the door. She grabs him by his collar and pulls him out of the doorway. He giggles. She glares at him for a moment and he scurries away then she turns to Bran and puts on her 'charming' smile. Never fails.

Bran nods. "Ms. Fischer. Hi. I'm Bran." He holds out his hand.

She takes it. "Please, call me Emma, Bran. So nice to meet you."

"Emma. Umm…" He offers her the bottle from his other hand, she relieves him of it, thanks him and ushers him in. A warm night, so no coats.

Bran enters the great room and spies Jofi and the two ladies arrayed about the intimate sitting circle in the big room, fireplace all aglow. Bran waves and smiles his hellos. In walks Matt from the kitchen with Eric trailing behind humming to himself.

"You must be Bran," Matt says heartily, and they shake on it. "I'm Matt. Welcome. This monster is Eric." He waves and smiles impishly.

"Yes!" pipes Bran. "We met."

Now all seated and served, pleasant small-talk follows which the ladies do well, but Jofi and Bran mostly just listen. Bran especially is clearly not comfortable with polite chatter but answers direct questions efficiently and with a discreet civility that Jofi and the ladies find quietly amusing, knowing him as they do. The only sign of the Bran they know being present is that he drains his wineglass too briskly compared to the others (hostess Emma is quick with the refills), and his attempt at 'dressing up' the ladies especially find endearingly inept.

But those ladies, now, they do look *fine*. Bran and Matt are frankly dazzled by their presence, Jofi – not so much. Emma and Daisy are basking all night in the wordless but obvious appreciation, and though Alma tries to hide it, she seems a little blue. She so wants Jofi to notice and appreciate her in that special way, and though he is pleasant, even attentive to her in conversation and as her host, she feels no charge from Jofi, yet she could hardly be more receptive.

Dinner is one of those difficult affairs for even a good cook – to make food that carnivores and vegetarians alike will delight in. But Emma has gotten pretty good at it. There is animal flesh on the menu most evenings at the Fischer home (Jofi doesn't care; he eats around it), but with Alma sharing

Jofi's vegetarian tendencies, there is none tonight. It is a tasty feast, nonetheless.

At dinner, both Matt and Emma are anxious to do a little probing into their guests' history and aims. Matt is curious about why Jofi has become involved with these three; Emma is most observant regarding matters of the heart, and she senses trouble on the horizon for Jofi and impending heartbreak for Alma.

Matt eventually asks, "So Bran, that head injury of yours. That all healed up?" What Bran hears is, *'You crazy fucking drunk, what the hell is wrong with you and why do you want to hang out with my 14 year-old?'*

"Heh-heh, yes. That's all better, thanks." Bran knows he needs to do this right. "Just so you know, that's the first and only time anything like that has ever happened to me. I usually keep pretty much to myself, but I got fired from the radio station that morning. I just sorta… lost it."

Matt looks at Bran and smiles. "I've 'lost it' a few times myself." They both laugh sincerely. Matt continues. "Did you find yourself again? That's the only important thing."

"I did," Bran nods. "Mainly with the help of your son. Actually." All chatting at the table ceases. The three ladies are especially all ears.

Bran's eyebrows go up and he looks around the table at the expectant faces.

"Umm… musically. Surely you know what a genius Jofi is."

Matt nods. "We do. And don't play chess with him."

"I don't know how or why he found me, or how he can do what he does…"

"We've learned to just roll with that sort of thing around here," Matt says. "We all hope to know more someday."

"Well… anyway, I was at a crossroads, I guess you could say, in my life. As a composer. Which is all I'm good for. And Jofi… got me back on track. In other areas, too. Because… I have a reason to do what I need to do now. With his gifts… he showed me how to do… what I need to do."

116

Jofi is human enough to blush, with all eyes on him, admirably. Daisy, sitting next to Bran, leans over and kisses Bran on the cheek. Now it's a regular blush-fest. Matt mercifully breaks it up by rising noisily and taking wine orders for the next course.

The drinks refreshed, and a new course laid before them, Emma, curious about the ladies, asks how they support themselves. Daisy opens her mouth to answers first, but Alma pipes up, "Daisy is an heiress."

Now, Daisy isn't much of a blusher, and laughs gaily at Alma's description. Bran was bringing a forkful of risotto to his mouth and stops halfway, wondering did he actually hear that correctly. Fork still hovering, he casts a slow sideglance at Daisy.

Eric points at Bran and laughs. "Bran didn't know!" he cries.

"Eric, shut up, please," Emma says nicely to her boy. He pouts and obeys.

"Really." Matt says to Daisy. "Tell us about that."

She says simply, "Do you remember Linna, the cellphone company in Finland?"

"Of course," Matt says. "Microsoft bought it some years ago."

"Right. My father owned it before it went public."

Matt nods appreciatively. "Well! That certainly must keep the wolf from the door."

"Were you born in Finland?" Emma asks.

"No. I was born in America. My family moved to Massachusetts when my mom was pregnant with me. We have many family members in the Upper Peninsula – more than we do in Finland, actually – and we were always visiting Michigan. Houghton is where I met Alma. And I decided that Ann Arbor is where I wanted to go to music school."

Bran has been staring at Daisy with a look of disbelief. "Wow," he says.

Daisy smiles. "Bran is wondering why I want to hang around with *him* instead of the fancy rich boys."

Everyone laughs, even Bran, who at the moment really is wondering exactly that. Well, not everyone laughs. Daisy looks quite serious now. She rubs the top of Bran's head as one would a dog's. "He's an amazing man. That's why." The laughter stops. "Jofi knows," she says. She looks at Jofi and gives him a smile.

"He is very much an amazing man," Jofi affirms. Jofi is pretty sure that the pair has been seeing one another a few times over the past week. This could not be just their second meeting.

"And you, Alma," Emma asks. "Do you work or just go to school?"

"I just go to music school. I'm not an heiress but my dad has saved to put me through college." Alma darkens a bit. "I think he wishes I picked something other than violin, but my mom would have been glad. She died when I was 15."

"I'm sorry, dear, that must have been so hard," Emma says, and after a pause, "I thought you had a scholarship?"

"I do! So, my dad's support goes for living. School is paid for by the scholarship."

"So, you're going to pursue the violin as a career?" Matt asks.

"Yep," Alma replies.

Matt looks at Daisy. "And you will pursue singing?"

"I will," Daisy says, adding confidently with a little smile, "I'm pretty good."

Bran agrees. "She sure is. We've been making music together at my house lots for the past week or so." (*I bet you have,* thinks Alma to herself.) "She has a unique voice. I accompany her on the piano, but I was always wishing Jofi was playing instead. That would be quite a matchup."

Jofi asks, "Alma, did you bring a violin tonight?"

"I brought both the baroque violin *and* my new one. They're in the car. I thought I might hear your harpsichord," she says with restrained enthusiasm. "That would be a huge treat."

Jofi is for once this night filled with enthusiasm himself, something he can really sink his teeth into, though Alma wishes fervently that that something was her.

And so there was much top-level music-making that night, an entire mini-festival with much variety.

All the guests are enchanted at the opportunity to meet Jofi's Hubbard-made double-keyboard harpsichord. They *oooo* and *awww* over it and cajole Jofi into opening the festivities with some appropriate prestidigitation. "Play Bach," Bran orders, then, remembering how Jofi cares not for being ordered about this way adds, "pretty please."

Jofi laughs and complies, sitting and wiggling his butt into a comfortable position *(just like when he was baby,* Emma observes) and launches into the *French Suite No. 5.* The sprightly work concludes with a jiggy fugue that turns the theme upside down, yet it all sounds so artless and natural. It is pure fun – the perfect overture. Nobody sits; all stand listening intently and observing Jofi's stunning self as he plays – a picture of physical perfection in perfect repose – and beholding the uncommon splendor of his instrument.

Daisy has never sung with a harpsichord accompanying her and is eager to do so tonight. She asks Jofi if he possibly has the keyboard reduction to the score of Henry Purcell's *Dido's Lament* in his awesome library. He does not, but he'll be damned before he disappoints Daisy. What he is considering is dangerous to do, even in front of these, his closest friends and family. It is far beyond a mere prodigy's achievement.

He reconsiders yet decides to go for it. "I've read the orchestral score to the opera it's from, so-"

"That's okay," Daisy says. "I can pick something else."

"No, no. I can distill a harpsichord accompaniment from what I recall of the orchestra score I read at the library. It'll be fine," he assures her.

Bran, Daisy, and Alma share disbelieving glances with one another. Bran breaks the silence. He doesn't understand, but he knows Jofi. "Dude… go for it."

Daisy is a little discombobulated, glares at Bran as if he's crazy, but finally looks at Jofi and nods that she's ready. Jofi smiles and plays an introduction.

A seasoned listener, an expert, a connoisseur, would have thought that the two had performed this together a hundred times. There is no awareness of technique or arrangement here – it is so transparent and assured – Dido's heartbreak in the throes of her apocalyptic romance is all that any listener could possibly think about or feel.

When they finish there is no applause, just a reverent stillness. Then something happens to Daisy that as an artist has never happened to her before. She touches Jofi on his shoulder, looking unsteady, then bursts into tears. Jofi rises in reflex, as if in rescue and she slumps into his arms. *It is as if she actually were Dido herself and has only this moment realized that Aeneas has truly abandoned her, and suicide is her only remedy.* She has sung this dozens of times, a specialty of hers, yet had never truly sounded its depths until this very minute.

It takes Daisy more than a moment to recover. She is quite embarrassed about it all, and this from a woman who doesn't easily get this way. Matt pours everyone a little Cognac, and that seems to brace Daisy a bit, enough to laugh at herself, but no one else laughs. They praise her exquisite performance. Bran embraces Daisy and looks over her shoulder at Jofi, fully understanding the profound nature of his achievement, nods, and smiles. Jofi gets it. They are grateful to one another.

Alma is busy fiddling with her fiddle, making sure the finicky baroque instrument is in tune and ready to roll, deciding not to replace her E-string and hoping she chose correctly.

"Do you know Corelli's sonata *La Folia?*" she asks Jofi, strumming the strings idly with her left hand.

"O! That's an awesome choice," Jofi says.

"It sorta requires a bass instrument with the keyboard, though," Alma ventures with a grimace.

Jofi smiles slyly. "Nahhh…"

Everyone laughs. They all have a strong feeling that Jofi can work around the challenge just fine, and they're right about that.

This 'sonata' is actually a set of the most ingenious variations on a majestic and quite plastic (in a good way) theme. Alma bends it, she shapes it, she is grave then serene, she noodles it and she doodles it, she rushes and caresses it. But at no time, as with every other performance all night long, is the brilliance of her technique ever even noticeable – only the music. There is *much* gay applause after this one.

That's how it is with musicians at this lofty level. Most musicians have poor technique, others only fair; a few have good technical skills. But there are two levels of virtuosity: some players dazzle you with their technique – all very thrilling; but the very best flaunt no technical skills whatsoever – they simply let the music speak without any discernable effort at all on their part.

Bran asks Daisy if she would like to sing another piece before Alma switches from her baroque violin and Jofi exchanges the harpsichord for the piano in the music room. She declines gracefully. Daisy, formidable young woman that she is, has still not sufficiently recovered from her total immersion into the tortured soul of the fabled Dido.

So, a little more brandy (only Jofi abstaining, and of course, Eric – who has been angelically good this evening, enchanted and diverted from mischief by the music-makers), and the seven of them repair to the music room to behold Jofi's pride and joy – his nine-foot Mason & Hamlin.

Brandy and conversation finished, and Alma's violin fine-tuned, she and Jofi launch into a movement from Cesar Franck's *Sonata in A*, one of the 'greatest hits' of the repertory. Alma says she knows the last movement "by heart," so they play just that. (Her teacher's biggest complaint: *You have a great memory but just for the parts you love.*) This is such an immediately appealing piece that it's enjoyable even when played adequately. But the performance here, like all the performances on this night, is breath-taking. No mere recording could possibly match the living magic in the room.

The evening of music closes first with a recovered and re-energized Daisy singing a song written by Bran himself, who accompanies Daisy at the piano, both performing from memory. The song is called *One Heart*, and she sings this beautiful aria so exquisitely that Emma cries, something that music has only rarely made her do before. Bran comments that he has never played a more magnificent instrument. It was, he says, the best realization of a work of his that he's ever heard.

The song and its performance are so affecting that Jofi at first refuses Bran's request to play, as the finale of the night, Beethoven's *Piano Sonata #32* (the last movement of which Bran's friend Li had requested of Jofi at Bran's home).

"I can't follow that!" Jofi says of Daisy's performance, but he is cajoled into action. The piece, Beethoven's final essay in the piano sonata format, is the only one he cast in two movements – struggle/peace, or samsara/nirvana, or perhaps earth/heaven. The effect is a transcendental, ecstatic and gracious crown upon the evening. A blessing – the already divine light of Beethoven shining forth through the lens of an Angel.

It is late, all agree. As the guests are packing up and making fond good-byes with promises of future gatherings, Emma pulls Alma aside and asks if she would have coffee with her tomorrow, and Alma agrees. This surprises Alma, as she had planned to ask Emma if there is a day this week when Emma might spare her a few minutes to discuss something important. Both women know what's on the agenda.

There was no place on the entire planet that night that music of such quality, variety and beauty blossomed forth with such unanticipated perfection than in that big house hidden across the river of the little town of Ann Arbor.

The night of my friends' first visit, I had another visitor, whom I had not seen in 14 years — my companion of ages, Metatron, who came in the night to me with many revelations and is there as always when most I am in need. While I work on my mission, it will be through music, specifically keyboard recitals and recordings, that I shall make my living and establish my independence. I shall also be permitted to be partner to Bran, Alma, and Daisy in the establishment of their own life's work. Before the dear one departed, I asked Metatron, desperately, for any encouragement that could be given me regarding finding the completely elusive Sam Morgan, for whom I am responsible and whose impact on the future of humanity's arts is so critical. I explained that I had no feeling that the man even exists, let alone where I may find him. Metatron's response was riddlesome. I was told that it was not just these humans who were being tested, and that I was henceforth forbidden to even utter the name of Sam Morgan, never again, even to Matt who had helped me look for the man. This instruction caused me much anguish, and I was compelled to ask my companion how it is that I should find this man if I am henceforth forbidden even to say his very name?! But Metatron simply smiled at me in blessing and was gone.

— from Chronicles of Jophiel, Vol. II.

"I feel that you want to come in, pig," Fr. Preston Holt says aloud, sitting at his desk. "So, do it." He closes his eyes and braces for the discomfort of the Ahri spirit to take possession of his mortal coil.

In the few days since Jofi's visit to the priest, Preston Holt has had quite an attitude change toward Ahri. He no longer grovels; he is no longer Sniveler. He treats the parasitical spirit with scant regard, and returns insult for insult, vowing never again to plead and cringe in the presence of the malevolent spirit.

He braces himself, but nothing happens; the spirit does not come forth. Preston feels compelled to snatch up his pen and begins to scribble on his notepad:

From this time forth
you will address me as 'Your Majesty'
or suffer for your impudence.

When he is done writing, Fr. Holt puts on his glasses to examines what he just wrote, and he is enraged.

"You go to hell, you filthy, pathetic swine! I will never again bow to you. Never! NEVER!"

When Fr. Preston Holt comes to himself again he is on his muddy knees in the muck of a nearby park on the Huron River. It is dark, and his sudden return to himself is more disorienting than usual. He blinks and looks up and sees the fat thug with the baseball bat in mid-swing. The bat strikes Preston's left arm midway between shoulder and elbow and breaks in half his humerus bone. He falls to the ground and the pain is the worst of his life. He screeches in agony.

"WHY DID YOU DO THAT!?" he shrieks at the man. "*O my god!* WHY?!"

The man is plainly confused. "Because you just gave me a bat and a hundred-dollar bill to do it, you crazy son-of-a-bitch." He gawps curiously at the priest writhing before him in agony. "What the fuck is *wrong* with you, man?"

And the fat man throws the bat into the bushes and lumbers away toward the railroad tracks.

27

I have no clue what to tell this poor girl, Emma thinks to herself, brooding over her latte at the downtown Starbucks. *This terribly young teenage girl.*

She looks at her phone. Almost 11 a.m. – she's early by six minutes. She's *always* early. Happily, so is Alma. She just walked in.

They say hi, Alma gets her drink, she sits and the two gush about the awesome fun and beauty of the night before. The smalltalk talks itself out in a minute or two, and Emma sits and smiles patiently at Alma.

Alma looks away, as if she's thinking. She turns back and says, "I need to talk to you about Jofi."

Emma broadens her smile. "I know," she says.

She needs to say this but looks away from Emma to get the words to come out. "I love him so much," she confides.

"Yes…"

"Is it that obvious?" Alma asks, regaining eye contact.

"It is to me."

"Does he ever talk about me? I mean… sometimes I'm not sure if he knows I'm alive."

"He's very fond of you, I think," Emma says. She shifts her position in the chair, and asks, "Why do you love him so?"

Alma smiles. "Because he's so beautiful and good. And a genius. And kind. I mean," she laughs, "what's not to love?"

"And you come to me for some insight into whether or not he might love you back as you love him?"

Alma simply nods at Emma, pleading with her eyes for a word of encouragement. Emma looks away and for a moment is deep in thought – about what she might tell Alma and especially how to phrase it.

She looks at the girl. "Jofi must be the one to tell you these things. Not me. You see… I trust you. Part of what you're feeling is the first flush of infatuation – all women feel it. They've never seen anything so beautiful outside of their wildest imaginings. Even men! They think he's a young woman and are constantly taunting him. But you – you I trust. I think you would be good for him. I think you were *sent* to him. That you would love him and protect him. And I think he would love and protect you. But as to the unspoken question *behind* your question – I cannot speak to that."

"I see…"

"No, I don't think you do… I don't know how you can," Emma says gently and leans forward intimately. "See… Jofi is unique, and he keeps so much to himself. If you would open this mystery… of this beautiful child of mine… you must be patient with him. Just love him. No demands. Just love him."

"That, Emma, is easy." She puts her brave face on. "I can hardly do otherwise."

"It may not be as easy as you think," Emma says, and Alma looks at her quizzically but does not question her further. "Just… just love him. And you may one day soon know more of him than he has ever told me."

There is little more to be said on that score. Both know this. They finish their drinks and after some light talk on issues less exigent, they go their ways, hoping genuinely to see one another again soon.

28

Emma didn't know how soon!

Over the next six weeks their home has become music central as Jofi takes each of his friends in hand and one or sometimes all four of them will be making music at all hours of the day and night. This isn't just recreation; this is serious career-molding business and, with Jofi's guidance, incredibly efficient without being in the least tedious. They all are first-rate musicians and they all know what they need to do to succeed: *perfect themselves, make recordings, play concerts.*

Emma glories in all of this; Matt less so, and his escapes to the other, quieter, wing of the house are getting more frequent by the day. But he doesn't mind. He knows something extraordinary is brewing and is watching his child become an adult. In unguarded moments he thinks of it as his boy becoming a man, but will check himself, oftimes sadly. In any case, Jofi is blossoming and Matt and Emma are glad.

Alma and Jofi are getting closer, as friends and as colleagues. Jofi never practices; he reads and plays. Alma has been concentrating on violin and keyboard sonatas – the Bach with Jofi on harpsichord, and the Mozart with Jofi on piano. They love being around one another. She touches him, and he touches back, but neither is sure what the other's touches mean, exactly.

Bran and Daisy are making music in many different ways, and sometimes at Bran's, or Daisy's (much nicer) home rather than Jofi's. They are very much in love and know *exactly* what their touches mean. When practicing they prefer Jofi's place for the excellence of the instruments, the luscious ambiance of the performing space, and the socialization in general. Their chemistry when all together is remarkable.

Daisy is learning every one of Bran's songs for female voice, and Bran has altered the lyrics of some of his male-voiced songs, sometimes rewriting them completely, just to hear her sing them. She can't believe this treasure is exclusively hers. (He promised her.) As relief from the seemingly infinite work Bran does on the *Anticanon*, he relaxes by composing new material for Daisy to sing.

At the end of the first six weeks of work, two major changes are proposed for the house – one by Jofi and one by Matt. Matt wants to sound-proof "the other half" of the house. "It's like living in a recital hall," he said to Emma, not bitterly, but with a note of fatigue. Even Emma admitted then that it was all getting a bit much. Eventually, Matt, Emma, and Eric will end up living on the other side of the house.

Jofi? He wants to turn the music room into a recording studio and knock a wall down to enlarge the space. The harpsichord would join the piano in that room. Jofi has consulted with studio designers now that Matt has generously given the okay, and the wall comes down next week, to be replaced with two pillars to preserve the structural integrity of the mansion. Bran, experienced in production matters, will be the engineer of the new studio and is in hog's heaven right now choosing hardware and software to make the place a reality.

Daisy wants to pay for the renovation, but Matt will hear nothing of it; he's a little insulted, actually, at the suggestion. They compromise, but only after Daisy becomes quite adamant. The others see a new side to Daisy here. She can be formidable when it's called for. So – Matt will pay for structural changes and Daisy will outfit the studio with the necessary hardware and software.

A couple of dusty weeks follow, and the renovations keep the mansion off-limits to the quartet of friends. They bounce among the other three domiciles to practice and socialize in the interim. The dust situation is a real bother to sensitive Jofi at home, so he has decided to spend some of these nights with Bran, who is happy for the company – unless Daisy is available and even Jofi is not so clueless as to encumber the two lovebirds.

Near the end of their two-week exile from the studio, Jofi is having dinner and music with Alma at her apartment. It is late, and Alma asks Jofi to spend the night there. He has never done so before.

She is outwardly calm, but frantic in her mind as to how to set this up. *Where will he sleep? With me? On the couch?* Honestly, she has been thinking about this scenario for weeks now but is no closer to clarity than before.

When it's time for sleep, clueless Jofi is open to any suggestions that would please Alma, or so he believes. She takes the initiative. She's terrified, but she does it.

"Jofi," she smiles, "would you sleep with me in my bed? It's nice and big. Nicer than the couch."

Jofi returns her smile and considers briefly. "Yeah," he says. "Sure. Why not?" On their way into her bedroom, she notes a change in Jofi's countenance. Reticent?

Alma turns on the lamp next to the bed, grabs a few things from closet and drawers, tells Jofi he can pick whatever side he likes, pops into the bathroom and shuts the door. Jofi looks at the bed with furrowed brow, pauses to think, *and without removing a single article of clothing,* pulls down the blanket and sheet and climbs aboard, tucking himself into the side farthest from the bathroom, pulls the covers up to his chin and places his arms stiffly at his side. At last, the gears in Jofi's mind begin to turn while he waits for Alma to emerge. *I wonder what's actually happening here,* he thinks, as his unsettled feelings begin to percolate to the surface.

Alma opens the bathroom door and switches out the light in there. She pads into the room and stops by the bed, herself bathed in the lamplight. She's got a negligee on that stops above her knee. It's a 'nice girl' negligee, sheer, but non-revealing. She smiles through her discomfort, not wanting to appear as if she's wantonly displaying herself, but still available for appreciative observations. Jofi senses this and complies chivalrously.

"Wow, Alma," he chirps. "You look really nice."

O the relief she feels! "Really?" she says. "This old thing?" (It's brand-new and painstakingly researched for just this specific application.)

"Yeah, sure," Jofi iterates. "Very nice."

In fact, any red-blooded actual human male would be drowning in a sea of saucy notions. Alma looks around the room. "Where are your clothes?" she asks, and then immediately wishes she didn't.

"Umm… I'll just sleep in them, I guess."

"O Jofi…" she shakes her head. "That sounds unnecessarily uncomfortable."

Jofi just laughs pleasantly. "It's okay."

Alma hops in beside him. She adjusts her covers and clicks off the lamp, but there is still enough light filtering through the unshaded window to discern features once they are accustomed to the level. She turns on her side to face him, she smiles. Jofi smiles in return and for a minute they simply lie there, holding each other's gaze tenderly.

In a fit of amorous courage, Alma scoots over and rests her head on Jofi's chest. In his frank affection, he strokes her hair, and she sighs. Alma is ecstatic yet calm in her bliss. Jofi's touch is so lovely. And loving.

"Jofi?" she whispers.

"Yes?" he whispers back.

She swallows and takes a deep breath. "I love you." She closes her eyes willing to surrender to whichever way this goes.

"I love you, too," Jofi says quietly.

Alma gasps quietly at this revelation. She picks up her head and scoots up in the bed to look into his eyes, her hair falling around Jofi's head. She drops down to kiss his lips. Jofi participates in this kiss, but Alms knows a 'sister kiss' when she feels one, full of love and affection and completely empty of ardor. She pulls her head back. Jofi smiles. He seems genuinely happy.

She doesn't know what to do. *If Daisy Lee were here,* she thinks to herself, *she would know what to do.* Alma sits up in bed and shuffles herself back so that she is sitting against the headboard. *What would Daisy do?*

Jofi senses discord. "What's wrong?" he asks quietly. He really doesn't know.

She looks down upon him, thoughtfully. She wiggles in place as she reaches down to tug at the hem of her gown, and pulls it over her head, then flings the negligee across the room.

Jofi beholds her. It was his favorite thing in the world, and he has not seen anything like it since he was an infant. "O!" he whispers. "What lovely breasts you have. How beautiful!" He's genuinely moved. "Thank you…"

"You don't have to thank me, Jofi," she smiles, takes his near hand and places it on her breast. He caresses her, and she closes her eyes, time stops for her as she blisses out.

In fact, Jofi is not so much fondling his girlfriend as he is reliving the best of his babyhood. Unlike a mere human, Jofi not only actually remembers nursing with Emma, in a way it was like yesterday, so perfectly vivid and pleasurable is the memory. This was Jofi's introduction to the nurturing, loving touch of human-ness. Most of us forget about this but Jofi has never forgotten even a single instant of it. From this act, he drew nourishment, affection, intimacy – human love.

He caresses Alma's nipple, so like Emma's were, but pinker. Alma's breasts are softer and a little smaller. She's fascinated by his attentions.

"The daughters of men are beautiful," he whispers. He withdraws his hand, now actually wiping a surplus of saliva escaping from the corner of his mouth. He stops. *Something is going to go wrong…*

Alma scoots down and resumes her head on Jofi's chest and he strokes her hair as before. But now he feels her hand slip down his belly and toward his groin. He seizes her wrist!

"NO!" His grip is a band of iron.

"Jofi! *You're hurting me!*" she cries, and writhes away from him as he releases her. She falls upon her back and covers her face in her hands and begins to cry hysterically. "*Jofi, I'm so sorry, I'm so so so sorry!*"

Jofi is paralyzed with remorse, and when he comes to himself he throws his body upon hers and holds her in a full embrace, begging her to stop weeping.

"Please don't cry, Alma!" he pleads. "You've done nothing wrong. We need… we need to talk. I need to explain…"

"No. You don't," she sniffles, pulling her hands from her face and looking shamefaced at Jofi. "I shouldn't have done that…"

"You don't understand," he croons in her ear, trying to be comforting. "Just please don't cry. Please. It's torture to me worse than for you."

She feels the trueness of this, and she stops weeping in order not to hurt him. Jofi relaxes his embrace and climbs off her, off the bed, and begins to pace the bedroom floor like a tiger. Alma asks Jofi to fetch her negligee and she puts it back on, rises from the bed to her closet and pulls on a long nightgown. She ties the front with eyes cast down in sad shame.

Jofi stops pacing. He closes his eyes and calms himself with deep shuddering breaths. He looks at Alma with a pleading face. "I have to tell you about myself," he says to her finally. "About who I am. What I am. It has to do with… with all this tonight."

Alma tries to smile. "The mystery at last," she says.

Jofi gives a puzzled look.

"'The Mystery of Jofi,' that's what me and Daisy call it."

"Ah. I see." He closes his eyes and nods. "I don't know how to even begin." He opens his eyes and looks at her intently. "And there are things even now which you must not know."

She has no reply to this. She just waits.

"And you must promise me never to share what I am about to tell you with anyone. Not even Daisy. Never. Promise me that or I will tell you nothing."

"I promise."

"This is not an idle vow," Jofi looks dangerously stern and Alma senses this. "I don't even know if I am *allowed* to do this. I was not expressly prohibited, but it just might be such an obviously wrong thing to do that instruction was not even *given* to the circumstance."

"Tell me what to do and I'll do it," she says, pleadingly. "Tell me how to behave and that is how I'll behave. I promise you."

Jofi hears this and feels that these are the right words. He decides to go ahead and share with Alma more than he has shared with any other. He points to the bedroom chair and she sits.

"Alma. My name is Jophiel. I am not a man; I am not a woman. I am, in a way, in my essence, much as what you are destined to become ages hence. I am *Jophiel – Angel of the Beauty of the Eternal Presence.* I have incarnated, I have an earthy body, because I have a mission that must be accomplished in this manner. In this human form."

Alma's jaw is open, and she is struggling for composure. She gathers her robe about her as if against a chill. "O," she says and waits for Jophiel to continue.

The Angel considers. "Do you wish to test me?"

"What?" she says, bewildered.

"Let me make this as easy as I can for you," Jophiel says. "Will you play along?"

"Yes," she says.

"All right," Jophiel says, kneeling in front of her and placing his hands on her thighs. "Now. Alma. Go back to a pleasant childhood memory. Okay? Just take a few seconds and think about some pleasant episode from when you were younger."

"All right," she agrees.

"Close your eyes."

She closes her eyes and after a few seconds she smiles and after a little while longer she turns sad and can sustain the vision no longer. Out of discomfort she comes back to the present and opens her eyes to her beloved and waits.

"Your grampa," the Angel says. Alma gasps and puts her hand to her mouth. "He takes you to the gem and rock show when you were six. He buys you a tiara. A child's replica of a famous piece of jewelry. You called it your 'princess crown.' You wore it all summer long. He died at the end of summer, and you snuck it into his funeral and wore it even though your Mom said you weren't allowed."

Alma starts to cry, puts her head down and covers her face. Jophiel is patient. "You're an Angel?" she whispers and raises her head. "That's how you can do all the things you do? And know all the things you know? And read minds?

"No. Listen," Jophiel hurries the information to her. "I do not read minds. I did it here to prove something to you. I *never* do it unless there is an emergency. I consider it rude. Unfair. Obtrusive. Crude. Unloving and unfriendly. Do you see? Do you believe me? I *hate* to do it."

"I believe you."

"That I am an Angel? Do you believe that I am the Angel Jophiel?"

Alma gathers herself, it takes a minute, and then poses a question. "Yes. But I have a request."

"Whatever I *may* do, I *will* do for you," Jophiel says.

"I want to look at your Angel body."

Jophiel considers this, and silently assents, standing to remove his shirt, socks, pants and, finally, his underpants, all very quickly and efficiently. Alma cannot but gasp at the sight.

In the half-light she sees a perfectly proportionate form, slim and sculptured, delicate but strong, chiseled, sinuous, unblemished by a single pimple or stray mark. Jophiel's human form is hairless, except for his luxurious brown locks. Standing with his legs apart, Jophiel says to Alma, "Come look. I know you're curious. It's all right."

And Alma drops to her knees in front of her beloved and studies with grave countenance the pubic region of the

Angel's earthly form, and after a few moments lovingly leans to kiss Jofi's belly in the twilight. She stands. She looks dazed but determined to behave as she knows is required of her.

"Why…" she whispers, "why are you here… Angel?"

"I must not tell you," Jophiel confides. "Of that, I am *quite* certain."

"I see," she says solemnly, then she tears up. "I still love you, Jofi," she says. "I love you and that will never ever change."

The naked Angel advances and embraces Alma, who is now quite understandably overcome by it all, and the dam inside her breaks. What woman has ever had to endure this?

Jofi is quite overcome also, but relieved. So much tension was wrapped up in all this. More than Jofi realized. He holds her until her shudders stop. Then, inspired, she looks up at him.

"Lie back down," she bids, all wet-faced. Jofi grabs his pants, but Alma stays his hand. "No, no," she says. "Just lie down as you are."

Jofi hesitates but complies. Alma quite unexpectedly removes her robe, her nightie, and her panties, and lies down in the near-dark next to Jofi, turning to face him.

"If you are an Angel, and I believe that you are   for it explains every single thing about you – why are you so fascinated with my breasts?"

Jofi smiles. "My mother breastfed me," he explains. "That was my true welcome into the world. It was the most wonderful thing I can remember." He smiles sadly. "It still is. I had kind of a rough start."

And at that, Alma cradles Jofi head and moves it to her breasts, moves Jofi's lips to her nipple. He remembers. He is remembering. He fastens on to Alma's sweet nipple and sucks, and she holds his head and kisses the top of it while she suckles him. For a while Jofi blisses out and relives his infant ecstasy. That same while Alma is losing herself in waves of deepest delight, and while Jofi enjoys one breast, then the other, she wraps her legs around him and presses herself into him, and after a full minute of this, she spasms into ecstasy.

This violence brings Jofi quickly back to earth. *His mother never did this!* It finally dawns on Jofi the Clueless what must be happening. He holds onto his naked girl for a space until her tremors cease, wondering what to do next.

She looks at him now with eyes shining in the twilight and strokes his cheek. She would dally here for hours in the bliss of her release but Jofi is not of like mind. She senses this, frowns and releases him. He sits up on the bed and dabs curiously at the wet spot she has pressed into his thigh.

"Are you unhappy because you didn't like what we did?" Alma asks, bravely.

Jofi turns and gives an ironic smile. "Hardly. I very *much* enjoyed that, but we can *never* do that again."

"But... but why?" Alma sits up on the edge of the bed. "That's the most wonderful thing I ever felt! And I could feel you enjoying it with me."

"It isn't right that I should be doing that. I can feel myself sinking into humanness at the expense of my own nature." He takes her hand. "I can't afford to be changed that way. I have enemies. I have responsibilities."

In her anxiousness, her mind strikes out for anything to keep him close. "Milk!" she says.

"What?" Did Jofi hear correctly? *"Milk?"*

"I can give you milk! I remember reading that this can be done. I would do that for you, and we-"

"No, no, no, no..." He takes her hand now in both of his and squeezes it in gratitude. "My dearest Alma, no. We must not go on with this. This is *sex*. I am not made for it, *literally* not made for it. I do not understand it, and I must not descend into it. Wine. Sex. *No. None of that.* I must not. These are... these are the earthly delights. They can only impede me."

She withdraws her hand and they sit in silence for a couple of minutes. Finally, Alma says, "Can we still be close? Can we still touch one another lovingly? Can we lie together… in affection? In rest? In sleep? Jofi, I will always love you."

Jofi leans over and kisses her cheek. "And I shall always love you, Alma. And I love being close to you. But only as I may. Only as my nature, and my mission, permits."

Alma leans to kiss Jofi's forehead, and in a few minutes, they are back under the covers, a few more and they are both asleep, Jofi on his back, Alma on her side snuggled against her beloved, her arm draped over his chest, each taking refuge in their separate world of dreams.

At a too-early hour, they are rudely buzzed awake by the doorbell. Annoyed, Alma slogs out of bed, pulls on her long robe and goes to answer. Jofi scrambles up and begins to dress.

It's Daisy. She storms in, oblivious to Alma's attempt to obstruct her. "I couldn't wait. I have to tell you in person!" Daisy cries, tramping into the living room and stopping abruptly with a clear sightline to Jofi putting his pants on in the bedroom. He waves.

Daisy puts on a big fake surprise face and turns to Alma. "Alma Pierce – *you little devil!*" She puts her hand to her mouth, pretends to be shocked and outraged.

Alma is *so* annoyed. "Just *stop* it!"

Jofi ambles out, fiddling with his shirt buttons and greets Daisy.

"Hey stud!" she says. "How's it goin'?"

Jofi gets it. He nods and smiles that lame smile that only Daisy seems to draw from him. "Fine, thank you."

"I'll bet! Well… this *almost* pre-empts my news – god, wait till Bran hears about you two – but not quite. And it's just as well you're *both* here."

"Well what?" Alma asks. "What is it?"

Big smile from Daisy Lee. She is radiant.

"I'm *pregnant!*"

30

When Daisy told Bran the Big News (he was the last of the four to know), he asked, "Really?" and she smiled and said yes. Then Bran stared out the window, all earnest and solemn, for a space, turned back to her and asked, "Will you marry me?" And Daisy smiled and said yes, and before two months had passed they had wed, in a small ceremony at 'Jofi's Fantasy Palace' (which the ladies still call it) where Emma and Matt insisted on hosting the event. Jofi was Best Man, natch, and Alma the Maid of Honor. There were about a dozen friends sharing in the celebration, mostly musicians from school. Both Bran's and Daisy's fathers were in attendance and got along famously, but they have no siblings between them.

After they had wed, Bran's lease on his little house was to expire that very month. The newly-married pair had decided that they would live in Daisy's home – at least twice as large as Bran's old place and not far from Jofi's home.

Bran had been working on the *Anticanon* now for almost four months and took a break from the task while he prepared to move his effects to Daisy's home. The night before the moving trucks were to arrive, Bran's home was engulfed in fire. Arson was suspected but there were no leads. (Jofi knew full well who was to blame but he would not reveal the identity of the arsonist to his friends, nor to the police.)

Bran was sad that he lost his piano, records, and his stereo, but what shattered his heart was that all the work he had done on the *Anticanon* was destroyed – the computer and his backup drive – burnt to a crisp. His backup to the cloud was not well-maintained (a fatal flaw since remedied), and his morale was sickened to the breaking point. Luckily, Daisy had all Bran's original scores for all his vocal and other instrumental music at her home. She moved them personally a few days before the scheduled move.

So, moving was an easy task, as Bran had nothing to move. He gave up on vinyl LPs and turntables and resigned himself to the digital world for future recording acquisitions, though he never returned to the collector hobby in earnest. His concern now was his own music and the music of his friends.

The stereo was replaced by another modest setup. (Odd how composers and musicians rarely care about top-line audio components for themselves. Audiophiles are rarely musicians. Civilians try to duplicate the reality of the studio or a live performance; the initiated know that this is impossible and generally don't bother trying that hard. It's the difference between being in a savage battle and watching a war movie on TV. They know that a *recording* of music will never be music, any more than a painting of a landscape will be an actual landscape.)

His beloved sweet little Yamaha piano, since charred to its metal skeleton, was replaced by a new Steinway Model D, nine feet of pianotastic ebony gorgeousness. Bran felt unworthy and still does, but you would have better luck separating a mama grizzly from her cub than to wrest that piano from Bran. He is working on becoming a fine accompanist to Daisy, and having a live-in pianist makes Daisy very happy. Bran sometimes accuses her of marrying him for this reason.

The pair get along beautifully. It's beyond love — they actually *like* each other. Daisy has moderated Bran's destructive tendencies to a large degree. (He is mostly unaware of this, but everyone except Bran notices this quite clearly.) Bran loves Daisy and he loves his work — until very recently, he had neither. Daisy's only spoken complaint is Bran's snoring, especially after party nights, the sound of which she has described to Alma as "like a donkey caught in a wood-chipper."

Daisy did not join in to the partying with the alcohol-swilling ways of her husband. She took very good care of herself in her pregnancy and she looked radiant throughout.

Tragedy struck hard for them one morning when Daisy woke up to blood on the sheets. She spent two days in the University Hospital, and she lost her baby. No one saw them for almost two weeks after the event. Jofi or Alma would call them every other day or so but had the feeling that their calls were an annoyance. That didn't stop them, and eventually, their reception was more civil and finally grateful.

After a suitable period of mourning (and long consultations with Jofi and Alma), Bran and Daisy rejoined their friends, making music together and soon healing laughter once again rang though the halls of the big house.

Bran started work anew on the *Anticanon*, and after a couple months even admitted that "this new version will make the burnt-up one seem crummy in comparison." Likely a typical Bran overstatement but everyone got the point.

Jofi and Alma are almost inseparable. Alma quit school (so did Daisy, for the same reason), believing (unlike Alma's Dad) that school was interfering with her music career, in which both ladies have the greatest faith, skill, and finesse to justify such a feeling. Plus, Alma has the most terrific accompanist in the world and she is always open to Jofi's gentle teaching and encyclopedic knowledge.

One of the new studio additions, courtesy of Daisy Lee, is a fortepiano made by Paul McNulty, to play music between the harpsichord and modern piano era. Now Jofi may accompany Alma as well as Daisy in music by Haydn and Mozart, even some Schubert and Mendelssohn and the gang, and have sounds come out that the composers themselves would have recognized.

In a year Alma has become very close, even daughterly, to Emma, confiding in her most of the details of her relationship with Jofi, minus the Angel stuff, to which only Alma is privy. Alma is committed to being Jofi's mate in life. She doesn't put it this way to herself, but she is sublimating her sexual impulses to the service of Jofi's needs and to her music career. She (at least not yet) does not find this difficult.

Jofi's parents want Jofi to live at home, "You're only 15," is their battle cry, but they have no problem with Alma's overnight stays with Jofi in his rooms and her extended sojourns at the Fischer home. (And they know that Jofi's peculiar anatomy makes Every Parent's Nightmare an impossibility.) She almost lives there, but not quite. Besides, this is where Jofi would live anyway, given his druthers, because he spends so much time in the studio. If he had his own place, it would only be a place for Jofi and Alma to sleep.

The studio is a masterpiece of the genre. It is only a single, albeit huge, room, with a vocal booth and an isolated control room adjacent. Very simple; very state-of-the-art. Bran was showing it all off to his cellist buddy Li (a frequent visitor) soon after it was complete. He pointed to a multiple-mic stand hovering over the piano.

"See that microphone stand there?" Bran asked. "That cost more than my entire old studio. And the mics? The cost of a new car. A *nice* new car."

"Jesus, man," Li said, "how do you justify that kind of outlay?"

"Because its design is perfect and it's effortless to use and I'll never have to replace it," Bran replied with a savvy grin.

That design philosophy holds true through the entire studio. The purchases were, in fact, so canny that, as pricey as it all was, nary a dollar was wasted.

Money without genius; genius without money – the story of every failed enterprises. But when both conjoin, what dreams are not possible to attain?

31
Ann Arbor

Jofi's main dream is this: finding Sam Morgan and establish his ascendency, but even he is convinced that he will never see Mr. Morgan. Unlike his other family and friends, he has never for even a moment felt Sam's presence on the same plane as his own.

Next is to make sure that Bran Englander finishes the *Anticanon*, and that it is given a worthy premiere. Finally, Jofi is dedicated to assuring the careers and well-being of Alma and Daisy. Not because he has to; because he wants to.

Perhaps unsurprisingly, the way that he raises up the women is by commercially establishing his own monstrous talent and authority as a keyboard player. Jofi is now 17 and is in growing demand as a solo recitalist as well as accompanist to the rising young violinist Alma Pierce. Jofi also accompanies Daisy when she performs early vocal music that requires harpsichord or fortepiano, though it's usually Bran who works with her when she tours with later music for piano and voice. Since many of these songs are Bran's own, he is the right man for the job.

Daisy has struggled mightily with the common problem of 'what is a newly-married woman to call herself?' She thought of keeping her name, Daisy Lee Saarinen; she considered changing it to Daisy Lee Englander; then flirted with the hyphenated solution of Daisy Lee Saarinen-Englander; or maybe just Daisy Englander? But it was her remarkable new agent who suggested the simple solution of – Daisy Lee. For a performer, for a stage-name, it works. (When Alma heard that her friend had adopted this stage name, she sniffed, "It sounds like a good name for a stripper if singing doesn't work out for you.") Daisy's sho-'nuf *legal* name? She hasn't quite solved that yet…

They have all started what at least *appear* to be promising careers giving recitals nationwide. They have an incredibly able and efficient agent/publicist who oversees all four of their careers. They are, in fact, his only clients. Daisy has made that demand a deal-breaker and pays dearly for it. His name is Jamaad Garrett, a savvy and street-smart black gentleman with the air of an aristocrat. Young Jamaad knows what makes the world go 'round and he knows it ain't love.

Bran is usually with Daisy even if Jofi plays her recitals, and Alma and Jofi travel together — sometimes as a violin/keyboard duet, or else she will simply go with Jofi when he plays solo piano recitals. In other words, the quartet often travels together from gig to gig enjoying new cities and reveling in each other's company, the money they make from the shows never (yet) coming *close* to covering their expenses. Though this activity takes up an increasing amount of their time, they still call the Ann Arbor studio at Jofi's house their base of operations and are all in Ann Arbor for most of the year. So far, anyway.

32

Matt and Emma are out for dinner, and Alma and Jofi are at the house now, sitting together in the great room of a summer evening. Bran and Daisy are expected to join them soon. They're celebrating. Bran has "some news."

Jofi is reading email on his tablet and starts to laugh.

"What's so funny?" Alma asks. She's online, too, but she's looking for fancier shoes.

"Well," Jofi says, "I finally got my first concerto request."

Alma puts down her tablet and shouts, "Yes!" with her fist in the air.

"Actually, no," Jofi says. "It's from Grand Rapids. They invite me to play Tchaikovsky. The First. Of course."

"You won't play that?"

"I *can't* play that."

Alma does not understand this. "What? Of *course,* you can play it."

He turns to face her, shaking his head no. "Tchaikovsky is about sex and death. I don't understand the former, and the latter I don't acknowledge. Scriabin, too. I'm just not that horny or terrified."

"I see," Alma says, laughing. "So, suggest something else."

Jofi keeps reading. "Nah. It says here it's for a Tchaikovsky thing they're doing."

The doorbell rings and Eric, now a hearty 13 year-old, attends to the door and ushers Bran and Daisy in.

"Hey kid," Bran says and gives Eric a playful slap on the cheek. Eric play-strangles Bran and they struggle and laugh until Jofi yells for Eric to desist. He releases his dreaded enemy, kisses Daisy hello and heads back to his room.

"Champagne!" Bran cries as he holds up the bottle. "I drink less these days, but it's one hell of a lot better booze since I got married!"

Daisy shakes her head in (mock?) disgust. "You're such a pig."

"And *you*," he continues, as he surrenders the bottle to Alma, "are the most beautiful soprano in the world."

Daisy pretends she's not flattered. "Just among the sopranos?"

Bran gets serious. "Well, actually," he confides, "there's this *amazing* French contralto-"

"Perhaps I'll have her killed," Daisy interrupts with a wicked smile.

"Will you guys stop that and sit down!" Jofi hollers from the sitting circle and the guests do as bidden. Alma follows with open champagne and four glasses. Jofi doesn't drink, but Bran has explained to him that "refusing champagne is anti-life," so he joins in.

The wine poured, Jofi asks, "Why do we have champagne?"

Bran slams a flash drive down on the table before them and says, "It's done."

Alma is all excited congratulations, but Jofi just closes his eyes and breathes, "Finally… it's finished," and slumps back in his chair looking all blissy.

Bran points to the flash drive on the table. "There it is – pdf's of the full score, parts, conductor's score and notes. Four years of work. Of course, I'll revise it a thousand times, but even if I die now I won't be ashamed of what's there."

Jofi's eyes get big. "Don't talk about dying now, please."

"Kidding, man. Chill," Bran says.

"We need Jamaad here," Jofi says. "Maybe meet with him tomorrow, eh?"

Daisy agrees. "I'll call him. Get the ball rolling."

"The obvious place to start is the Ann Arbor Orchestra," Alma opined. "It's a fine group. They're up to this. Lots of young people, music students. They're not hidebound; they're flexible. You *must* have considered this."

Bran looks like he's about to vomit, eyes crossed and tongue hanging out.

Jofi laughs. "What's wrong with you?"

"The conductor is an asshole. I'd hate him if I ever gave him a thought," Bran explains.

"Oooo – do tell," Daisy says.

"I brought him my first symphony years ago. I called and asked him if he'd look at it and he said yeah, so I went to drop it off." Bran hits on the champagne and sighs with pleasure. "So, I go to the office there on Liberty Street and this midget waddles up to me and smiles. I dunno who he is, I never saw the guy up close before. Daniel Cohen is his name, y'all know that. So, he gets pissed that I don't recognize his magnificent maestro-ness, and just sort of snatches my stuff from me. And I leave."

"Yeah, so?" Jofi says.

"So, three days later I open the mailbox and there's an envelope with my stuff in it and not a goddam word from the son-of-a-bitch inside. Not a 'no thanks' or a 'go to hell' or 'why did you write this crap' or anything."

"Hmm…" Alma muses. "That *was* kind of rude."

"But what the hell did I expect?" He counts on his fingers until he runs out of fingers. "He *never* plays contemporary music, has no understanding of *anything* after Stravinsky, likes Mendelssohn *way* too much. He's great with fundraising, and the phony smile, and the children's concerts, and the Mostly Mozart crap, and the blue-haired ladies like him. But he must be the most mediocre person in the entire *world*. Fuck 'im. He's the 'Peter Principle' incarnate and Ann Arbor is stuck with him."

Daisy smiles. "Cohen doesn't deserve your work. A good way to get back at him would be to hire the orchestra out from under him."

"Yeah," Jofi chuckles, *"you* conduct it."

Suddenly Bran stands up, strikes a noble pose, tosses his head back in abandon and runs his fingers through his luxurious long mane (which doesn't quite come off as he wears a crew-cut these days to hide a growing bald spot), and with his invisible baton he cues up the orchestra in a passionate flourish!

Everybody has a big laugh at his parody but suddenly Bran sits back down and looks at Jofi all serious. *"You* conduct it," he says.

"Me? Why me? Why not you?"

"Because…" Bran thinks about how to put this, then gives up and says, "because… *you 'da man!"*

Jofi snickers and considers this for a short space. "Sure! Okay."

"I'll have Jamaad call the orchestra tomorrow and see if they'll agree to it and what it'll cost," Daisy says.

"To rent the orchestra without the conductor?" Alma asks. "And the theater?"

"Yep," Daisy says, "and three rehearsals. That's the plan."

The maestro is enraged and indignant at the mere *suggestion* and *will not permit it!* He threatens to return to Israel to teach, where he is *properly* appreciated! But the orchestra is, like most, in dire straits, and the board is more eager for the revenue than they are to placate the mediocrity over which they are having a growing amount of unpublicized buyer's remorse.

Jamaad knows how to play the hand, and the only concessions he makes to get the deal are that the concert not be considered part of the official season, nor would the orchestra use their assets to publicize the event. They all agree, and the still-outraged conductor is bent back into humiliation.

It's yet another gambit that will cost Daisy plenty – *but they have set a date!*

33

"Friday night, September second, 2022, and we have the theater from noon to midnight," Alma reads from the agreement. "We have to use their union people for techs and house people, blah blah blah…"

A few days have passed since the contract was negotiated. All four of the group are present again, eating a swell lunch that Emma made for them all. Matt has taken Eric with him to the gym – his usual routine.

Emma feeds them a lot, but Daisy buys a lot of food for the house. Matt and Emma pretend to be annoyed by Daisy's thoughtfulness (though Matt knows well that Daisy could buy and sell him a dozen times over), but they aren't bothered, really. They very much respect the young woman.

"The *Anticanon* is only a half-hour long," Bran observes between bites. "That's a pretty short concert."

Jofi suggests filling it with Bran's pieces that the four of them can play – songs sung by Daisy, a fantasy for solo violin that Bran wrote for Alma. "I can play Bran's piano pieces," Jofi concludes.

"Better than I can," Bran admits with a twisted smile.

They happily decide on a 'Bran Englander Mini-Festival' for that evening. That meant the added expense of having Jofi's piano moved into the space for use that night. Later, Matt – citing his interest in promoting Jofi's career – would convince Daisy to split the total bill with him. Daisy would not give in easily but was secretly pleased at Matt's offer. She knew all this would be expensive, but the final tally really rocked her. She's trying to keep *some* sense of balance.

"We need to get Jamaad cracking on publicity for this thing," Daisy says. "TV and radio, internet, even print – that was Jamaad's selling point to us, remember? He claims he's a real new-media guru."

"Well…" Jofi adds, "We'll soon see."

The *Anticanon* is finished, the premiere is scheduled, and Jofi is overwhelmed with concern for the well-being of his family and friends. *The adversary may strike hard between now and September,* Jofi ponders, *in some way to prevent the premiere.* He decides to make a visit to a new friend, and a primordial enemy.

Climbing the steps of the rectory, Jofi notices that the door is open, and Fr. Holt stands smiling to greet him, standing tall, looking healthy. They embrace and Preston ushers Jofi into his office and closes the door, taking his customary seat. Jofi does likewise.

"I know what you're enduring," Jofi says. "How are you holding up?"

Preston shrugs. "As you see," he smiles wanly.

"Things are at a crucial stage. Do you have any way to conceal yourself from Ahri?"

Preston shakes his head. "Impossible. If I did, there is no way that that beast could succeed in any of his stratagems."

Jofi suspected this to be the case but needed to confirm.

"In fact, Ahri says that if I let anything like that slip to you he'll put out one of my eyes. He says, 'that's next on the list.' He'll do it, too. So far, he's had my arm broken, and the day the cast came off he had my ankle broken. And so on. And most recently –" Preston holds up his left hand, revealing a bandaged stump where his little finger used to be. There are no tears anymore. Just the facts. "But Jophiel – if you need me to talk to you about what I know I'll do it anyway. It's all pretty horrible… but I will not fail you. It's actually better now than it was… even with the excruciations."

"I don't, and won't, ask such of you. *And Ahri already knows that,*" he says, peevishly.

"Even if I so much as *think* about things he may have planned while I'm in your presence, he'll torture me. Because he knows you can read me if you want to. My mind."

Jofi holds both palms up. "I'm not reading you and I won't. He knows that, too."

Preston lowers his head and breathes heavily. "He's right on the brink…"

"Let him through. Let Ahri through."

"He doesn't wish it," Preston says.

Jofi's countenance darkens. He looks furious. "Loathsome spirit," he rumbles. "Come through now or I'll *rip you through!*"

"*'Loathsome spirit'?* Really, Jophiel? So charmingly *biblical!*" Ahri says, all sunny. "Anyway, so nice of you to pop by, but I'm afraid your visit will be of little use to you. I'm simply not feeling chatty."

"I came to warn you," Jofi says.

"Against what?" Ahri clutches at the arms of his chair and pretends to be afraid. "Am I in danger!?"

"You shall be if you hurt any of my friends or family."

He waves that off in a bored gesture. "O just relax, Jophiel. I have a job to do. There's no other assigned to this case but me, same as you. One of us will succeed, the other will fail. I don't have to hurt your friends to do it. Totally unnecessary effort. It's all very simple, really."

"Then why do you torture the priest? Your esteemed colleague would never do this. It's not even like *you*. Why do you do this?"

Ahri leans back and fixes Jofi with a dazzling smile. "Oh, it's not about my *former* Sniveler – he's nothing; it's about *you*, Jophiel. See… I know you feel his pains worse than *he* does. And this distracts you."

"We'll both do fine through all this."

"Perhaps…" Ahri changes the subject. "Say, ever wonder just *exactly* what happened to Sam Morgan? The main point of your mission? Your *huge* failing? Your eternal embarrassment? Because you know better than I do that you will never even *see* him, *because he's nowhere to be seen.*" Such a malevolent smile… "You ever wonder if *we* had anything to do with that?"

"I don't feel that you did," Jofi says, unable to hide his uncertainty.

"Come now, Jophiel. You know all your efforts are useless without him."

"Heed my warning." Jofi stands to take his leave. "If any of those in my aura of protection so much as *stub their toe,* I'm coming after you."

"Perhaps you should think less of what I plan for others," Ahri snaps, "and wonder instead just what I have planned for *you.*"

"I don't care about me. *You can't hurt me.*"

"Hah! You'll care about *this.* You'll care *plenty.*"

34

Jamaad Garrett personally designed the website and social media strategy for the upcoming concert and presented a comprehensive media campaign proposal that went a long way toward making Daisy feel that she bet on the right man for the job, and so she had no problem authorizing a paid assistant for Jamaad.

There were internet and print interviews for Bran coming up locally, also in Detroit, Grand Rapids, Flint, and Toledo. So far, the way has been welcoming and smooth for their new agent.

"They don't expect someone like me," Jamaad explains to the quartet at a breakfast gathering a month after the deal was sealed with the orchestra. "First of all, I'm black. Nobody expects that in the lily-white world of western orchestral music."

Alma notes that this is less and less the case these days, but Jamaad raises his palm to calm her down. "Yeah, yeah, I know. It ain't as bad as it used to be, that way. But still, it's a shocker to these folks."

He sips at his tea, resets the cup and tugs at his lapels. "I'm tall and trim and I got style and I can talk the talk. After the army, I taught college clarinet and bassoon for six years before I started my agency and I know musicians. I don't grin, and I don't suck up. My secret is," – and at this, he leans forward and looks comically conspiratorial. The others lean in, hanging on his every word – "that it is *I* who am condescending to permit *you* to *possibly* have a share in the goodness to come, through *me*. I never patronize or hit 'em over the head with it, I keep it under the conscious level of perception, but I get it across that it is *they* who are the lucky ones. For there are many of them but only one of me, and I have granted them audience."

"Wow…" Alma whispers.

"And I have *hypnotized* you, little Alma," he straightens in his chair and smiles broadly, "and that's the name o' *that* tune!"

All the laughter breaks Jamaad's spell and they continue their happy breakfast.

Six weeks later now, and a letter appears in the editorial section of the *Ann Arbor News*, and all state-wide affiliates. Its outrageousness sent it viral through the entire state, and in the music world, nationally. It's the sort of thing that just isn't done.

6 May 2022

I am Daniel Cohen, music director and conductor of the Ann Arbor Orchestra, a post I have held with pride for almost 20 years. There is a scandal afoot, both musically and organizationally, that simply must be dragged into the light, and I am the only one in position to report on the situation with the proper knowledge and sense of objectivity.

The Ann Arbor Orchestra, against my express wishes and council, has agreed to sell itself to do the bidding of a charlatan by the name of Bran Englander. He has written a 'symphony,' if the word can be debased as such, and has purchased the favors of the orchestra to perform this piece in lieu of a previously-scheduled concert of two Mendelssohn concertos and a Bernstein overture.

Why is this a concern? Let me tell you about Mr. Englander.

* He has no education. He claims to be a composer yet has never taken a music lesson in his life. He has no idea how to score music for an orchestra even if he were to stumble upon a cogent musical thought, which I do not believe he has ever done.

He doesn't know how to compose music. I am one of the few people in the world who has actually seen and analyzed (which took less than a minute) Mr. Englander's two 'symphonies.' The first of these I thought was a joke. I actually thought someone was playing a joke on me. In its totality, the work – composed entirely of eight-measure building blocks, lasts about one septillion years, or about one quintillion times longer than the current age of the universe. I was expected to extract a 'performing version.' And that bit of absurdity was just for starters.

How could it get more bizarre than the previous? A look at the second of these 'symphonies' (the desecration of the term makes it painful to type) sports 100 instruments playing 100 different things all at once with no relation of harmony or key structure or any notion of orchestral colors – the three glories of western orchestral music that have taken centuries to perfect. It is, succinctly put – a half-hour long jumble of the most deliberately offensive noise imaginable. Note this: deliberately offensive.

And finally, if the freak show isn't grotesque enough for you, please note that the 'conductor' for the event will be a local boy – not a man, a boy – named Jofi Fischer. Note too, that young Jofi has never conducted before and has never taken a music lesson in his life.

I am NOT making this stuff up. How could I NOT bring this to your attention?

How can anyone take pride in an orchestra, an organization, that would do this to itself, and more importantly, to its patrons? An orchestra, formerly of the highest standards, that will lay down like a cheap w***e for any Tom, Dick, or Bran with a few bucks, and then give a child a baton to beat time with. The Ann Arbor Orchestra can no longer be trusted to act with your artistic welfare in mind.

This Bran Englander would be a danger to the entire realm of Art if he actually had any talent, but I can assure you: in that regard, we are quite perfectly safe.

The Ann Arbor Orchestra has not authorized this letter, and I'm putting myself in danger of rebuke. But I am doing it for the listeners and patrons of the art of music in Ann Arbor, and in the desperate hope that the orchestra leadership will rescind its deal with Englander and restore some semblance of sanity.

The Angel Jophiel

If the orchestra allows this event to come to fruition – then save your ears, your time and your money. Stay home that night.

Daniel Cohen
Music Director and Chief Conductor
Ann Arbor Orchestra

The administration rebuked him, all right. They *fired* Cohen the day it was published.

Reactions among the crew, as Jamaad reads aloud to them the letter as posted online the day before, are varied.

"Ah, man…" Bran is annoyed. "This truly sucks. That stuff about my first symphony… I think people believe this guy."

"He told lies!" Daisy notes. "That Mendelssohn concert was all up in the air because one of the soloists backed out. *He had to know that!* We probably weren't taking anything away from them that night!"

"Well," Alma adds, "at least they fucking fired his worthless ass." All are silent, staring in wonder at Alma's bitter use of the profane – not her style! "And he's going to be 18 when he conducts! The bastards!" Crossing Jofi seems to bring out the nasty in the girl.

But Jofi is just smiling, staring at Jamaad. Jamaad catches Jofi's eye, and they grin and nod at one another in recognition of the true consequences of the letter and firing.

"What!?" Alma demands. "Jofi. And Jamaad. What the hell are you smiling about?"

Jamaad gives voice to it. "Alma, darlin', we couldn't buy publicity this good for a million dollars. This is great news!"

"Plus," Jofi observes, "Ann Arbor gets rid of its bum conductor."

So, word was out and in a big way. No longer did Jamaad have to *ask* for interviews and features. The media came to *him*. It was a regional *cause célèbre* for all the thinking class. And all the way from Chicago and Buffalo, Cincinnati to Marquette and points in between, the art music world was buzzin' like a beehive. The crown of it all was a piece the next month in *The New Yorker,* which so rarely condescends to acknowledge the existence of flyover country. They talked to all four of them for the article, also the conductor, and though the group feared a hatchet-job, the consensus among Jamaad and the quartet was that it was priceless publicity that could have been a lot worse.

35

Oberlin College heard about Jofi through the invisible college gossip grapevine – often merciless in its jealousy and cynicism – and engaged the unlettered youth to play a recital of modern piano works of his choosing. They were hearing rumors out of Michigan (and read *The New Yorker* feature) and sought to investigate the suspected charlatan and quash his reputation in the bud. This is one of the ways that some academics assure themselves of their own worth.

But their satisfaction was not to be, for the program Jofi chose was to immortalize him in the annals of piano recitals and recordings. It's what made him famous, at age 17, and launched his career. There were six pieces on the program. He played them all from memory:

Xenakis	*Evryali*
Nancarrow	*Study No.37*
Feldman	*Palais de Marie*
Nancarrow	*Study No.21 (Canon X)*
Englander	*Poetry of π*
Xenakis	*Herma*

The controversy about Jofi's performance centered about this fact: *at least three of these pieces are unplayable by humans.* The two Nancarrow pieces were never conceived for humans to play in the first place. They are so far removed from the possibility of human execution that one needs to outfit a player-piano to do the job; and that first Xenakis piece forces the player to make a performing version for oneself because, as written, one would need three hands to play it. Also, there is a note in the score that is too low to be played on a standard piano, but the recording picked it up. In the recital, *Jofi sounded a note that was not on the piano.*

The audio recording proved that Jofi played the pieces brilliantly, every written note in place, but the video failed to reveal how he could actually have done so. Four cameras were set up (by an inexperienced student technician) to record him: one in gorgeous profile; another head-on from the back of the piano; a third with a full shot from mid-auditorium, and the fourth positioned behind and above the pianist's head to capture in detail his hands on the keyboard. *That fourth camera, though functioning seemingly perfectly during the recording, rendered nothing but static and noise upon playback.*

With but two human arms and hands, and ten fingers, what was possible to actually play, and the sounds that were actually heard and recorded, presented a dichotomy that was not possible to rationally resolve, and persists to this day. The young technician took the brunt of the blame for the failure of camera four but insists, and still insists, that he was not at fault.

Knowing that, if he were to ever repeat this program in concert (as he was often petitioned to do), people would be completely focused on the mechanics of *how* Jofi did what he did, and cameras would be busy recording the movement of his arms, hands, and fingers. Listeners would be caught up in all the spectacle and controversy at the expense of attending to and appreciating the *music*.

So Jofi never played these pieces in public again and the mystery persists.

"Jesus, Jofi… You made Xenakis sound like Chopin."

After the recital, Bran is sitting in the dark with Jofi in Bran and Daisy's hotel room near Oberlin. It's late. Daisy is asleep; Bran is drinking.

Jofi senses that Bran is upset. "Well, not quite Chopin, but I know what you mean," Jofi says. He has a guarded feeling about this conversation and approaches it carefully. He knows Bran is too savvy to be diverted. "When difficult new music is performed, players often behave as if they've done the world a great public service to be able to simply bang out the notes. As if to proudly say, 'There, I did it, see?' But that's usually worse than not having played it at all as it rarely represents the composer's wishes. There is *poetry* in the mathematics of Xenakis."

"I never knew how much. I just thought it was just ballsy and violent and intricate," Bran says.

Jofi explains that he didn't so much 'make it sound like Chopin,' he just brought out the poetry in the score. "And the only way to do that is the only way to effectively play *any* music by *anyone* – technique needs to be an absolute nonissue. That's why literally *no one* plays this music well and so people think they hate it. To enjoy it, to let the music speak, the notes need caressing, and you should not hear any effort."

Bran gives a heavy sigh. He's known Jofi quite a while now, but he has never seen or heard anything anywhere quite like this. It sticks in his craw. He can't get beyond it.

Bran wants the truth and he dives in. "Was that difficult for you? The hardest music ever written?" Bran asks pleadingly. He fully comprehends what Jofi did out there tonight, yet it does not sort with his ideas of reality. *Bran understands without a doubt that what he witnessed Jofi do at the piano was simply not possible.* "Was it? Difficult? At all? Even the Nancarrow?"

"No. It's nothing," Jofi quietly admits, and sighs. "It's literally nothing."

The two friends sit for a while in silence. At last, Bran drains his glass, rises and stands behind Jofi with his hands on Jofi's shoulders in the darkness.

He says, "I love you, Jofi. Meeting you, you literally bringing Daisy to me – these are the most important things of my whole life. But there's something about you that is… deeply… terrifying to me."

This jars Jofi; hurts him. He turns his head to look up at Bran. "Terrifying?"

Bran thinks a space. "Inhuman," he whispers.

Shall I tell him? Or can he sense it? Jofi ponders. *Can there be two that know?*

Bran squeezes Jofi's shoulders. "You were magnificent," he says. "No one will forget tonight." And Bran heads to his room.

36

It's concert day, and almost everything is in place. Conductor Jofi has of course memorized all the parts for the *Sinfonia* and the *Anticanon*. His three rehearsals over the last month had been all that was needed, and the players love him.

Bran included his earlier *Sinfonia* "just to prove that I can write *normal* orchestra music," and there is little there of a challenging nature. But no one anywhere had ever seen or heard anything like the *Anticanon*, and it was a challenge to put together, even for such as Jofi.

The players need to attend to two things only – the emotional contour of the piece, and they all need to listen to one another, even though there is no harmonic connection or even a strict time connection among the parts. By the end of the first rehearsal there was confusion and angst and even some tears as they tried to come to grips with this unique style; by the end of the third rehearsal they were masters of the technique, even reveling in the glory of the sounds they were making – such sounds they had never heard before.

They find Jofi's charisma to be overwhelming – beautiful, gracious, knowing of every detail of every line, and none of the players can recall another maestro in their careers with a more natural authority and greater perfection in communication.

The rest of the program had been fleshed out.

Englander	*Upon Reflection* – sinfonia for strings
Englander	*Queens* for soprano & piano
Englander	*Prism Partita* for solo violin
Englander	*3 Crane Songs* for soprano & piano
	-- intermission --
Englander	*Anticanon* for orchestra of 100 players

Bran, it was decided, will accompany Daisy in the songs. Jofi will conduct the two orchestral works. The multi-talented Jamaad has taken to his role as concert producer and emcee like a duck to water.

Tickets were sold out two months in advance. The adverse publicity and general oddness about the entire proceeding has assured maximum visibility, even in this very regional of settings. Critics from all metro media within a radius of a couple hundred miles are all in for this event, and *The New Yorker* magazine has promised a follow-up article to its original feature. Every classical and art music and orchestral music site on the web of any consequence has sent emissaries to evaluate the outcome.

They all seek the answers to the same questions: What is the deal with this gaggle of total unknowns who have presumed so much? Is the apparently untalented and decidedly unlettered Englander's new work really that inconceivably dreadful? And what's up with this Jofi character? First, he was a teenage nobody with no music training, then he's the most mind-blowing virtuoso in almost a century, perhaps ever, and now the kid thinks he's a conductor? And, speaking of conductors, will the judgment and dire warning of sacked maestro Daniel Cohen be vindicated?

Most of these industry scribes are praying that this is the biggest art music fiasco in decades. They're professional critics and they are just now at their most cheerful – *they smell blood in the water.*

It all happened so fast.

Jofi and Bran are in their dressing room, waiting for Jamaad to finish his introduction to the packed auditorium. They can't hear exactly what Jamaad is saying to them all, but they can catch the odd bout of laughter from the crowd, and then applause. And then – nothing.

An observer in the aisles would have noted a big man in uniform walking down the center aisle to the edge of the stage and stopping, beckoning Jamaad for a word, who squats down to listen to the man in uniform.

Jofi feels it. He can tell something is wrong. He motions Bran to stay put and, in a moment, has joined Jamaad on the stage. The three share a few more words and Jamaad makes an announcement to the capacity crowd.

"Ladies and gentlemen, our fire marshal has alerted us that it would be prudent to exit the auditorium immediately. There appears to be no immediate danger, so there is no need to rush. Just head to the exit closest to you and file out of the theater in a nice orderly fashion. I repeat – there appears to be *no immediate danger.*"

The crowd does not go peaceably. Urban violence has been overspilling the fringes of Detroit for months now and people fear the worst. No one is seriously hurt but scrapes and bruising falls abound as the crowd hustles to safety, the spectre of recent regional calamities in all their minds.

Jofi goes back to the dressing room to discover Bran pacing anxiously.

"Jofi! What the hell is wrong out there?"

"We have to leave," Jofi says. "There's been a bomb threat."

"What the fuck!"

"The found a device that may or may not be a bomb in the tunnel, and the call they got says there are more devices inside. C'mon now, let's go."

"The ladies!" Bran says.

They bolt to the ladies dressing room, but the women have left. They find the pair outside the stage door, in tears.

The evacuation is complete. There are no casualties. And, of course, there shall be no performance.

As they are all hustled away from the theater building so the bomb squad can do their work (which lasts well into the night, though no other devices are found), the words of the possessed priest echo in Jofi's ears – *I have a job to do, same as you, and I don't have to hurt your friends to do it. Totally unnecessary effort. It's all very simple, really.*

37
Detroit

Looking back on it all, it was a godsend, really. There was way more silver lining than cloud. Music aside, there was a major healing event in the lives of Jofi's family.

The doorbell rings and Eric answers the call, tugging open the heavy door and beholding a pretty woman there who looks a lot like… his mom?

"Hello," Eric smiles.

The woman smiles in return, but Eric sees that she's started to cry. Flustered, she wipes at her eyes.

"You must be Eric," she sniffs.

"I *am* Eric," he says, and waits.

"I'm your Aunt Janet."

Janet had returned – Emma's beloved sister and only remaining family, Matt's former fiancé, and Jofi's aunt, whom he vividly recalls. She had gotten wind of Jofi's conducting debut from *The New Yorker* feature and was one of the first to buy a ticket. Alas, only a single ticket.

Janet had obtained a divorce a year ago in London and moved back to Baltimore a few months ago. They had not seen her at the aborted concert, and she had simply driven to the mansion the next night.

It was hard to imagine anything lifting the depressed atmosphere in the house that evening-after, but Janet's reappearance transmuted all the pain and frustration into gladness, for the family at least.

Matt beholds Janet as she is ushered by Eric into the great room, rising from his chair he is speechless, not really believing his eyes for a moment. Emma is standing near the fireplace and actually has to sit down, jolted into instability by the apparition.

As soon as he is able, Matt hurries to Janet to embrace her and they stand there in the middle of the room holding one another with closed eyes and faces so full of bliss that it looks like pain to bewildered Eric. At Emma's impatient bidding Matt releases Janet to her and they embrace for long moments.

Jofi, in his room studying, feels a disturbance in the usual evening ambiance and decides to investigate. He wanders down and discovers his mom hugging… Janet!

Janet spies him over Emma's shoulder. "Jofi, honey!" she says. "It's me. Your aunt Janet. You… you probably don't even remember."

Jofi rushes to her. "Of course, I remember," he says as they hug. "I remember everything…"

She breaks the squeeze and holds him at arm's length. She wears a look of awe. "How can you be even more beautiful now than when you were a baby? I've never seen the like."

Jofi smiles. "Just lucky, I guess."

They sit together till the wee hours, talking and sipping wine, but none for Janet. She tells them about her ex-husband, the London architect. They had many years together, happy ones, but Janet would not go into detail about what led to their divorce. "Some other time," she promises.

Jofi long abed, and it's almost time to end the party. Janet makes a bathroom visit. While indisposed, Emma asks Matt, "Can she stay?"

"What?" Matt is taken aback.

"Just till she gets settled," Emma amends.

"She didn't say anything about moving back to town," Matt says.

"I know… but I'll bet she wants to. It isn't the same Baltimore she used to know. It's a war zone."

"Well… I'll ask."

Janet is back, "You'll ask what? Me something?"

"Umm… yeah. Emma just asked me, and I never thought about it, so sudden and all, but she asked if you could stay *here*, and I think that's a *swell* idea, but… well? What do you think? Got plans?"

Janet looks at the couple, one to the other, and holds her head with eyes closed as if with a splitting headache. "O my God… the memories…"

Emma pops up and goes to sit beside her, drawing Janet to her embrace. Matt looks very sad.

Janet is crying and embarrassed. "Well, I can't blame the wine," she sniffs into Emma's shoulder. "Not anymore."

Matt laughs a strange little laugh and rises from his chair, standing in front of the ladies on the couch. "Remember, so many years ago, when I proclaimed my great idea that we should buy a house and all live in it? Well… I guess I'm doing it again – under drastically different circumstances, but the spirit behind it is the same. Janet, we missed you, the three of us, so much. I've been so worried about you… we *both* have… since you left. You're more than welcome to come back to town, it's nice here, and to stay with us on any basis that pleases you. For a while… or for keeps."

Janet is deeply moved, wiping away tears and smiling. "Well, certainly for tonight. If that's okay."

Emma looks at Janet and says, "This is where you're loved. Where you'll always be loved. Maybe this is where you should stay."

Well, it's Grand Central Station around here anyway, Matt thinks. *May as well have my dear Janet back with us.*

It's bedtime.

162

38

Now afternoon the next day and the adults are all out to lunch together, along with young Eric. Bran is in the studio with Jamaad, sitting and talking. The other three pals are on their way over. Jamaad has something to tell them, but he wants some facetime with Jofi before the rest arrive. After some light chat he gets to the nub.

"Who called in the bomb threat?" Jamaad asks, studying Jofi.

Jofi is taken aback by the question as well as how it was asked. "Why are you asking me?"

"Do you know?"

Jofi clams up. He's unsure what to say.

"It wasn't Cohen," Jamaad says. "The cops jumped on that right away. He's *happy* about it, but the cops say it wasn't him. And the plague of urban violence that's kicking Detroit's ass and growing by the week? Not here. Not in quaint little Ann Arbor. At least not yet. So that ain't it."

"Ah!" Jofi responds as if to dismiss the subject. Doesn't work.

"So," Jamaad repeats, "do you know who it was?"

"Why do you think I would know this?" Jofi asks.

"I think it's interesting that you won't answer me. It's one of them 'yes or no' deals, Jofi, know what I'm sayin'? Simple question."

After long seconds pass, Jofi says, "I can't answer you."

Jamaad drums his fingers atop the table, staring at Jofi. "Do you have any idea how bizarre that sounds?"

"Yes…" Jofi breathes.

"I mean… you're telling me that you *do* know, but you don't want to say that. You won't even *lie* to me! It would have been *so* much simpler to just *lie* to me! You just expect me to be okay with that strange-ass answer of yours. Right?"

"Again: why do you think I know?" Jofi wonders aloud.

"I dunno but that I think you do," Jamaad says. "I think you know *lots* of things."

They hear the doorbell, and Jofi rushes to close the discussion. "I won't ever lie to you about anything, Jamaad, so I'll tell you this – the agent behind this is untouchable, and it will do much more harm than good if anyone knows about this. I wish you would trust me on this."

Jamaad nods sagely. "Okay… you da man," he says. "You *are* the man, you know?"

Jofi looks down and sighs. The door opens wide and all three friends file in and say hello.

Much of the last 20 minutes or so was mere emotional unloading on the events of the night before. Outrage mellowing to sadness, finally to quiet. Bran keeps mostly silent through it all, the ladies providing the bulk of the indignation.

"So why did you want to see us all today, Jamaad," Daisy asks, "so soon after?"

Jamaad is silent for a moment. He starts carefully. "You lost a lot of money Daisy Lee."

She shrugs. "I *have* a lot of money," she answers, but she can't hide that this put a real hurt on her from the perspective of a concert producer. She feels a little stupid.

"Well, some *good* things have happened," Jamaad says, "and I know we all need to hear about that."

Affirmative mumbles all around.

"I talked to the orchestra this morning," Jamaad says. "As you know, they all got paid, but they actually feel our pain."

"What do you mean?" Alma asks.

"They want another shot at it," he replies.

"O god…" Daisy moans.

"Listen, this is weird. The orchestra has agreed to do it for *nothing*, over the objections of the union, which, if I know orchestral musicians, is probably the first time in *history* that offer's ever been made. They knew what they had going," he looks at Bran, "what you gave them. They could feel that it was important. Only the union rep, one of the bass players, objected and wouldn't join with the others."

164

"Yes," Jofi says. "I know who you mean. No great loss. He isn't very good but he's impossible to get rid of."

"My god! What did you tell them?" Alma asks.

"I told them how grateful we all are, but I told them no thanks."

The chorus of "WHAT?!" is unanimous. Jamaad actually starts to laugh as he tries to calm everyone down.

"Because…" he holds up his palm and waits for a little calm. "Because… before I talked to *them*, I got a call from the Detroit Symphony." That gets their noiseless attention.

"They want to host the concert. Same program, same conductor."

"Terms?" Daisy asks.

"No charge. You know how once in a while they do something off the subscription roster? Usually it's a modern thing. They were thinking about adding a concert this season, wasn't settled on what it would be, and then this fiasco happens. They're pretty hot about it. And they will, unlike Ann Arbor, *publicize the hell out of it."*

Bran, silent up till now, stands up, fills his lung in a big long whoosh, and unleashes a piercing howl, like a wolf, except it's a real human sound, not like he's trying to sound like an animal. He wails, the ear-splitting yowl echoing through the mansion spaces. It is actually terrifying in a hair-standing-up-on-the-back-of-the-neck sort of way. Primal. Atavistic. After almost a whole minute of this, he storms out of the room.

Daisy rises up to follow her man. She is crying.

"Daisy!" Jofi calls to her. She slows. "Maybe let him be?"

She freezes and considers… and sits back down. All are silent for a space.

Jamaad (who is so good at this sort of thing) breaks the spell. *"Wow!* Is he happy? He *seems* happy." He looks at the others for confirmation and decides he nailed it. "I think he's happy."

It's 10 p.m., the family had returned from their outing many hours ago (Janet is still with them). The guests have long since departed, all save Bran, who is sitting by himself in the studio, in the dark. Jofi slips in quietly and watches Bran from the doorway.

"Contemplating the vagaries of the cosmos?" Jofi asks.

Bran turns, annoyed. "What?" He reruns Jofi's question in his mind and smiles. "Yeah… I guess I am." They both start to laugh. Bran loves how Jofi can make him laugh in a way no others ever can.

Jofi enters and sits at the table with his friend. "So, what have you been doing in here for hours on end?"

"What time is it?" Bran asks. Jofi tells him. "Jesus… really? I've just been sitting here. Thinking. Contemplating – how did you say it? – 'contemplating the vagaries of the cosmos.' That's *exactly* what I was doing. But I had no idea it was so late."

"Daisy was worried about you," Jofi says. "I told her you were happy, just a little overheated by the events of the last couple days."

"Thanks, buddy. *Heh-heh* – 'overheated.'" They sit in silence for a minute. "I'm wonderin' though."

"About what?"

"Whoever's doing this. This… disruption. What are they going to do in Detroit?"

"The Detroit people said they'd be 'on guard' against that sort of thing. Whatever *that* means."

"Who's doing this, Jofi?"

Here it is again. Same question. "Why do people think I know the answer to that?" Jofi sounds exasperated.

"I'm sorry, bud." Bran laughs softly. "I just wonder… do you have any ideas?"

"Well… I think you and Daisy are safe. If anything happens to you the symphony will become the hottest property imaginable and would be performed everywhere. That would seem to defeat the purposes of those who oppose you."

"But it will be performed. The harder they try to stop it the more assured that is. It's starting to have a life of its own. They must know this."

"Agreed," Jofi says. "So, let's try to think like them."

Bran's face changes. "You know, you never told me exactly why it's so goddamn important that I wrote the thing to begin with, and that it gets a performance," Bran says, a little hotly. "Maybe now is a good time to spill the beans, eh?"

Jofi rises and starts to pace the room.

"Why are you upset?" Bran asks. "Just fucking *tell* me."

Jofi stops and turns to him. "The *Anticanon* will cause something important to happen."

"What?"

"I don't know!"

"You know who's doing this, don't you. You know who's trying *to fuck us up! You know who burned my fucking house down!"*

"Yes! I know!"

"Who? Who, goddamn it!? and if you say you can't tell me I'll… I'll…" both fists clenched in front of him, he can't finish that sentence.

The silent deadlock is brutal for both of them. At last an exasperated Jofi breathes, "Bran… don't you believe I would tell you if I could?"

Bran closes his eyes, then slumps back into his chair, defeated. Composure recovered, he says, "Yes… yes, I think you would tell me if you could…"

"Well, let's just try to think this through, then," Jofi says, recovering his seat at the table.

They sit for many minutes in silent darkness, thinking. Finally, Bran says, slowly and carefully, "The thing that would be even worse than stopping the next performance, since there would only be another try by somebody else, would be to make people not care about it… to discredit me…"

"Stop it in its tracks in Detroit and make people feel foolish that they even bothered to pay attention to it in the first place," Jofi adds, sitting up with attention.

"Right… sabotage it."

"Not grossly, or completely, because that would just impel another group to take it on," Jofi says.

"Right. But enough to enforce the idea that I'm a total boob and don't know how to write. That the work is deliberately offensive, like Cohen claims. And that Cohen was right all along."

Jofi agrees. "That would do it. That would destroy the work, and your reputation. Maybe for the rest of your life."

Bran nods. *"That* is what we need to be on guard against."

39

The Senator scores again. Another term is his. He worked hard and his law-and-order message hit a nerve. Phil Powell, the man behind the message, is now the Senator's Chief of Staff – a fitting reward for a tireless worker whose very face has become the emblem of efficiency to D.C. insiders. Both he and the Senator know that the real goal is less than two years away – President of the United States. Presently, the Senator is the front-runner, and he owes much to Phil Powell.

There is much celebration in the offices this morning, though the election wasn't even close. The 'law and order' effort has been rebranded internally. Phil came up with 'Safety through Sacrifice.' The staff mostly likes it, but it sends a shiver up the Senator's spine. He keeps that shiver to himself.

But all eyes are on the Senator now. If he's elected President, people will expect the terror to stop. They will expect a plan to deal with the rioting. They're tired of words, and they want action. *The Senator may not understand this,* Phil thinks to himself, *but I do. And that ought to be enough.*

40

The concert by the Detroit Symphony is scheduled for almost exactly a year from the aborted local attempt. Jofi will be 19 and (legally anyway) no more of this 'boy-conductor' nonsense. His personal piano recital schedule over the next year will be no more hectic than it's been of late, just more lucrative and in more prestigious venues. He stays far away from much of the so-called 'Romantic' repertory (obsession with sex and/or death he simply cannot process with any genuineness), and he avoids most modern works that employ serial or '12-tone' technique. He finds that philosophy artificial and based in sterile intellect rather than upon true and organic inspiration.

He also had his first concerto engagement (with the Minnesota Orchestra). On that occasion, he played two modern concertos on the same program – Samuel Barber's Piano Concerto and the Piano Concerto No.3 by Bela Bartok. It was a huge success. Not only was the concert covered by much of the music media, but it all caused even more interest in the upcoming *Anticanon* premiere because the word is out – Jofi makes his conducting debut there.

Jofi bought a car. With the wide world of automobiles from which to choose at his feet, no one who knows him was surprised by his choice of an off-lease Honda Accord.

"Dude, what is *wrong* with you?" Bran grumbled at him when he heard the news. "This thing has no character. What. So. Ever!"

"It's reliable and well thought-out," Jofi said, knowing this was just egging Bran on to greater indignation.

"It's the automobile character equivalent of a *toaster oven*, for chrissakes. Why didn't you consult me? Me. Your pal Bran. The car guy."

Jofi strokes his hairless chin, pretending to think hard. "Remember the old Jaguar XJ sedan you used to drive after your Dad's old Caddy died?" Jofi asked. "The 'touring car'

[Jofi makes quote signs with his hands] that you could never actually go on a trip with because it wouldn't go a hundred miles without breaking?"

Bran's face was turning a nice shade of road-rage red. "Yeah. What about it?"

"Now *that* car had *lots* of character," Jofi said with a grin.

Bran walks off, flipping Jofi the bird behind him as he does, and calls out, "You wouldn't know character if it bit your ass."

One reason Jofi is in such demand is because he limits his solo performances. He gives equal time and effort to the careers of Alma and Daisy.

Jofi has asked Alma to move in to the mansion and live with him. He has done so out of concern for her safety, as the adversary must know by now how close and dear she is to Jofi. He fears they may attack him through this connection. Jofi did not tell her his true motivation, but she was so thrilled by the request that she never pressed it. Matt and Emma are glad to have her and, in truth, have felt parental toward the young lady in an in-lawish way for quite a while now. The living space is enormous, so that's not an issue. Alma is clean and helpful, smart, lovely and cheerful – so what's not to like?

Jamaad has done well by both the ladies, procuring them more and better concert dates as time goes on. Jofi and Alma tour this year with music for violin and fortepiano – classical-era stuff – that have gained good notices. It won't be long until Alma is offered concerto performances of her own, initially with third- and second-tier orchestras, but she is in no hurry. She loves her life.

Lyric soprano Daisy Lee is more impatient, a *prima donna* in the bud, a newborn killer-queen. She's murderously competitive. She knows who her competition is and she would like very much if they all got tonsillitis. Daisy is, by any measure, a musically and technically awesome soprano with that one elusive but essential quality without which stardom is but a hopeless dream no matter how 'good' one is – *her voice is*

170

unique and instantly recognizable. Also helpful, career-wise, is that she looks like a Scandinavian love-goddess.

Jamaad has Daisy's career doors springing open left and right. Bran is a good accompanist, but not a performer in the same league as his wife. So now she *practices* with Bran, and she *concertizes* with Jofi – an arrangement that Bran is just fine with. Daisy loves baroque and contemporary opera, and Jamaad is angling to get her a shot in Monteverdi's *L'Orfeo* in Houston. She is also badgering Bran to write an opera – as a vehicle, custom-composed with her voice in mind.

Bran travels with the other four (as Jamaad is usually there with them, now an indispensable and entertaining member of the crew). But Bran's main occupation is the constant re-visioning of his *Anticanon.* The others – except Jofi, who thinks this is hilarious – are always unnerved when Bran announces yet another major revision, crowing on about how terrible the previous version was and how he has finally achieved perfection! This happens so often it kinda makes them wonder…

When they aren't traveling they are relaxing in Ann Arbor and recording in the studio. Jamaad wants his own recording label, and in truth, no company ever started up with a more promising stable of artists. Already there are dozens of state-of-the-art recordings just waiting for a proper distribution channel. Jamaad is on it.

Back at the ranch, Janet is also part of the family now. She no longer works or wants to. Her divorce has provided her with plenty of money. She does volunteer work of various sorts that keeps her busy for long hours – nothing supervisory, just hard manual toiling for the benefit of others. It's almost as if she is serving a sentence, trying to repent of some terrible thing she's done. She has changed in this way. She's quieter, oddly sweeter, seems more preoccupied than before. But she feels the love there at her new/old home. She wraps herself in it and gives herself over to it.

Eric, now a normal annoying teenager, has developed quite a loving attachment to his Aunt Janet, and she him. He doesn't share the musical genius of his brother and, via normal annoying teenage rebelliousness, asserts his differing musical tastes in ways that annoy Jofi to degrees he had never before thought possible. Jofi finds his brother's musical tastes to be unspeakably crude and vulgar (actually, they would be considered pretty normal) and tries hard to be tolerant, but suspects (correctly) that the harder he tries the more Eric pours it on.

One might think that Matt, with his need for quiet and order, would find it difficult to adapt to a household that includes himself, his wife, an adult child, an exasperating teen, his kid's girlfriend, and his ex-fiancée. Add to this the almost constant music-making, and one would be right – it *is* a challenge for him. But he loves them all and would not have it any different. It surely helps that there are intervals throughout the year when the musicians are touring and it's just the four of them.

Janet was most hesitant to move back 'home' on Emma's account, but Emma is so happy to have her sister close that it was mainly her insistence that compelled Janet to rejoin them. Matt is very affectionate toward Janet and senses that she is far from the erotic-minded girl she used to be, and in fact Janet is not seeking such liaisons. More to the point, she is actively avoiding them. Her daily work rounds put her in contact with many men throughout the day, and for a woman in her mid-fifties, she is still very attractive though she tries to hide it. She always makes it clear early on to anyone interested – that she is *not*.

Emma is the family's anchor. She is always the same. Placidly beautiful and tender in all her ways. She still plays her little Yamaha with regularity and much enjoyment. (She won't play Jofi's pianos, and Jofi never touches Mom's except to tune it at her request. An unspoken pact.) She and Matt still enjoy their few close friends and their society pleasures. She loves her garden and takes true pleasure, as she always has, in life's little things. She worries about Jofi. She intuits whiffs of menace and peril but knows better than to press the issue with her loving child – the shining mystery of her life.

41

"Man, I wish I could give them the music to the new version of this score," Bran gripes as he peruses the stack of papers. "It's so much better than the last version." General moaning from the group.

"O *pleeeeze*, stop!" Daisy laments. "I just *know* I'm going to have to listen to this every week of my *life! What did you do? Change an F to an F-sharp?*"

"No… lots of stuff…," Bran mumbles lamely.

"You'll do this till you *die!* It'll *never* be good enough!" Daisy and Bran seem to fight a lot these days, the others are noting.

Jofi chuckles and Alma looks crossly at him. "It *is* getting annoying," she whispers.

"Alma, why do you always think I can't hear you when you whisper about me?" Bran asks Alma. Everyone laughs, so Alma doesn't have to answer.

"Ladies and gents," Jamaad interrupts, holding up a hand, "let's stay on track now. Is everybody all set for tomorrow night?" He pauses and looks about the studio. No response. "Any little thing?" Still no takers. "Good. My job here is done. Meet you all here tomorrow at 2 p.m." He grabs his fedora and heads to the door. "That's fourteen-hundred hours in the army, which you people sometimes make me wish I was still in."

Raspberries and catcalls from the peanut gallery follow him out the door.

They were granted three rehearsals, not the four Jamaad asked for, and they pretty much mirrored the Ann Arbor preparations; the first was a tense near-fiasco, the second was a breakthrough and by the end of the third the orchestra was broken in and eager to present. They, too, are enraptured with Jofi as their leader for the night, but it was a rocky road getting there.

First of all, he knew all their names. He had seen a chart with pictures before rehearsals. When Jofi addressed his comments to them personally they suffered a strange mix of being grateful for his courtesy, melded with a certain unsettling disbelief.

Many of the musicians seemed annoyed at first that Jofi did not use a score but did the rehearsals from memory. It took them the entire first rehearsal to fully understand that Jofi had committed 100, separate, half-hour long instrumental parts to memory. This is, of course, unbelievable, so it was inevitable that some smartass wag would test him. The fourth second violinist pretended he couldn't figure out if the B in measure 87 was marked a natural or flat. Jofi reflected a moment and replied, "There is no B in your part for that measure." The player thanked him, and the other members looked in furtive amazement at one another.

Near the end of the first rehearsal, Jofi was having a difficult time getting an oboist to properly phrase one of his lines. In frustration, the gruff old fellow finally called out in indignation (oboists are good at that, as they are for the most part holding their breath), "Maybe *you* should play the line and show *me!*" This brought uneasy titters from his colleagues. With a cordial smile, Jofi stepped down from the podium and tooled over to the oboist, asked for his instrument, which he surrendered, and then proceeded to play the phrase to perfection. The player's eyes widened as he took his oboe back and nodded in understanding. Jofi stayed put in front of him until the player repeated the phrase perfectly. "Ah!" Jofi exclaimed, "it sounds so much better from a pro! Perfect! Thank you, Adrian," he concluded, using now the first name of the musician instead of his surname, as if they were old pals. Well… now they *are*.

Finally, there was the now-legendary episode of the silk scarf. There is a passage in the *Anticanon* where it is the softest

174

and sweetest, dozens of heartbreakingly exquisite melodies played so quietly that they can barely be discerned. Try as they might, Jofi remained unsatisfied, the passage lacking the last ounce of finesse. It seemed they were at an impasse. Suddenly, Jofi brightened. He asked the concertmistress if he could borrow the lovely silk scarf from about her shoulders. She consented with a frown as Jofi called over a nearby technician and asked him to climb a scaffold in place on the stage to its highest point, then drop the silk scarf into the air. The entranced orchestra watched the scarf's protracted, graceful flutter. It took *so long* to fall so silently to the floor. Jofi beamed. "There," he declared as it settled in a soft heap, "play it like that." And they did.

So, it goes very well so far for fledgling conductor Jofi Fischer, but in truth, slick young concert producer Jamaad Garrett is highly annoyed. He is on the cusp of the big leagues now, but Detroit insisted upon their *own* producer for the concert. Jamaad is billed as 'assistant producer.' And to clarify – 'assistant producer' is French for 'please just stay out of our way, pal.'

42

There are guards everywhere, some in plainclothes, some in uniform. Matt himself has joined the security team, but only Matt knows this. He's always preferred to work that way.

Canine teams have cased the joint, and video of security cameras have been scrutinized for more than a week. Orchestra Hall is, as they say in the biz – clean.

Jofi has a deep dread but says nothing to his peers. There's nothing he can put his finger on, and he knows he may be wrong. He hopes desperately that he is.

The first half of the show goes off without a hitch. Jofi feared disruption would come during the first piece, Bran's harmless and well-designed orchestral piece *Upon Reflection…* but there was no interference and the piece was well-received.

The songs and violin piece by Bran went over furiously well, especially the songs, Daisy Lee proving that she has a reach far beyond the footlights. Her aura mesmerized peasants in the second balcony as effectively as the aristocracy in the box seats. A notable, and noted, debut.

The first half of the concert alone should establish Bran as a composer of note, Jofi thinks to himself in his dressing room. *The second half ought to immortalize him.*

Bran, who has been fretfully pacing all evening hither and yon, strolls in to commune with Jofi before the second half commences.

"You did a great job with the sinfonia, Jofi. Thanks," Bran says.

"So you've said. You're welcome."

"How do you feel?" Bran asks him, as if Jofi is a boxer between rounds.

Jofi chuckles. "I feel fine, Bran. Just relax."

Bran sits. "Relax. Right." He sighs. "The butterflies in my stomach are vomiting."

Matt wanders in on the pretext of wishing Jofi good luck. Jofi knows better but plays along.

"Everything good?" Matt asks heartily. "Anything unusual?"

Jofi smiles. "Everything's great, Matt."

Matt returns the smile, wishes Bran a fond good luck and heads back, probably not to his seat but to who-knows-where to keep a good eye on the proceedings. The chimes ring for the house to get ready for the second half.

Jofi comes on stage to great applause, which he acknowledges humbly and takes the podium. He calls for another tuning, even though the band tuned up before Jofi came on stage. As the strings tune to concert-A, Jofi points to one of the first violinist in the back row who thinks he is in tune but Jofi begs to differ. The fellow tries again and Jofi finally smiles in satisfaction.

All are silent, waiting for Jofi's cue.

The *Anticanon* begins with 100 instruments calling out at once in their own voice, in their own keys, at their own distinct tempos. No one has ever heard anything like this.

Some are shocked, a few are entranced, others tense with the sonic onslaught and the newness of the experience. Some are already angry and mumbling to seatmates after the opening bars. After a few minutes, it becomes clear that a story is being told by the orchestra, for no matter how disconnected each instrument is from every other in rhythm, no matter how unrelated the harmonies are, how different the tempos – the emotional contour of the piece is intact and flowing in the same direction.

A section soon begins of calm and quiet sounds, and the audience seems to be more and more receptive to what is unfolding. But now come rude noises. Low farting bassoons, out-of-tune tubas and mocking trombones. *These sounds are not coming from the orchestra.* The players on stage are not all aware of what their audience is plainly experiencing. Jofi's keen ears detect that the disturbance is not coming from his band, but he keeps them playing, wondering how to respond and when the interference will cease.

The obstructing rude sounds grow more insistent. The audience is sure that these loutish noises are originating in the orchestra, that the composer wants this vulgar and offensive face on his offering.

People begin to react. From various places in the hall there are boos and objects being thrown onto the stage, as if some of the patrons came ready to protest what they knew, or dearly hoped, would be a fiasco of a high order.

An older gentleman in the middle seats is dismayed to hear the man behind him heckling the music. The old fellow stands and faces the seated offender. "You goddamn sissy!" he shouts at the mocker. "When you hear strong masculine music like this, get up and use your ears like a man!"

"You deaf, old man?" the heckler yells back. "He's using the orchestra to shit in our ears! He's as bad as they say!"

The old man stands, listening, and finally sits back down looking chastened and confused.

The unruly brass instruments are blatting noises that are so frankly obscene that Jofi stops the music. The offensive onslaught stops a few seconds later. Jofi turns to the crowd, now standing and yelling their protests, objects hurling through the air at Jofi and his players. Jofi, without a microphone, is trying to tell the audience that those horrible noises were not part of the performance. No one is listening.

Jofi turns and dismisses the players who file hurriedly offstage for their own safety. Jofi follows them out. The hall is still not calm. At least half the audience is on its feet yelling and booing, the stage bedecked with what looks like rotting vegetables. *Who keeps a store of rotten vegetables to take to concerts?* Jofi wonders as he looks out from backstage.

Security takes a hand in the proceedings now, and order the hall cleared. There are lots of uniforms in the aisles and it is, for the most part, an orderly egress for all. The musicians grab their wraps and hurry away from the scene. Ten minutes later the hall is empty and silent. Empty except for Matt, Emma, Janet and Eric near the front, still in their seats. Matt looks mad; the ladies are pale with heartbreak; and Eric... well, he's awestruck and rather enjoyed the spectacle.

Jofi spies them from behind the stage and walks out, stands front and center and spreads his hands in front of him in a display of surrender to the horrors of the day. He just stands there with this hurt look. No one has ever seen Jofi look like this.

"Those noises..." Jofi says to his family, "we weren't doing that... we weren't making those horrible sounds..."

Matt stands up. He has other concerns. "You okay?"

Jofi nods.

"We'll see you at home, son," he says, as the others rise and Matt shepherds them out of the hall, his right hand inside his coat. Jofi has seen that shoulder-holster before.

As they leave the auditorium, Jofi notes that there is another man near the rear of the hall just now standing and putting on his hat. Jofi looks closely and confirms his vision: it is the good priest, Fr. Preston Holt. He waves at Jofi and makes his way down the aisle. Jofi squeezes his eyes shut and does not wave back.

Jofi heads back to his dressing room; no Bran. He finds him in the ladies dressing room with the two women and Jamaad, all sitting together on chairs and benches, wearing blank expressions. They look like mannequins.

Bran looks to Jofi. "Jofi, where were those noises coming from? I was backstage and could hardly hear them but apparently the audience heard it really loud. What the hell?"

"They were only audible to the audience, not on stage… for some reason," Jofi says.

"I've never heard uglier sounds," Alma mused in a dreamy voice.

"Jofi," Jamaad says, "Do you think these are the same people that have been messin' with us?

Jofi closes his eyes like he's really tired and nods. "Yeah…"

"It had to have been a *recording* of instruments," Daisy says as if to herself. "None of the players were making those noises, right? And they weren't muffled, like if they were off-stage. So, it must have been coming over the speaker system."

They look at one another then rise as one and hurry their way to the seating area. Jofi spies a fellow who just entered from backstage (it's the same guy who dropped the silk scarf at Jofi's bidding) and Jofi calls to him. The man freezes in panic and flees backstage. Bran follows him in a rush but soon returns. The man had fled out the stage door and Bran could not follow. The five walk down the center aisle about halfway and stop. Alma starts to talk but Jofi silences her. They listen through the silence. Nobody hears it but Jofi.

"Listen," he whispers.

"What?" Bran says after a few moments. "What are you hearing?"

"Listen!" he repeats. They all just shake their heads.

Jofi points almost straight up. "An electrical hum… from behind that grill in the ceiling. You know what's above the ceiling?"

No one answers.

"A crawl space. Usually used to set up microphones and lights and such. Putting a couple speakers up there would easily blast those sounds into the hallspace so just the audience would hear."

Daisy had narrowed it down, and Jofi had pinpointed it. There must be speakers or acoustical horns behind the grills in the ceiling that are not part of the hall's speaker system which had been shut off and carefully guarded during the concert against sabotage. The placement was ingenious – it would be impossible for the musicians onstage to hear the rude accompaniment while they were playing but the sounds were projected loudly and obnoxiously to most of the audience area. The stagehand was going to tend to the evidence but was caught red-handed and fled.

Now they had the 'how.' And Jofi had the 'who.' But this data would do them no good whatsoever.

They moped all night – what else were they going to do? It was not the time for deep thoughts or strategies on how to move on. They were drained and utterly disheartened. This was an ingenious attack against Bran that could ruin him for life.

They sat for a while together at the mansion, drank wine and talked little. They made plans to meet again after breakfast the next morning when, they hoped, things would be a little clearer.

By 10 p.m. everybody had gone home, the family abed, Jofi and Alma sitting in front of the fireplace, staring into the flames, silent and inert.

43
Washington, D.C.

The next morning held little more promise. A disheartened aura permeated the studio, where sat the five in mostly
soundless interaction. It's nearly noon, Jamaad having waited
for Bran and Daisy to finally make a showing before he
speaks. The others note how beat the pair look. Bran looks
terribly hungover but is not, just so demoralized he is actually
sick; Daisy looks rumpled and almost frumpy, so very oddly
careless about how she looks today.

Bran is especially downcast. He has another burden which
he will share with no one. His heartbreak of the events of the
night before almost pales in comparison to what he
discovered in the bathroom trash that morning – an empty
plastic shell of birth-control pills with Daisy's name. But they
were supposed to be trying again! Careless of her. Or was it?

So, what is Jamaad waiting for? To share the reviews of
the concert. Like they don't feel bad enough.

The reviews are universally brutal. The glowing promise
of the concert's first half notwithstanding (which only half of
the reviews even bother to mention), the focus of the notices
is on the catastrophe of the *Anticanon*, and the worthlessness
of Bran. None of the notices, not one, mentions that the ex-
traneous nausea-noises that sparked a near-riot were not being made by the orchestra. The critics did not pick up on this.
Also, none of the writers wondered how it was that the small
army of antagonistic revelers was so eager to blast forth their
venom at once and on cue, and how was it that so many rotting vegetables were so close at hand and ready to launch?

"None of these dumb son-of-a-bitches picked up on any
of that," Bran sneers. "Can you *believe* that?"

Jamaad chuckles bitterly. "Yes. Easy to believe. They came
for blood, and they got it and they got so much of it that it
blinded them from any real analysis. The long-knives are out
for you, buddy. You're an outsider crashing the gates."

"Listen to this!" Daisy announces, holding up one of the handfuls of printouts. "It's from the Detroit Press –

"*In some ways, Ann Arbor Orchestra's music director Cohen's evaluation of Englander's unfitness as a composer was somewhat disproved in the first half of the concert. Englander proved to have solid gifts as a somewhat traditional composer, technically and musically. But Cohen deservedly nailed Englander to the wall when he spoke of the Anticanon as 'a half-hour long jumble of the most deliberately offensive noise imaginable.' This reviewer, after 37 years of criticism, has never actually felt personally insulted at a piece of music (no matter how badly conceived or rendered in performance) but that is how I felt last night. Englander's creative mind tends dangerously to monstrous indecency – filth, really – and unfortunately, that seems to be the extent of his original music-making. For this, I believe, is his true voice. And the parts of that piece that weren't terminally uncouth were nevertheless written with no sense whatever of harmony, progression, logic or human feeling. I believe – I pray – that we've heard the last of this wretched fraud.*"

"You think that's so awful – you better not read the rest of them, Daisy Lee," Jamaad warns.

"The New Yorker?" Jofi wonders.

"Pretty much the same," Jamaad says. "Minor comments on the first half, major evisceration on the *Anticanon*. But mostly an intimate dissection on the evils of one Bran Englander."

Bran puts his head in his hands. "I'm fucked for life," he says. "Whoever the hell we're fighting… they beat us."

Everyone in the room wants desperately to object to Bran's comment, but no one can think of a single thing to say, and the room goes quiet.

Emma made lunch for everyone this Saturday morn (she so wants to cheer them somehow) and invites them all to the table. They sulk away in unison heading toward the food, sit, drinking ice-tea in sulking silence, nobody touching the platter of sandwiches she made.

No one hungry, everyone tired from a night of little or no sleep, the group decides that today is not a good day to start thinking about how to proceed. Jofi suggests that they wait until Monday to reconvene and use Sunday to just try to tune out the world and reboot. All agree, except Bran, who is asleep in his chair. Daisy nudges him gently awake. They stand to get their wraps, but the doorbell rings.

Emma answers the door, opening it to a tall gentleman and the pair have a short exchange. Emma bids the man to enter the great room, then goes to the dining room where she announces, "Jofi, a Sir George Cavendish is here. He wants to talk to you."

"No *way,*" Bran says.

"What the hell…" Jamaad breathes.

Daisy sprints to the bathroom, terrified to be seen as she is.

"Stay here," Jofi gestures to them. "Don't go yet," he says as he heads to the great room. He sees a tall man standing, facing the fire, warming his hands. He turns.

"Jofi Fischer?" his voice is surprisingly deep for a man his size, tall but thin, regal and elderly, but no vibe of infirmity. He is still in his overcoat.

"Sir George!" Jofi says. "You must know what a surprise this is."

He nods, looking grave. "I'm visiting my ex-wife who lives safely north of Detroit on one of your many beautiful lakes. I know about this ordeal of yours, and I thought I'd take in a concert that I didn't have to conduct! Haven't done that in a while. Years."

"It's an honor to have you here, Maestro."

"I saw the video of your first piano recital. I don't know how you did what you did – considering that it was impossible. Perhaps, if we get to know one another better, you might share your secret with me." Sir George allows a hint of a smile now, putting Jofi at some ease.

"That would be interesting, Sir George. Perhaps-"

"Those people in your dining room," George interrupts, "they are the cast of characters from last eve, are they not?"

Jofi nods. "Indeed, they are. That's the lot."

"I'd like to meet them if they wouldn't mind."

"I'm sure they wouldn't mind. I'll get them." Jofi steps into the dining room and beckons the group to follow him to the great room.

They all stand while Jofi makes the introductions. George is silent until Bran, at last, is introduced.

"So, you're the man of the hour?" Sir George asks.

Bran's 'Authority Figure Hatred Reflex' is activated. He looks daggers at Sir George and fumes, "You don't know what happened last night."

Sir George stares at Bran and nods slowly, his eyes scanning him contemptuously from head to toe and back up again to meet Bran's icy look.

"When you speak to me, you will address me as 'Sir George' or 'Maestro.' *Is that clear?*"

Bran doesn't answer. The two men stare at one another for long uncomfortable seconds until Bran says uncommitally, "I hear you."

Sir George, unsatisfied, is about to deliver further rebuke but Jofi cuts in. "Why don't we all sit?" Jofi suggests.

"No," Sir George orders. "I don't want your relaxation, I want your attention." He looks first at Jofi. "You, young man, are a special case. Unique, I suspect. There's little I can teach you and I have nothing to say to you. Today. That will change."

He looks to Daisy and cannot help but smile. She has luckily recovered some sense of style for this encounter with royalty and no longer looks like a bag lady. "Ms. ... Ms. ..."

"Daisy Lee... Saarinen, Maestro," she says.

"Good lord, you sing when you speak!" Everyone smiles, except Bran. "Take care of your voice and pick repertory gracious to your voice and you will be unstoppable. Learn what not to sing. It's even more important than what you sing. You realize that you are still too young for some repertory that might tempt you right now because of your level of sophistication. Intelligent and ambitious singers right about your age have damaged their instruments with bad choices. Be careful. Call me if you need to."

"Thank you, Maestro. I will be careful. Did you like the songs?"

His smile disappears. He ignores Daisy's question and turns his attention to Alma. "Chamber music at an orchestra concert, eh?" He laughs. Alma is blushing fiercely. "And a solo to boot! It worked out very well... I'm not criticizing. You realize that there are hundreds of very fine violinists out there, don't you, young Alma?"

"I do sir. I mean, Sir George."

"You must differentiate yourself from the pack. You can't be merely fine, or even great." He points at Jofi. "If anyone can steer you right it is probably Jofi. I hear that your recitals with him have been flawless and the programming most imaginative. But you'll still need a little something extra. Do you know what I mean?"

"Did you enjoy what I played, Maestro? Bran's *Prism Partita?*"

George bluntly ignores her query and turns to Bran.

"When I heard your little orchestral opener on the first half, *Bran,"* he said his first name with emphasis, "I thought you were pulling a Prokofiev on us. You were, weren't you?"

Bran waits a space, and said, "Yeah. That's right."

George just stares at him... keeps staring... won't stop staring...*very uncomfortable now...*

"That's right... Maestro," Bran says. Finally.

"Ah," George continues as if the most awkward thing ever didn't just happen. "So, like Prokofiev did with his first symphony, you dashed off a little music that you wrote essentially to prove to any doubters that you could write normal, nice, pleasant music if you have to. So, when you removed your mask and revealed your true self, as Prokofiev did with the rest of his face-melting symphonies, people couldn't conveniently dismiss you as a hopeless hack."

Bran nods.

"How'd that work out for you?"

"Not too well last night… *Maestro."* Bran fairly spits the word out.

Sir George laughs heartily. "You call me 'Maestro' the way many of my men in the army used to call me 'Sir.'"

Wanting more than anything in the world not to soften and smile, Bran softens and smiles. And curses himself.

"Listen, Bran. I know those sounds last night… I know they weren't from your pen," George turns to Jofi, "nor were they from your band, Jofi."

"Why does no one else seem to know this, Maestro?" Jofi asks.

George considers. "You can't blame them, really. The journos – well, bugger them, they're always out for blood. One reason *I* knew is because I had a glimmer of what Bran was trying to do. It made no sense for him to sabotage himself this way. The other reason I was sure you all had no part in that fiasco is much more mundane. I left my seat and got a view of the brass section. I could tell it wasn't coming from there. What I was watching them play with their fingers and what I was hearing was quite completely unrelated."

"I'm glad you understand that, Sir George," Bran said. The Maestro turns on Bran and fixes him with an angry look.

"I understand a *lot* of things, Bran. I understand that what you're trying to accomplish flies in the face of everything in my life that I have held dearest."

Bran is befuddled. "I'm sorry… what-"

"I sat and listened, until the horrors began, to the greatest musical instrument ever conceived by man – the western symphony orchestra – and I listened to you tear it to pieces. With malice of forethought. Our greatest musical achievement – harmony – consigned to oblivion;" Bran was turning pale as he listened.

"The matchless beauty of the palette of instrumental colors and textures – shat upon by some nobody who finagled an orchestra to ruin for the night-"

"How dare you tell-"

"SILENCE!"

Bran clenches his fists and looks about to spring upon the Maestro.

"Never presume to interrupt me again!" The maestro continues his harangue. "And *finally,* as if the preceding were not enough of a felonious assault on a thousand years of musical development – no instrumental part synchronizes to any *other* part! It's a mess! *A total mess…"*

"What the hell are you doing here, *Sir George?"* Bran asks, his voice ashake with rage.

The Maestro calms himself and says, "It might be… it might be a *divine* mess." He pauses to gather the words. "I heard a… a *species* of beauty… that I've never encountered before. A school of possibilities, of potential. *If* you're doing what I think you're doing… it needs a hearing. There's so little that's new that actually… has beauty. No one even aims for it anymore."

With this sincere acknowledgment, Bran's rage dissolves into a puddle. He is overcome and starts to tear-up from days of stress, fatigue and now relief.

"Your aim *was* beauty, Bran. Was it not?" George asks softly.

"Yes, Maestro," said without irony, "That was my only objective." Bran wipes at his eyes and stands, ashamed at his tears, looking totally beat.

"I see…" Sir George has a proposal, or rather, a decree. "I want Jofi to conduct your work in Washington. The Concert Arts Center next season. The National Orchestra, *my* orchestra." He sighs. "I worry a bit that if *I* don't conduct it people will think I'm even a bigger old fuddy-duddy than I actually *am* – but I think it's more important to give a boost to young Jofi here, rather than be too concerned with my vanity at this very late-"

Bran lets loose with a whoop that actually hurts ears. It's long and piercing, like screaming but it has a joyful cadence. He paces the room, howling long and short, like a wounded banshee and scaring holy hell out of their visitor. After a few laps around the great room he heads for the studio, wailing like a soul in torment along the way, but everyone (except George) knows he is actually overcome with joy.

"Sweet Christ!" the maestro exclaims. "Does this happen often?"

Daisy laughs. "Only when he gets ecstatic life-changing news."

"I see… well. It's been a pleasure meeting you all," the Maestro says, in a big hurry all of a sudden. He reaches into his pocket and whips out a business card. "Here. Take this. My people will be in touch. Umm… please instruct Bran to send me a copy of the score as soon as he can, all right?"

Daisy assures him he'll have it by tomorrow. Jofi ushers Sir George out the door to the echoes of Bran's last few fading gale-force squawks of joy.

The adversary's efforts to keep the Anticanon from being heard had backfired so badly that it would have been better if no effort at all were spent in trying to obstruct its premiere. Only the locals would have heard it, and whatever impact it might have made would likely have quickly fizzled, leaving it far short of the critical momentum it needs to achieve in order to become somehow influential.

A performance by the National Orchestra in Washington would be the international musical event of the year, and the tricks that stopped the first two performances would never be a threat in such a carefully protected venue as the Concert Arts Center. Washington D.C. is the most carefully-policed region in the world right now.

But I could not find comfort in this scenario. My enemy is possessed of infinite cleverness and no strategy would ever be considered too cruel or underhanded. I needed to pay a visit, a final visit, to the good priest and the parasite that infects him.

I have, to my eternal shame, already failed in the primary purpose of my incarnation – to find Sam Morgan and protect him so that he might fulfill the glories of his calling. He may already be dead, the adversary's hint that they have

already disposed of him may have some veracity.
I simply do not know. At very least I must not
fail to protect the Anticanon and help bring
Bran's vital creation to life.

— from Chronicles of Jophiel, Vol. II.

44

Jofi had planned to seek out Fr. Preston Holt at the church rectory the very next day, but he woke that morning to a message from the priest. It seemed Holt no longer lived at the rectory, in fact, he had abandoned his priestly duties there.

Dearest Jophiel,

I am no longer serving at Holy Trinity Church. I was demoted to assistant because my many injuries eventually prevented me from carrying out my duties. Therefore I was replaced as pastor. Ahri has made my life so very miserable that I decided the best thing to do for my congregation and myself — was to simply walk away. I packed a few things and left.

I live now in an upper flat on 1516 Lawrence Street in the student ghetto. I have a side-door entrance and have placed a key under the mat for you to use if you require me in any way.

I venture out only rarely, driving for miles to do the simplest errands lest I be found out by a parish member. I spend my time in meditation and prayer.

Ahri will not permit me to reveal the details of the Detroit sabotage to you. The only antidote to the poisonous shame I feel is your sweet promise that I am helpful to you and if I persevere I shall eventually be released from the penitential anguish that defines my life.

Please visit me if you can. Just to behold your beautiful face is a heavenly balm of healing and joy to me.

Love and devotion in Christ, always —
Preston Holt

Jofi did not have to resort to rooting out doorkeys, as Preston Holt was downstairs holding the door open for him when Jofi arrived that morning, after a quick breakfast at the diner and a stop at the bank.

"He usually tells me when you're coming," Preston calls out with an attempted smile as Jofi makes his way up the driveway.

Jofi shakes Preston's hand and gives him a hug. "Well, at least he can be helpful sometimes," Jofi says, releasing the priest and climbing the stairs to Preston's very un-fancy new digs.

Coat off and settled on a kitchen chair, Jofi accepts a cup of tea all ready for him. Preston sits across from Jofi and leans toward him conspiratorially. Jofi holds up a hand and Preston stops. Jofi pulls from his breast pocket a large wad of hundred-dollar bills; 250 of them.

"When this runs out, let me know," Jofi says.

Preston closes his eyes and radiates relief. "Thank you, Jophiel. That takes so much worry away."

"You merit it."

Preston recovers himself and leans forward. "I am to tell you, on instructions from the thing that so often possesses me, that any attempt to stop the premiere of Englander's piece in Washington – or anywhere else – is 'off the table,' to use Ahri's words." Preston feels an actual chill from Jofi's intense stare as he speaks. "Ahri realizes, I believe, that the more he objects to the work being made known, the bigger the disaster. From his point-of-view. This has caused him considerable embarrassment in certain circles."

Jofi wears a stern face. "Let him through."

"He won't come," Preston says, with a note of fear in his voice.

"I'll rip him through!"

"You will have to," Preston closes his eyes and surrenders to a most unpleasant procedure. But Jofi reconsiders.

"He'll vent only lies," Jofi whispers, as if to himself. "I won't get a word of truth from him." He stands and says loudly, "I need the truth. Now! He's hiding something from me that is monstrous! I can feel it! *What is it?*"

"Jophiel! You know what will happen to me if I-"

Jofi rises, hurries around the table and violently snatches Preston by the front of his shirt, out of his chair as if he were hefting a featherweight toddler, and slams him up against the kitchen wall, facing him nose-to-nose. Jophiel presses his forehead against the priest's and bores into him with his burning sapphire eyes.

"NO! NO! NO! NOOOO!" the priest screams as Jophiel does that thing he so hates to do, that belies his humanity and will cause a hapless human so very much future agony.

Suddenly, the priest is quiet, open-mouthed and entranced, slack against the wall as the Angel scours the contents of his soul. The Angel meets the full might of the adversary's resistance and Jophiel cannot achieve the clarity he seeks here, only the outlines and even these but through a glass darkly. After a few moments, he slowly releases Fr. Holt, who sinks slowly to the floor as his legs have no strength to stand on their own. Preston sits there, against the wall, slowly coming back to himself and starts to weep, then, realizing that he is in the presence of the Angel, stifles his tears and bows his head low in silent supplication. Waiting. He knows what Jophiel has uncovered.

"Why?" Jofi wonders to the ceiling. "What is this – revenge?" He looks down at the priest, still cowering before him. Jofi paces the small yellow kitchen. "Why would he… how could even *he*… what does *she* have to do with any of this? This won't affect anything! *It's mindless cruelty! What is the reason!*"

"I don't *know* the reason," the priest whines. "You know what I know."

Suddenly, Jofi reaches for his coat and phone and bolts from the house. By the time he gets to his car he gets Daisy's voicemail. He tries Bran. No answer. He climbs in, buckles up, starts the Honda and calls his dad. Matt picks up.

"Jofi, what's up?"

"This is important. Have you seen Daisy?"

"Not today, why?"

"Someone's trying to kill her. Can you get to her house? You're closer than me…"

"I'm on my way. Any other information?"

"That all."

"Anything. THINK."

"No, Matt, nothing. Just that. We have to see that she's okay!"

By the time Jofi arrives at Daisy and Bran's home, Jofi notes that Matt's little car is parked well down the road from their house. Jofi parks his car behind Daisy's little Porsche Boxster right in front of the home and he gets out, noting a pair of long legs poking out from beneath her car. Jofi notes that the shoes are Matt's.

"Hi, son!" Jofi hears the muffled cry.

"Matt? That you under there?"

"It is."

"Everything all right?"

Matt scoots out from beneath the little car and quickly pops to his feet, a few tools in one stained hand, a small wired package in the other. "It is, now."

"Is Daisy okay?" Jofi asks.

"She's fine. The two of them are in the house. Go on in," Matt says. "Let me put this stuff in my car. I'll meet you inside."

Daisy has been crying, Jofi notes upon entry, as she throws herself at him for a long, anguished embrace. She releases him and he looks over at Bran standing near, who simply nods in greeting. He looks scared. Matt enters and closes the door.

Bran looks at Matt. "Is that what I think it is?"

"If you think it's a car bomb, you are correct."

192

Bran sits on a bench in the foyer. *"Holy shit,"* he exclaims. "Matt, how did you know to check for a car bomb? Did Jofi say that?"

"Nope. Just that someone was trying to kill Daisy Lee. That was a no-brainer for a guy like me to check as fast as possible once I established that she was alive and safe. And hadn't used her car today."

"O my god," and poor Daisy is just now getting her bearings back. *"A car bomb."*

"Pretty standard stuff. With enough of a punch so that the result would leave little doubt that whoever tried to start the car would be dead." Daisy puts her hand to her mouth and gasps. "Professional job; really well done," Matt said with a hint of admiration in his voice. "No chance of failure."

Bran looks edgy. "Why... Jofi? Jofi, how did you know to call Matt? What the hell is going on?"

"I had it out with our enemy. I choked it out of him," Jofi says.

"Who *is* the enemy?" Bran demands. "Tell me, so I can choke something *else* out of him."

Jofi sighs deeply and looks resigned, maybe even relieved. "Let's go back to my house. You all deserve to know more about all this. I'll explain."

"Good!" Bran cries. "Finally!"

It took almost a half-hour to drive the few miles to home. Downtown Ann Arbor traffic was at a standstill due to a demonstration at the Federal Building that got out of hand. There were two dead and suspects on the run.

Emma and Alma were waiting for them when they all arrived. Everyone wants to hear Jofi explain, and all but Eric are in attendance, which is just fine because neither Matt nor Emma wants Eric to be privy to any of it. They are now all arrayed around the big dining room table with Jofi sitting at the head.

Bran is impatient. "Jofi, who is this guy?"

Jofi has been considering how to discuss this while in the car. He knows it's going to be a tough sell. "He's not a man."

Emma is confused. "A woman?"

"No, no. Nothing like that. Let me start over, and don't interrupt. Please, everyone. This is hard enough."

They agree to be silent while he explains, as best he can, what they are all up against.

"There is a priest here in town, who… well, he shares a body with another spirit who possesses him from time to time." Jofi notes that this is not going over well, his auditors sharing furtive glances of disbelief, but he continues. "The priest is a good man; the spirit is the enemy. He tortures the priest if he resists. This spirit has a job to do. Much as I have a job to do. I have failed at my main job, but that's another story. My secondary job is to guide Bran in the creation of the *Anticanon* and to make sure the work is performed. The job of *this* spirit is to prevent that from happening. Or at least it *was*. He claims that's no longer the objective."

Bran raises his hand, schoolboy-style. Jofi nods to him in resignation. "So, this is the guy who burned my house down, sabotaged two concerts and *tried to kill my wife?*" He was barely keeping it together.

"No," Jofi says. "The spirit that occasionally possesses the body of the priest makes these things happen through others – various local thugs and whoever – but neither the spirit nor the priest, are the actual agents who do the deeds."

"I can tell you that it was no priest who put that bomb together," Matt says.

"Why does he want Daisy dead?" Bran demands.

"I don't know. I was told that he has given up trying to stop the premiere of the piece and killing Daisy or you would only bring more notoriety, so that would be stupid. And he's not stupid. But other than the upcoming concert – I don't know what it could possibly be about. I think he's still trying to stop that premiere. I just can't think of another reason."

"Umm… you mentioned just now about killing *me?*" Bran asks.

"That's right," Jofi says. "You are *both* in danger."

"Why don't you kill *him?*" Bran asks. Matt nods as if to say, *not a bad idea.*

"If I do, he'll simply find another host for himself, that I'll feel responsible for, *but we won't know who it is.* That's why I was willing to play the game… at least before it became a matter of life and death."

"Well," Bran says, "now that it *is,* what do you suggest?"

"Daisy and Bran need to be kept safe," Matt says. "That's job one. I need to get to the priest so I can-"

"NO!" Jofi cries. "That spirit can *hurt* you. Hurt you in ways you have *no idea.* You have no defense against those weapons. I need to go back there." Jofi stands up.

"And do what?" Matt asks.

"We need to think of a way to… lock him away… something like that," Jofi says, unconvincingly and unconvinced.

"He won't be there," Matt says flatly.

"What? Why not?" Jofi asks.

"You said he wasn't stupid. If he stays there – he's pretty stupid. The game has changed. He won't be there."

Jofi considers this and looks deflated.

"I'll drive; you go in and see if I'm right," Matt suggests.

"And if he's there?" Bran asks.

"I'll see if I can find out any more than I already know," Jofi replies. "I had to hurry out of there when I got concerned about Daisy." Daisy blows Jofi a kiss.

"Glad you did, brother. Glad you did," Bran says. "I gotta say, though…"

Daisy leaned against Bran. "Say what, my dear?"

"I think it's downright bizarre that we all just listened to Jofi explain all this and we all *believe* him. I mean, *I* believe him, and nobody else seems to have a problem with an explanation that's so… *bizarre,* that rational people would just laugh out loud!" He looked around at all assembled and noted smiles and nods from them.

Daisy laughs. "Well, getting to know Jofi…" and she hold her hands up as if in surrender to the strangeness of life. "He was even harder to believe than *this* stuff!"

"Wow," Bran concludes. "What the hell next?"

They took the drive. Jofi found no key under the mat, but the place was unlocked and there was no one upstairs, the few effects that the priest had were gone, no clothes in the bedroom or any bathroom effects, and Preston's car was not in the carport. There was, however, a note on the kitchen table.

My Dearest Angel,
I hope you keep them from harm. You will never find me now — Ahri is making sure of that. He will take my eye now. I hope my end is soon. I've tried my best to serve you, but I am only human. Please stay mindful of me.
In the Love of Christ,
Preston

After long discussion that lasted most of the afternoon, things shook out like this: Bran and Daisy would stay close; meaning, that to 'send them away someplace safe' made little sense if there were no one around to protect them. This same security was also deemed wise to extend to Alma.

Jofi agreed that this was a good idea but flatly rejected Matt's suggestion that Jofi himself be included in the security scheme. Matt groused about this. So did Emma. "This is my fight," Jofi said.

Matt, because of his success in the professional arena of protecting people (also his natural inclination), felt pretty proprietary about all this. He would arrange 24/7 security on the three and would like to see them cancel their concert activity "until the heat is off," though of course, when that might actually *be* was not clear. They decided to go with the idea that the adversary was still trying to prevent the premiere of the concert.

196

It was decided that this would be a year of recording projects in the studio. It was a good solution. After the concert in Washington, they would re-assess the situation. This troubled Jofi, Alma and Bran not at all, but Daisy was upset that her career might be damaged by abstaining from concerts at this delicate point in her ascension. Bran noted sagely that if she were dead it might be even more difficult.

Until then, Bran and Daisy would have living space at the mansion and split their time between there and home – not unlike the current regime, just more of it at the mansion. All three would be at all times under armed and chauffeured guard when they traveled to and from either location, for even the most trivial errand, and two guards would be stationed at Daisy's residence when they are at home, with another watching their house when they were away. Matt would hand-pick the personnel for all this and Daisy would foot the bill.

Matt also counseled them that this was not going to be an easy 11 months or so – that they would get sick of the routine and perhaps long to weasel free on the odd occasion. He warned against this as precisely the opportunity the opposition may be hoping for.

Everyone gets the message, and everyone is down with the plan. In the meantime, both Jofi and Matt had decided to try to track down the priest, each using his special tools to do so, and each having decided to keep their efforts to themselves.

45

As the months unfold, the new regime is perceived by the group as almost unendurably brutal. Daisy seems to suffer the worst though all have complaints that, in Matt's mind, reflect a petulance that is hard for *him* to bear, though he has had much professional experience safeguarding people who groused and even resented being protected.

But Daisy – she is the least temperamentally well-disposed to such lifestyle restrictions; add to her 'outraged heiress' persona the fearful certainty that her once-promising career is needlessly evaporating before her very eyes! An uncharitable person, for example, might suspect that Daisy is just acting out in order that the others will take pity on her tragic state, and prioritize her recordings in the schedule so as to soothe her heartbreak. Bran doesn't mind so much since most of Daisy's material was written by him, but Alma has a bee in her bonnet over it all and is often sulky and bored.

Janet (much to nephew Eric's distress) is deteriorating. She is losing weight and the family suspects that she is depriving herself of food. She has become absent-minded and spends more time alone in her rooms than before, and when she emerges from her chambers her eyes are red-rimmed, and she is somber.

Eric has asked Jofi to speak with her. Up to now, Eric had never acknowledged big-brother Jofi's 'otherness' in any way but humorously. In his request to Jofi and the respectful way he made it, it was clear that his love and respect for his older brother was immense. He had faith that Jofi could relieve his beloved aunt's misery no matter how weighty or how deep. Jofi was touched by this and said he would speak with her.

Jamaad finds that his own worst fears of being minimized at the Washington concert will not be realized. He is a paid liaison for this event, and with very little on his concert schedule until then, is happy to have some way to justify his salary.

It was made immediately clear to Jamaad that only Bran and his *Anticanon* will be featured on part of the Concert Arts Center concert – this would not be a 'Bran Englander Festival' by any stretch. Bran's *Anticanon* shall be the sole piece on the second half. Part one shall feature Maestro Cavendish conducting Stravinsky's ballet, the *Rite of Spring*. This news depresses Daisy and Alma even more.

On the bright side: Daisy, Bran, and Alma are still alive. *They seem to forget that little detail,* Matt muses to himself. The crew he has assembled is first-rate and the routine is a good one. *Amazing*, he thinks, *how they all just take this for granted.*

There has been no suspicious activity noted by any of Matt's people since the start of the project. Both Matt and Jofi search in their own ways for the renegade priest and the pest that infects him, but to no avail. Matt's formidable tracking skills have dead-ended, nor can Jofi sense the adversary's hiding place. Unlike the catastrophic failure of his search for Sam Morgan, he can at least feel that Fr. Holt is here in this world. He just cannot locate him.

46

"Two up, bacon and wheat," Harriet says to the new short-order man, who snatches a couple eggs, breaks them skillfully in the little buttered pan and rams two slices of wheat bread into the toaster. It's the slow part of the morning and Bobby is glad of it.

The cook's real name isn't Bobby, it's Preston.

He's a good cook. Learned his chops while he went to college, before the seminary. He worked then in a diner very much like the converted double-wide he's in now, except that one was in Green Bay; this one is in the Pocono Mountains of Pennsylvania in a little berg called Canadensis. The town is tiny, but the diner is a popular destination, especially for truckers.

They all love sweet, shy little Harriet and are protective of her. She's deaf and speaks the dulled and blunted speech of the deaf. Most everyone here remembers the stranger who stumbled in from the bar across the street one rainy day last spring and made mooing sport of Harriet's unmusical voice in a hurtful way. To his dread, the stranger watched as the truckers actually pulled high card from a deck to see who got to beat the living hell out of the man out back of the place. He left in an ambulance and was never seen at the diner again. Harriet never knew.

Preston, er… Bobby, is a little in love with Harriet and thinks she's beautiful. She pushes all his buttons, buttons Preston had almost forgotten he had, and hadn't had pushed in decades. He wonders as the toast pops up and he scoops soft butter from the tub *am I really a priest anymore?* She's very nice to him and blushes when she catches him looking. That little bit of adorableness sends him over the moon! She even told him that his eyepatch makes him look like a scary tough guy. Ha! Imagine that.

It occurs to him as he sets the toast on a little plate – *this is the happiest I've ever been in my life.* So he takes the bacon slices and bends them into a smile and places them below the sunny eggs' yellow yolk-eyes. Harriet laughs as she whisks the plate away.

The dreaded and loathsome Ahri, after he took Preston's eye (as he promised he would), has had absolutely no contact with Preston since. He feels him inside, but for the first time as a dormant thing, not as the ever-active, ever-scheming parasite that has for so many years dominated his life. It has been four months now and there has not been a single stirring within. He wonders, especially when his gaze alights on the lovely shape of his little colleague – *am I free? Has Ahri given up the struggle? May I have a new life?*

Near quitting time yesterday, he was nearly overwhelmed by such a hopeful thought, and he wrote on the little whiteboard with a red magic-marker *Will you go to the movies with me Friday night?* and you know what? She said Yes!

47

It's nighttime and it's snowing, and Alma is sad. She's lying in the big bed she shares with Jofi, who is in the studio comparing versions of Bruckner symphony scores. She looks at the clock. It is almost midnight.

She is sick of the isolation and the routine and there are six more months of it unless they find that damned priest.

She feels bullied by Daisy, even though Jofi has convinced Daisy to take next week off so that Alma can record the *Rosary Sonatas* by Heinrich Biber. Jofi on harpsichord and Bran's pal Li Ming on baroque cello will accompany her. Quite a project, that. *And Daisy Lee acts like she's doing me a favor by taking a break!* Alma seethes.

Alma is 23 years-old, and she feels her womanliness more vividly than ever before. Her love for Jofi is undying but these days she is trying to come to grips with feelings that she interprets in herself as vulgar and crude, and unworthy of her Angel's regard. She wants, she *needs*… to be *filled*. Her hand drifts under the blanket and under the elastic of her panties and she presses down, and sighs.

She shares no sexual intimacy with Jofi since he worshipped her breasts that unforgettable night that she repeats in her mind over and over. She is now so wetted by the raw charge of that memory and she strokes herself languidly. They were so close in those moments. *Closerthanthis.* Her burst of orgasm will offer her some release, and these come more easily and more frequently these days, *but she needs to be filled up.* Her orgasms are easy but the void that wants filling is never satisfied. Daisy has her toys (as she calls them) and wants to take her shopping *but they won't work for me. I just know it.*

She tries to fill this void now with two fingers and as she approaches climax, she thinks of her beloved Jofi and brutally squeezes her nipple, and this drives her hard over the edge and into her ecstasy.

She doesn't know if she is finished. She catches her breath and lies still, opening herself to the thoughts and feelings that always bubble up afterword. *I want a family,* she thinks. "I want babies…" she says aloud. She starts to tear up but stops herself. This is no time for self-pity.

She is consort to an Angel. How many women in history could make such a claim? O how she would love to meet them. What a sisterhood that would be! But for all the glory of such a thing, the woman in her is unfulfilled. The void in her is unfilled. Shall it always be thus? Alma, at last, lets the thought open up in her – *I need a man to love me, and I need a man to love.* The thought is oppressing and liberating at the same time. She caresses again the center of her wetness and moans in frank wantonness. It's become a need like food or water or breathing. In a moment she will cry out. But not too loudly…

Loudly enough. Jofi is still in the studio, well out of earshot of his ecstatic partner, but the Bruckner scores lay closed up in a pile and Jofi stares straight ahead forlornly at the foam-padded walls in front of him. He does not *hear* Alma – he *feels* her soul crying out and bleeding into his and he opens himself to this.

For some time now Jofi has accepted what Alma has only now begun to fully understand about herself – *she needs a man to love her, and she needs a man to love.* He sighs and counts it as yet another failure in his mission. He should never have brought her so close.

48

Jofi has put off speaking with Janet. He doesn't know what to say or how to go about it. Eric has just left Jofi's room, where he has again presented his petition. Eric (as well as Emma and Matt, in whom Janet will not confide) believe she is getting worse. Jofi decides to let the words come to him, and he goes to Janet's door, closed now as usual, two hours after dinner had ended. He knows he is about to interrupt the solitude she protects, but he knocks anyway.

In a few seconds the door opens, and Janet stands there in her robe, red-eyed, an attempt at a smile on her pale visage. "Hi Jofi, honey. Come in, dear," she bids him, and he enters. She closes her door and turns the lock. "Sit there next to the bed." Jofi sits and Janet takes a seat on her bed facing him, seeming glad at the intrusion. "What's new with you?" she asks.

"I'm worried about you."

She looks to the floor and frowns. "O…"

"Also, Eric is very concerned."

"He's such a sweet boy," she whispers. "I don't want him to be upset."

"I'm sure he knows that, Janet."

They sit in silence for a space. Jofi breaks it.

"Would you share with me whatever is so upsetting to you?"

She looks up at him and laughs softly, bitterly. "It's hopeless. It's hopeless, Jofi."

Jofi rises from the chair and gets on his knees in front of his aunt. Looking up at her, he says, "It's not, Janet. I promise it isn't. You're looking from such a dark and distorted and fearful place, and light will help dispel the torture you're feeling."

She starts to cry. Noiselessly. Tears just streaming down. "The light will make it worse!" she says. "You have *no idea!*"

"Well… maybe just admit that it's possible that you're wrong about that. Nobody knows-"

"That's right Jofi," she interrupts in an ugly, scolding voice. She can't meet his eyes. "Nobody knows about these things, not even *you*. Now please. I'm tired. I want to rest."

Jofi gets it. He stands and leans over to kiss his sad aunt on the cheek, then heads to the door and unlocks it. He opens it and turns to face her. "I'll come back tomorrow evening. You can throw me out then, too, if you feel that's best." He smiles and shuts her door. He hears the lock snick.

Jofi turns and spies Eric in the hallway. "How'd it go?" the boy asks.

"Fine," Jofi smiles.

"So, what happened?"

"We'll know more tomorrow."

Eric looks confused and Jofi heads for bed.

49

The unthinkable happens the next day. Trouble in Paradise – the five become four.

Bran and Daisy called to say they would be late to the weekly meeting that Jamaad likes to have. He keeps them abreast of developments about the upcoming concert and they discuss bookings for the next season when they all hope to be free of their travel constraints. Then he consults privately with Daisy about the bills.

When they arrived Bran looked hungover, but he was not. Daisy looked all business, but there was a brittleness behind the façade.

Hellos all said, rather perfunctorily, and now settled around the big diningroom table, Daisy asks Jamaad if she may speak first. She stands.

"I'm going to Houston to sing the role of Eurydice in *L'Orfeo*. Bran is… Bran is staying here." She coughs and takes a breath. "Things are not really working out for us. I'm leaving tomorrow morning, and-"

"What?" Alma is shocked into interrupting. "O no! You're leaving? *Really?*"

Daisy bows her head and covers her face in her hands, not making a sound. In a moment she drops her hands and raises her head. "I promised myself I wasn't going to make a scene… but… between me and Bran… it's all very personal and I don't want to talk about that."

She looks at Jofi. "I know your dad will do everything in his power to dissuade me, and I know these guardians of mine will not back off until he tells them to. But he must. He can't legally hold me here. I need to travel and be on my own and go about my life as I see fit. If my life is still in danger, then that's my problem. No one else's."

Alma bursts into tears and Bran looks like someone has torn his heart out. In fact, someone has. Jamaad is in shock; Jofi seems oddly detached.

"So Jofi," Daisy says, "I need to speak with your dad."

Jofi nods. "He's at the gym with Eric. When he gets home I'll have him call you. He'll release you, of course. He knows he must if you ask."

"Thank you," she says. "Now, I know you all have things to discuss, but I would like to take my Jamaad time now, just me and him, so we can work a few things out. I'll be withdrawing my level of support for what we've done together so far, but everything is in place and that oughtn't be a hardship. I don't regret a single penny that I've spent. I'm proud of everything that's happened. It's just... it's just time..." She stops trying to explain.

Alma has been reduced to sniffles, but Bran still looks like hell and has said not a word through all this. They stand to leave Daisy alone with Jamaad, but Daisy is not quite finished.

"I hope you know that working with you all has been the best thing in my life. Knowing you all... has been..." and now the tears she swore she would dam. She sits and covers her face and lets the tears come.

Daisy still wants Jamaad to manage her affairs. He has agreed to this. She did not ask him to come south with her or to abandon the others to concentrate solely on her career. If she had, Jamaad would have cut her loose. She, even more so than Jofi, is by far his most obvious money-maker, but he would not have hesitated to quit her.

She wants the studio masters of all her recordings, and there are many, and all rights reverted to her. Jamaad refuses, gently and politely, insisting that they would come to a mutually agreeable arrangement. But not today. Daisy acquiesces, knowing it was a longshot.

A few more nickel-and-dime issues settled, and Daisy gathers a few of her things from the studio and departs, with no additional goodbyes.

No further business transpired that day. Matt tried his best in his phone call, asking to meet with her in person to discuss the issues, but realized early on that he was not going to win. He released the guardians and chauffeur.

The next morning Daisy boards a plane to Houston without incident. She feels free, and terribly, indescribably alone.

The day is far from over. It's evening, an hour after a somber family dinner, and Jofi raps softly upon Janet's door. She unlocks it and invites Jofi in. He notes that she has placed two chairs face to face a few feet apart as if anticipating a discussion. This lessens Jofi's anguish, and he sees a sweetened aspect to his aunt's face that was absent in their last encounter.

"I need to say I'm sorry about last night, Jofi," Janet says quietly as she takes her seat across from her nephew. "I was rude, and I hate rudeness. So… I'm sorry, dear."

Jofi smiles. "What I asked from you was incredibly personal and causing you pain and stress. I came to you out of the blue with all this…"

"Listen, Jofi… I need this to stay between you and me. At first. What I mean is… I need to be the one to tell the others… if I do. Okay?"

Jofi smiles and nods his understanding. They are silent for a space. She is about to speak but Jofi heads her off. "You know, you might want to only do this once. I mean… it might be easier, now that you feel you can unburden a bit, to do it once and for all."

Janet looks confused, anguished. Jofi senses that Janet may have perceived his efforts as a trap. He continues. "I mean… Matt and Emma – they love you as much as I do. And they've suffered even more than I have. And for a lot longer."

Janet has her eyes closed. She makes the jump in her mind. Now she nods her head stiffly, eyes shut tight as she sends Jofi approval through her pain with profound effort. He rises and heads out to bring Emma and Matt to hear Janet's account at last.

In a minute the trio is in place, standing around the empty chair smiling with a hopeful tenderness at Janet. Matt and Emma are in their robes, obviously full of expectant sympathy that they find hard to hide.

"I have something to tell you," Janet begins. "I know I've been quite the pill lately. And getting worse over the months. It's not been fair that I have countered your love and generosity with my stony… silence. And self-pity… that-"

"Janet," Matt speaks, "we don't care about that. We just love you and want to know why you're so sad all the time."

"You need to know there is nothing that you could do that would make us stop loving you," Emma says.

"Thank you. All of you," Janet says with a touch of formality. She takes a deep breath and begins her story.

"When I left Ann Arbor… this house… all those years ago, I went back east and got a job in a little hospital where I worked for a year and then met a man from London who was in town visiting relatives. He was an architect, very successful back in England. I was a mess when I met him, but I suppose I hid it pretty well. I've always been a drinker, but I really hit it hard after I left here. John didn't mind that – he was a bigger drunk than I was. One of those three-martini lunch and golfer types who are very successful in spite of it all. A real society guy.

"I went back to London with him and a year later we married." She pauses here. "I'm not really cut out for drinking. I mean, I'm not a good drunk. Not like John and so many others like him. I became… well, I became an embarrassment to him. I can't believe I'm saying these things out loud. I never put it out loud into words all that happened…" Janet clears her throat and reaches for the water bottle on the table next to her bed and drinks.

She replaces the bottle, takes a big breath and continues. "Anyway – you know how I can't get pregnant?" The others nod. "Well, I got pregnant."

Emma covers her mouth. "O my God…"

"And I was hoping for some joy from John about it all. And he was *happy*. He had an *heir;* he never thought he would. Everybody was excited for him. I quit drinking. I took care of myself. About the fifth month, he stopped touching me. He was revolted. 'Not while you're pregnant,' he would say to me. He's good with the ladies and they like him – good-looking, rich, a fun guy… younger than me. I started suspecting him. Soon he didn't even bother hiding it. I started drinking again. And then it was a terrible spiral down. I turned into a total mess of a woman. John stopped talking to me. He wouldn't come home for days, and when he did he was so repulsed he would leave again, screaming at me how terrible I looked, how my drinking was hurting the baby – but I didn't care. I stopped eating. I was drunk all the time. I would wake up at night to drink and if I didn't I would get the shakes so bad…"

She is beyond weeping. They have the feeling that there have been so many tears in her life about all this that she has just about dried up.

"I hated John even more than I hated myself. I got back at him, though. That's what I thought. Take THIS you son-of-a-bitch! I thought. O! I knew how to *hurt* him!"

She stops talking and sits with head bowed in silence for an entire minute.

"And so, then I…" and she raises her head to look at the three who love her. She looks like she is about to die of grief. "I… I had an abortion." She puts her head back down, in deepest shame. She cannot look at her family as she continues. "I was so goddamn drunk that I don't even remember it. I killed my baby for *spite!*"

She looks up. Her tragic, ruined face frightens them. *"For spite! I murdered my own child!"*

They are wrong about her tears drying up, for she bursts forth bawling terrible sounds, in her wailing she sounds not like a woman weeping but like an animal being tortured. Emma runs to her and smothers her with herself. Janet now clinging to her, squeezing Emma, clawing at her in her agonies, thrashing in her chair and making those terrible sounds.

Matt stands open-mouthed with tears streaming down his cheeks, watching the two women he has most loved in his life tangled in grief. *Is this my fault?* he thinks. *Did my love for Emma cause all this? How can Janet not hate me as much as the louse she married?*

Jofi just watches. Standing still. Observing all. He decides to leave the three alone. This is not about him. He goes to the great room and sits. Waiting.

A full hour later, Matt and Emma emerge from Janet's room and Jofi goes back to her door, knocking softly. She answers. She looks serene. Jofi enters and she embraces him, and they stay in their sweet hug (he can feel some lightness in her grateful heart) for a long time before Janet releases him.

"I know it's been quite a night, Janet, but there is one thing I need to tell you before the night ends."

She nods, ushers him in and closes but does not lock the door. She never again puts a lock between herself and those who love her.

He bids her sit on one of the chairs and she does. He kneels in front of her and takes both her hands in his. He looks into her eyes and she into his.

"What I have to say will sound strange to you, and you will do with my words what you will. But what I tell you here is true."

Janet nods. Curiosity is on her face, touched with apprehension.

"Your baby forgives you," Jophiel says. He feels her try to pull her hands away, but he holds them tight. "You'll have another chance with him."

"Him?"

"Yes. Your baby would have been a little boy. Did they not tell you that?"

"Yes. They did. But how did-"

"This is a soul very dear to you over many lifetimes, and who needs next time for you to be his mother. He'll wait for you. You didn't murder your baby; you destroyed his body in a fit of diseased addiction. But his soul, and his need to incarnate inside you has not been changed. He feels only love and compassion for you and he'll enter again when your own life is renewed. He will wait. He waits with love for you and nothing you did to him has hurt him in an unrecoverable way. He's a wise soul and will give you much joy in the fullness of time."

She blinks, for the first time since Jophiel began speaking, as if emerging from a spell. "How do you know all this, Jofi."

He stands and smiles… and says nothing.

"Ah," says Janet with more than a little indignation, slipping her hands from Jofi's grip. "I can bare my soul to you, but you won't share at all with me? Is that how it works?"

Jofi considers this and says flat out, "I'm an Angel."

Janet smiles the slightest smile and keeps Jofi in her level stare. "Yes… umm… I see…"

"One more thing," Jofi says. "Forgive your husband."

Her whole aura knots up and she looks away, hurt.

Jofi says, "Think of what one of your philosophers once said."

"One of *mine?*" Janet looks back and smiles.

"He said, 'Hating someone is like drinking poison and waiting for the other person to die.'"

Janet looks down and nods.

Jofi concludes. "Forgive him and be free of him. Let him go. Don't let your anguish gnaw away at you from the inside. That's a real disease that you don't want."

He leans down and kisses Janet on her forehead. "I love you, Janet."

"Thank you, Jofi," she says with quiet gratitude. "And I love you too, you wonderful, beautiful boy…"

Janet is slowly getting better, healing though never 'cured.' She doesn't want to be cured; she knows what she did. The memories shall never leave her, but the love she had been shown allows her to slowly dissipate the self-loathing that has crippled her and sapped her life force; and Jofi's strange words, though baffling, have solaced her to her very core.

But the joy in the house is alloyed by the misery left in Daisy's wake. Bran and Alma are devastated. Daisy left Bran her house and put two million dollars into his bank account, but he would rather be penniless and live in the bus station if only she would return to him. Alma is so distraught that she hasn't had a tear-free day in the month since Daisy "ran away." (This is how Alma thinks of it.)

Their common pain has cleaved Bran and Alma together. Bran's sad associations keep him from the house that he now solely owns, so he and Alma are always at the mansion together and often in one another's company. Jofi sees them embracing from time to time, losing their grief in the other's empathy. But there is something else there; Bran kissed her. Jofi is relieved by all this and hopes to see them grow even closer.

He had dissolved his old bond to Alma (before the kiss) and freed her from her unofficial role as consort. This is a great relief to both, though Alma pretended she was saddened and Jofi let her pretend. With this in mind, Jofi has moved out of the big bedroom and into a smaller room, leaving the suite to Alma. She fought heroically for the little room, but Jofi would not hear of it. It pleases him that she should have it. She loves the suite – all the space and the big bed and beautiful bathroom and closet space – and Jofi could not care less about the niceties of his accommodations.

Jofi has explained these new changes to Bran. He made sure that Bran understood that Alma was free and there was nothing but friendship between Alma and himself. "It was never going to work out like she wanted it to," Jofi told Bran.

Jofi also let Emma and Matt know what was going on. Matt takes it in stride, but Emma seemed saddened by the news. He's also given his parents a heads-up on the possible budding romance between Alma and Bran, hinting that they should welcome such a development. He senses that they would but would be less than enthusiastic if the new couple ended up playing musical bedrooms while living there. Jofi hoped they would be discreet, and so they were for the duration of their "imprisonment," as Alma calls it (only half in jest).

In just a little over two months the concert will be upon them. It was not the easy sell to the National Orchestra's board that Sir George thought it would be. At first, they suspected that the maestro's attitude toward Bran and his work was further evidence (to some) that he was getting old and going around the bend. But his advocacy was intense and his argument strong. By now it had become well-known that the Detroit concert had been sabotaged, much to the embarrassment and professional detriment of the many journalists who saw blood when they should have been listening more carefully. Bran's "fraud" has instead become the hottest ticket of the year.

Manager/Producer Jamaad has been exemplary both in his role as facilitator for the big event as well as friend. He never fails to lighten the load of his suffering companions. He can always make Alma laugh and Jamaad's presence seems to click her into a different gear. He has the odd trait of being a different person, depending on who he is with. He would never speak with Bran as he does with Alma, nor act with Jofi as with Bran. But he never comes off as disingenuous, for he is not.

But the big news these days is Jamaad's management of the recording label they have created – *Seraphim Media* – which has enriched them all in a modest but growing way. The list of recordings is extensive, and the reviews have been uniformly excellent. It hasn't taken long for every collector of art music in the western world and beyond to know the label and revere it for the virtuosity and authority of the performances and the realism of the recordings.

The offerings include Jofi plumbing the core keyboard repertories in addition to accompanying Alma and Daisy; Daisy Lee has many song cycles of the greats including vocal pieces by Bran; and Alma has freshly explored the realms of the violin from Renaissance to Contemporary, both accompanied and unaccompanied. When they need a cellist (as they often do for the early works) they are happy to include Bran's and Jofi's pal Li Ming. Collectors worldwide are begging Alma to record the Bach solo pieces – the crown of the repertory – but Jofi thinks it's better to drive them all mad with anticipation. "Make them wait," he says, laughing. "Let them dream."

The lull in concertizing has hurt them, and not just in the pocketbook. Agents are tired of waiting for them, and aficionados are getting very impatient. But all that should end after the concert. Only ten weeks to go till the prison doors open.

I needed to feel again my divine connection.
Never have I felt so forsaken, though in my heart
I knew that such could never truly be so. In
compassion, Metatron, my companion of ages,
came to me again as I was most in need. In our
reverie, I saw that there would be trouble ahead,
for we were not yet free
of the adversary who dogs us.
Metatron's directives were very strange. I was
instructed to have a special conductor's baton
made for the event. I protested that I do not use a
baton and would find it an encumbrance rather
than an aid to communication. But Metatron
insisted that I have it made and that I should
keep it with me at every moment at the concert
hall, and not to play easy with these words but to
obey explicitly. The specifications were odd – 18-

*inches in length with a shaft of steel and handle
of wood. On this Metatron was most adamant.
I asked again about Sam Morgan, who needs to
meet Bran and is destined to become a savior of
the arts in this time of humanity's great need. I
needlessly reminded Metatron that finding Sam
Morgan and keeping him safe was at the core of
my mission, yet I could not even sense his
presence on this Earth. Was I too late? Had the
adversary snuffed out his light as was implied?
My ageless companion had no answer for me.
Instead, Metatron beamed a smile of infinite
mildness and bade me have faith through the
coming travails – for faith would be my only defense to avoid drowning in sorrow, submerged in
a sea of deepest human sadness. The warning
was plain, and it was hard for my dearest
Metatron to utter to me these brutal tidings.
There was odd comfort in this, for I now knew
beyond doubt what I had only suspected.
But how does one prepare for grief?*

– from Chronicles of Jophiel, Vol. II

51

'Bobby' is putting the finishing touches on a BLT. It's
beautiful. It's perfect, actually. It looks like a sandwich in a
foody magazine, or what a fine chef would make for his own
mom. Nicely packed but nothing rudely poking outside the
toast, mayo not too much not too little, lettuce as crisp as the
iceberg it's named after, and the tomatoes – well, it's past season so best not dwell on the tomatoes – and the rye toast is
still crispy and warm. When he serves it up his ladyfriend
Harriet will be all smiles and appreciation.

You'd think the last thing Preston would want to do on his day off is cook, but Harriet is hungry, and she has a real nice kitchen, a pleasure to cook in. Not a single dull knife. Plus, she's his girl!

Yessir, these two are quite the item locally. Everybody is happy that Harriet has a beau, and everybody likes the nine-fingered renegade demon-possessed former-Catholic priest-in-hiding with the limp and gouged-out eyesocket they like to call Bobby.

He slides the BLT in front of Harriet onto the plaid place-mat. She looks up from her seat at the little table and gives him a sweet smile, then pulls him over by the arm and kisses the hand that made it for her. He can't believe this. More than two months of bliss with this wonderful girl, the demon of old seemingly uninterested in his doings to the point where he is starting to forget the horrors and make some big plans.

Big plans. He feels the ringbox in his trousers. It sticks out in his pocket when he sits but she can't see under there. He's going to wait till she's done with her lunch (he isn't hungry), and then by god he's gonna do it. He's going to ask her. His upbringing and training lend him a brush of regret over not waiting till they were wed before he made love to her. He doesn't think she was a virgin, but she might have been. He figures don't ask. It was probably the best night of his life. He wants her again. And she loved it, man, she *loved* it.

She dabs at her mouth with the paper napkin and her pretty face darkens. "What's wrong, Bobby?"

Preston's face is flushed scarlet and his good eye is popping from its hollow. "No. *No. NOOO!*" he shrieks.

She hops up and scurries to his chair across from her. "Honey, what's the matter! My god!" she moons in her vacant voice.

He yelps, "No! *You motherfucker!*" thrashing in his chair, "*You will not have me! You will NOT!* slamming his fists so hard on the little table that he breaks a board in it. "*You rotten piece… you fucking filthy… Never! Never again! NO!*"

"Bobby! What's the matter!" and she throws her arms around his neck and presses his convulsing body to herself. He stops. He's calm. It's quiet. She thinks it's the magic in her embrace.

He reaches to his chest and carefully pulls her arms away. She straightens and looks down on him, then recoils in fright.

"My god, Bobby!" she moans. "What's wrong with you. Why are you looking like that?"

He smiles a smile she's never seen. "Everybody's gotta look like *something,*" he says flatly and pulls himself up unsteadily, getting his bearings and looking around the house. "A coat…" he mumbles. "He had a coat, right? That's where the carkeys probably are…"

She points to the rack near the door, too rattled to speak. He walks over, unhooks the coat and puts it on, zipping up tight and patting the rattling keys with an assured grin.

"Where are you going?" she asks, as if in a trance.

He looks at her as if he has only now just seen her. "Gotta go to work!" he says with that awful grin, snatching up the long boning knife from the butcher block as he turns from her.

"But… but it's *Sunday…*" she brays as he walks out and shuts the door.

52

The Oval Office is dark except for three candles. The President loves his candlelight. It's late, and it's only himself and Phil, starting to work out the details of the fateful speech. They are discussing the news of the day. Sporadic rioting and a mass shooting in California. The President is staring off into space, considering who-knows-what, and Phil looks appraisingly at him. In the candlelight, he reminds Phil of the great leaders of legend who have sat in that very seat, doubtless with the same expression and burdened with like cares.

"It's a first draft, but we've still got a week," Phil says, waking the leader from his reverie. "The networks and cable have been given a heads-up. They want to know more, and frankly, a few of them are reluctant to give up prime time for the address. We're working on the stragglers. They have no idea yet…"

The President nods, takes the first page from the small sheaf and snicks on his desk lamp, destroying the candlelight effect. He grimaces, puts on his glasses, and reads.

"It's pretty much the same as we've been discussing over the past few weeks. Just cleaned up a little," Phil says.

While the President peruses the document, Phil lays it on as thick as he can without sounding too soulless and mercenary. As usual, he fails. "The massacre this morning in L.A., though a horrible tragedy, couldn't have come at a better time, considering what we're about… I mean, what *you* are about to tell the nation, sir."

The President peers at Phil over his spectacles with a look that says, 'please shut-up now.' He continues reading. He looks at Phil.

"The first, second, fourth, and tenth amendments. That right?"

"Yes. As we discussed. And only temporarily, sir. We need to suspend them only for 12 to 18 months. That's our best estimate at this time."

"Have you ever heard of a right taken away 'temporarily?' Amendments one, four and ten… that's just on emergency order by me and new enforcement procedures, but do you really think that the military is going to help disarm Americans in their homes? I mean… the other stuff we can work around, but this seems like it could blow up in our faces."

"It's only in select locations, sir. No one is going to try to disarm some farming community in the Dakotas. But the major metro centers – these people are out of control. That's why it's so important that you remove the generals on the list I sent over yesterday and replace them with the ones we indicated who are more… elastic and amenable to our aims here. In fact, that move alone will alert the networks and cable holdouts that they need to free up the airtime to find out what's going on. All of America will be watching that night."

"It makes me nervous…"

"Sir, all due respect – how many times must we have this conversation?"

"As many as I deem appropriate. You forget yourself, Philip."

"And I apologize, sir." Phil pouts and looks chastised. "What may I clarify for you here? Our troops have all been vetted on this issue and we'll only use the ones who have indicated that they will obey orders on this matter without question."

The President replaces the sheet atop the little stack, pats it with his palm and yawns. "Leave this with me. We'll talk tomorrow."

Phil stands. "Very well, sir. Good night."

Before he reaches the door, Phil turns and reminds the Chief. "Ten o'clock with the cabinet, sir." No response. Phil turns and departs.

The President snicks off the annoying light, takes off his glasses and sighs, basking in the candleglow. He meditates for a short space on the horrors he's about to commit, and conversely, on the horrors that will continue if he does not act. At length, he blows out the tapers and heads for bed.

53

Bran points to Jofi's new baton and cackles uproariously. Jofi is not amused. Bran snatches the stick – *"yoink"* – from its velvet-lined box. Bran points at the box and laughs even harder.

"Velvet!" Bran pretends he's wiping at the tears in his eyes. "O my god… this is too much. Jofi." Bran holds the baton up. "What the hell is this *for?* You don't use a baton. The thought of it is *hilarious.*"

218

"Evidently," Jofi grouches.

Bran examines it further. "Jeez… wait… what's it made of?" He wipes at his pretend wet cheeks. "Metal? A metal baton? *The perfect tool for the discerning young conductor!* – said nobody, ever! Who the hell uses a metal baton?"

Jofi snatches it back from Bran – "*Yoink yourself*" – returns it to its snuggly velvet home and clicks the case closed. "We have a rehearsal in an hour, Bran. Excuse me. I gotta get ready."

Bran heads toward Jofi's hotel room door, still chuckling. "Yeah… you mean you gotta practice with your fancy stick in front of the mirror!" He flashes a big obnoxious grin and shuts the room door.

Jofi frowns after him. *Humans…* he broods.

They got their three rehearsals, and they needed them. Maestro Cavendish runs a tight ship, but the average age of the players is on the elder side, and they aren't quite as flexible nor receptive as the young Ann Arbor group, or even the Detroiters. The first session went poorly, and Sir George had to assert his authority with some scolding after the rehearsal when Jofi had left the hall. As obviously fine a musician as Jofi is (they all know his righteous rep as master keyboard virtuoso), they nevertheless resented his youth, and the nature of this newfangled music angered and eluded many of the old guard. They were also upset that he did not use a score but did it all from memory. *A mockery! Such a thing is just not possible!*

The dressing-down from old Sir George motivated the players to open up a little and give Jofi the benefit of the doubt, which was, of course, all the wedge Jofi needed to make Bran's work come alive and, by the end of the third rehearsal, shine like the sun. These are pretty much all old-school musicians, but they *get it* now.

And Jofi never did use the baton. His orders are to keep it with him, not necessarily to actually *use* the ridiculous thing.

54

After the second rehearsal, Bran takes Sir George up on an invite to his nearby home, a modest retreat in Georgetown. "I live in London," the maestro explains as he unlocks the great front door, "but when I come to Washington this is my base." They enter and Sir George points to his left. "The kitchen is pretty much for show."

"I know how that works," Bran quips.

"So many good restaurants here and I'm too damned busy to cook. But this," he opens a pair of French doors that reveal a cavernous room in which Bran would happily spend his last days on Earth. "This is where I *live.*"

"Yeah…" Bran breathes. "I can see why you would want to live in here."

It is *exactly* like Bran's room at every dwelling Bran has ever called home. The only difference is the quality of the few constituent items. Where Bran had a little Yamaha and now a lovely Steinway, Sir George has a Fazioli *and* a Shigeru Kawai concert grand– in case one needs to play some nice duets; Bran's stereo might have set him back a grand or so, but that would not be enough to replace the stylus on the maestro's tonearm cartridge or even the wires connecting the speakers to the amp. And the speakers! Bran thinks that, combined, they might be bigger than his first car, and that was a Cadillac. His writing desk is magnificent in size and construction, and his TV isn't *on* the wall, it *is* the wall.

Bran is dazed as a slackjawed yokel on a spaceship. Sir George is laughing at him. "I felt the same way when I saw my mentor's home for the first time."

"You mean Malcolm Crowley's house?"

"I mean *Sir* Malcolm house, yes," the maestro says with a wry smile and a sidelong glance.

"Right." Bran corrects. "*Sir* Malcolm."

"It made me see what was possible," Sir George says. "And he enjoyed it to the fullest, just as I do here. But it took me years to know his secret, without which no true enjoyment is possible." Bran waits for it. "If it burned to the ground tomorrow I could not care less."

At this Bran is inspired to a gesture that made him hesitate, but then he figures what the hell. He recites:

> *"He who binds to himself a joy*
> *Does the winged life destroy;*
> *But he who kisses the joy as it flies*
> *Lives in eternity's sunrise."*

Sir George is stirred and delighted by this. He put his hand on Bran's shoulder. "Well, that's one quick way to a Brit's heart – an American friend quoting an old English poet. Thank you for that. It was well said." He studies Bran's face. "I think you may be a remarkable young man, your rough edges notwithstanding – just a froth that can be skimmed away."

"Huh." Bran says, uncomfortably. "Well… possibly."

They sit across from one another in the two comfortable chairs. Sir George looks deep in thought for a moment, then smiles and looks at Bran.

"Call me Skip," he says.

Did Bran hear that right? Nah. "Maestro? What did you say?"

"Call me Skip. That's what my family and friends call me. Since I was a kid!"

"Skip."

"Right. Skip." The maestro adds, "But please god only in *private*. Can you remember that?"

"I can, and I will. Skip."

"Very good. And now that I've read it through," the maestro says, "we need to talk about your symphony."

Bran nods. "All right."

"The more I read through the parts and notes on the work it occurred to me that your success, if indeed it comes, and I think it will, will be based upon that same formula that all the real masters employed."

"And what is that?"

"They *stood on the shoulders of giants.*"

"I *sit on the faces of midgets,*" Bran counters sagely. "But that isn't working out too well, so maybe I'll try your way."

The maestro tries to look appalled in that veddy English way but fails and blurts a guffaw so hard that it sets them both to long laughter.

The maestro covers his face with his hands and shakes his head. "Ah, Bran… was there ever another like you?" He drops his hands, stands and holds out a hand to Bran, who takes it and rises likewise.

"Brandy and cigars?" Sir George asks.

Bran looks so grateful. "O Skip," he says, "I love your life!"

They make their way to the library, the maestro's arm around Bran's shoulder, giving an affectionate squeeze. "Well, as you Yanks say, 'Hang in there!'"

And they discuss Bran's symphony, and all that it implies, and well into the night.

55

Jofi's contingent has a block of rooms in the nearby New Jefferson Hotel. Nice place; ultra-swank. Matt and Emma share a room; everyone else has their own. But one of the rooms remains unoccupied throughout their stay – Alma's. She sleeps with Bran in his room.

Daisy Lee sent personal emails the day of the concert to her old friends. She explained that she wanted to be there with them, but tonight is the final rehearsal for her debut in *L'Orfeo*. She was not contrite or sad, and one would have to have read much between the lines that were not there for even a hint of regret. She is a natural-born Diva with all, pro and con, that this implies.

Unlike Jofi, Matt does not need to be told that there may well be trouble tonight. He is armed and on high alert, scanning audience members as the hall slowly fills with the capacity crowd. Matt has already made a liaison with the relevant agencies associated with the Concert Arts Center and briefed them as much as he thought he could on what they may be up against. There are plainclothes and uniformed agents all over the place. Matt is the first one in and he's looking for a priest but knows it could be anybody.

Emma will join Matt in his seat near curtain-time. He thought about asking her to not come tonight out of concern for her safety but quickly dismissed the effort as an impossibility. She would be angry at him for the mere suggestion.

The first half of the concert is a performance of Stravinsky's *Rite of Spring* ballet score. This piece caused something of a riot on the night of its premiere way back in 1913, and in truth, Sir George longs for those days (well before even *his* time), when a mere piece of music could actually set a fire in the souls and the bodies of men. Such seems impossible today.

Maestro Cavendish is leading a performance of such vitality that no one would guess it is being ramrodded by a man in his eighties. Sir George does indeed use a baton, made of ivory with silver fittings and given to him by a king. He loves his podium, his tuxedo, his long shining silver hair, his brilliant orchestra and the thunderous applause. He is the epitome, the archetype, of the old-school idea of The Symphony Orchestra Conductor. But there is almost a sense of desperation in his performance tonight, as if in a rage against the dying of the light. He will not go easy when his time comes, and this is a foreshadowing. The man who was once the swaggering revolutionary prodigy is now… a grey eminence.

When he finishes and the last few barbaric bars of the work have had their say there is thunderous applause, worthy and sincere… but none of it is dangerous. There is no riot in the air. Everyone has heard it all before. What was at one time an incitement to rampage is now… classical music.

At intermission, Sir George seeks out Jofi and asks if he might say a few words before Jofi comes on stage in the second half. Jofi naturally agrees to this.

During the break Matt visits backstage, finding Bran a nervous wreck and Jofi the coolest of cucumbers. Matt saunters here and there, peering into corners and dark places, then to the stage door where he tells the agent assigned to the stage door area that he wants to step outside for a smoke. (Matt doesn't smoke.) The agent knows who Matt is and lets him pass. Matt steps outside and strolls about, taking the air. At no time does he note anything out of the ordinary, just a little mutt eating what looks like a donut still in its little bag. Matt leans down to pet the grateful little dog. "Stage-door doggie," Matt says affectionately as he strokes his head. Or her. He rises up, knocks on the door, the guard admits him (but not the heartsick dog who had pinned high hopes on his new friend).

Matt upbraids the sentry. "You never even looked," he tells him. "You just opened the door and let me pass."

The agent is annoyed. "I figured it was you. I know my business, pal. Piss off."

Matt swallows the urge to cuff him a good one and heads inside. He is soon back in his seat next to beautiful Emma. Next to her sit Alma, Eric, and Janet on the end. All are terribly excited.

Matt gets the attention of his family and points up to the boxes high up to the right of the stage. "Look," he says. "The President is here." The fam is duly impressed. There sits the prez himself, surrounded by a gaggle of aids and guardians.

The orchestra seated and tuned, and Jofi Fischer – world-renowned piano virtuoso – is expected to take the podium for the first time as the lights lower and a hush falls. But it is Sir George who enters to a smattering of confused applause and climbs the steps to the podium.

He turns and waits for the clapping to cease. "Don't worry. I'm not conducting the next work you are about to hear," he begins. "Not because I have at last achieved such a lofty measure of fuddy-duddyism that I can no longer conduct contemporary music (although there are some who will disagree), but because Maestro Jofi Fischer has earned this tonight. We have not seen his like as a performer since Glenn Gould flashed on the scene in the 1950s. In fact, Maestro Fischer's achievements are even more flabbergasting than the great Gould. It will be a pleasure when he returns later this year to concert halls around the country and the world." The maestro pauses at the smattering of applause.

"I doubt if the symphony you are about to hear would even exist if Maestro Fischer were not a devoted friend of the composer, for it is due in large part to Maestro Fischer's friendship, advocacy and musical mastery that Bran Englander's *Anticanon* has become reality. For better or worse is for all of you to decide.

"When I first heard the opening of the *Anticanon* at its aborted premiere in Detroit, I was mortified by the work and felt I needed to root out this sacrilegious man who claimed to be a composer and set him straight about a few things. This was odd, because Bran was a total unknown with a dodgy reputation anyway so why was I stirred up? Why not just ignore him? You know… ignore it and it goes away.

"Because he offended everything I had held dear all my life long. That's why. Englander was a living offense to harmony, to orchestration, even to the idea of basic tenants of ensemble playing. And I'm not comparing him to those talentless zombies of the '60s and '70s of the last century, to 'composers' who thought it was a profound idea to have cats walk on harpsichords or that radio static was just as aesthetically valid a sound as a Beethoven symphony, or that there was some value in crawling inside the vagina of a living whale and calling the resulting sounds *Danger Music.* Yes. You laugh. Do a web search. I only *wish* I were making that one up.

"No. Englander's music seemed infinitely more dangerous and even more revolting to me than *that*. On my way over to confront him I had calmed myself enough to examine my response and found it to be… hysterical. Anyone who knows me will not include hysteria in any litany of faults and vices they could possibly assign to me. Many, many other nasty and embarrassing traits but not that one. So, I pulled off the road and I considered my thoughts and feelings.

"Orchestras are dying all over the world. There is nothing truly new in what we present. Nothing truly alive. Not a thing that one can point to without having its precursors spring immediately to mind. We play the same pieces over and over again, and when we venture to something new our expectations are always low. So much of it is trash, and what isn't still fails to inspire. That which once offered a spring of living water had become a museum, and finally, a morgue. And this is not just true in music. It is the same in painting and the plastic arts. The sense of ennui has become overwhelming. Even physics and philosophy have been affected by this tedium and stagnation.

"Gradually it began to dawn upon me, sitting there in my car on the side of the freeway, exactly what it was about Englander's music that had revolted me to my core. Quite simple really. It was *alive*. It *dared* to be alive. Not a resurrected corpse, not a pretty museum piece. This was a living, breathing musical monster that sought to devour me to my last piece of gristle without so much as a 'pardon me.' It doesn't ask permission. It breaks the bones that hold the brittle old world together and it does so with grace and humor and a great big heart and good will. In fact, that's what the *Anticanon* is about. It's about individuals singing together in love. A hundred individual voices singing out and joining together – not with artifice! not with studied counterpoint or textbook rules of ensemble – but joined together by the shared adventure of our existence, and by hope and love, in a sea, an overwhelming *ocean*, of melody.

"Englander is not just showing us a way *out* of the deadening stasis of the past; he's showing us a way *forward*. Not the *only* way, but a genuine and historically justifiable approach to thinking about the art of music with an eye towards its future. It ties up the loose ends of the old era and hints toward the new.

"And his work is being offered to you tonight by the best orchestra in the world – you can take my word for that – and presided over by the greatest natural musical genius that I have ever known personally or by reputation: Maestro Jofi Fisher, in his debut as conductor. How many ways is this concert an historical occasion! I thank the God I question the existence of that I have lived to see it. And that the many years I have waited, cursing in the darkness for some new light – these were simply necessary fallow decades, not the black night of a formerly great culture in its demise.

"Whether you enjoy what you are about to hear or not doesn't matter. It's bigger than you are. It's bigger than I am. And Englander's voice shall be heard and reckoned with. And just as importantly, just as inevitable, his voice will be joined by a chorus of genius from every discipline as the transformation from the old to the new gets underway. Mr. Englander, I'm guessing, is a forerunner to all that. A harbinger of things to come.

"We need this new impulse. We are desperate for it. We live our lives in quiet desperation that's buried so deep we don't even consider the issue consciously – but we *crave* a new impulse and I say to you tonight… my god, I sound like an old preacher… I say to you that there is hope for Beauty. Across the board! Beauty is *not* dead; it's *not* just in the past; it's not a naïve hallucination, not just a desperate hope, it's a *living thing*. All this has made the old fellow you see before you… young again. In my heart. Which is the only place that matters.

"So, I congratulate all of you in the audience tonight. You are all present at a moment in musical history that will never be forgotten as long as western music exists.

"Thank you."

Bran, listening intently backstage says to Jofi, "We're fucked."

Jofi chuckles. "What do you mean?"

"He oversold it. Right? Ah shit. Didn't he oversell it? How can anything live up to that?"

Jofi peeks through the curtain at Sir George leaving the stage and looks back at Bran. "That's not for us to say, Bran. We won't be the judges of that."

The applause for the old maestro finally dying down, Jofi starts through the curtain but Bran stops him, embraces him and kisses him on the cheek. Hard. In a guy way. Bran looks down at the stick in Jofi's hand.

"You're not gonna use that thing, are you?" Bran says with an added look of horror for good measure.

Jofi smiles. "You have to call me 'Maestro' from now on, you know."

"Sure thing. Up yours, *maestro*."

Jofi is laughing as he steps through the curtain into another world.

The applause is deafening (many are standing) as Jofi makes his way toward the podium, stopping to shake hands with the concertmaster and to greet the orchestra before ascending to the pulpit. They are glad to see him. Jofi looks as radiant as always, just dressed a little better. Eschewing the traditional black monkey-suit, he sports a loose, collarless black shirt, black pants of relaxed fit and soft black loafers and no jewelry. He acknowledges the applause with a bow to the audience. He turns to the band and places the dreaded baton on the ledge of the podium, not to be touched during the performance.

He calls for another tuning. He detects no defects. He holds both hands in front of him, palms down, waiting for that pin-drop level of quiet that all conductors wait for. And there it is. He gives the downbeat and they're off.

There is no 'beating time' required of the conductor in this piece, as the parts are not that closely synchronized within the numerous sections of the work. So why a conductor at all (many have been asking this question for centuries), especially in a work like this? Because the work moves through different emotional states, and though each individual instrument has its own say, the emotional content unites them all. Jofi, through gestures and his force of will, keeps them all on the same expressive page, so to speak, as the work unfolds.

He also needs to be sure that the proper level of dynamics is being attended to, that each instrument is playing, at any one moment, the distinct level of loud-or-soft that is specified in the score for each individual instrument. This particularly is why every other conductor in the world would use a score to keep track of this flood of information that Jofi simply remembers from study. With this in his mind he can subtly and with ease shape the performance into the structural and emotional contours that the composer has specified for this particular presentation of the piece.

The other thing that Jofi is doing here is one that only the best of the breed can make happen – he is personifying the content of the piece as it unfolds through his very presence, through his gestures and expressions. Not as a drama-queen or exhibitionist, for this trick works only when the effects sneak into the beholder's perception under-the-radar.

The audience is spell-bound, though it is evident from the get-go that not everyone is pleased about it. Some look like they have been transported to a heavenly realm; others as though they can't avert their eyes from some terrible train accident unfolding before them. And everything in between.

For some, the half-hour speeds by in an ecstatic trance; for others, impatience has given way to frank expressions of anger, so that when the final bars fade away reaction breaks out almost immediately.

It starts with boos. Five or ten loud hoots of derision from all over the hall. Then some clapping in counter-reaction to the disfavor. Then more boos to contradict the claps, then cheers to challenge the booers. This culminates in a colossal amalgam of clapping, cheers, boos and hisses that haven't been heard in the Concert Arts Center in… ever?

When Jofi emerges to acknowledge his first curtain-call he has Bran in tow, and the pandemonium increases by an order of magnitude. There are scuffles in the aisles. (Old Sir George will be pleased.) Jofi turns to the orchestra and bids them rise up to be recognized, and even that gesture cranks the heat up another notch.

The President, awed and excited in his box, is standing and clapping. He turns to his aides. "I have to meet this composer," he shouts to be heard. "Right now, Phil. Backstage. He needs to know the consequences of his work. I know now what I have to do tomorrow."

"I advise against it. It's pretty wild out there, sir."

"Then get these guys off their asses and make a way through for me."

"It'll take a few minutes to get there through all the commotion, so let's get started," Phil says. He swiftly mobilizes his crew and they start their way down to the main floor.

There are no injuries, just a few shoving matches, and in four or five minutes the rage dies down, the performers have left the stage and the crowd begins to evacuate, much to the relief of the various security agencies and especially Matt, who assigns agents to watch over his still-seated family while he ventures backstage.

Meanwhile, there is a knock on the back door of the stage exit area and the agent assigned dutifully opens the door. He once again neglects to I.D. the knocker, but that's not a problem. Why, it's just a friendly-looking priest who gives the agent first a big smile and next a long kitchen knifeblade between the ribs. Preston drops the blade, lugs the body to a dark corner nearby and notes that the little 'stage-door doggie' has snuck in, grateful for the warmth. Preston ignores the dog and steps toward the dressing rooms. He parts his coat and takes a gun from his hip holster – a .45 pistol with suppressor attached.

Bran is in his dressing room with Jofi and Jamaad and the celebration has begun. The dressing room door is half-open, and Preston sees the three men quite clearly a few yards from where he is standing in the hallway. Bran has his back to the door, pouring champagne.

The President's men have cleared a path and they are now in the backstage area, on the far side away from the dressing rooms. They are making their way down the corridor.

Matt climbs the stairs to get backstage and hears through his headset that the dead agent's body has been discovered. He rushes down the hall to what he thinks is the dressing room and enters, but it's a storage room, adjacent to the dressing-room and well-lit. He spies the open door that adjoins the two rooms and rushes in.

Preston now has a clear shot. He raises his pistol and calls out, *"Englander!"*

Jofi, still holding his baton, bolts for the doorway and out into the hall as Bran cheerfully turns to the sound of his name and as soon is Jofi is out of the way Preston fires three rounds in rapid succession. The priest next tilts the gun for a shot at onrushing Jofi but cannot get a shot off before Jofi plunges the steel baton into the chest of the assassin.

He pulls out the bleeding stick, steps back and cries, *"Get thee…"* and with a thrust of inhuman might, "OUT!" he drives the stick home through the center of the priest's sternum and out again in back through the middle of his spine. The business end of the metal wand is sticking well out of Preston's back and aimed exactly – at the hapless little dog. The animal's eyes meet Jofi's glare. In an instant the dog is in seizure, barking hysterically and bouncing off of walls, now spewing ropes of white saliva and attacking anything and everyone around him, until someone opens the stage door and the frenzied creature disappears howling into the night.

The priest opens his eyes. "Angel?" he mutters. "Is it over?"

"Yes, it's done," Jofi breathes.

"Did I do well? Will I… be free? Tell Harriet… that…" Jofi lets Preston's body slip to the floor as death overtakes him.

Only now does he become fully aware of the commotion in the dressing room. He paces toward the door, expecting that his human heart will burst when he sees his friend. He senses death in the room as a certainty and tries to prepare himself.

Jofi is followed into the room by his family rushing in behind him and now exploding in anguish. He sees Bran kneeling on the floor, hovering tearfully over Matt, who has been shot three times in the side and is clearly no longer among the living.

"He pushed me out of the way!" Bran cries to Jofi.

Jofi bursts into tears. "O Dad!" he moans, getting to his knees and hugging the chest of his dead Dad. *"O no!"* And he weeps there while his mother, his poor broken little brother and his aunt sob alongside him as they try, uselessly, to come to grips with the horror dawning upon them. Alma and Jamaad sit nearby in a trance of shock and misery. The room erupts in activity as law-enforcement and medical personal burst into the room.

At the sound of the gunshots the President was immediately ushered out away from the disturbance, never himself in danger.

But he never did get to meet Bran.

56

It's the morning after and the leader of the free world is sitting at his desk. Across from him sits his Assistant Chief Douglas Moore. Standing in the background are two special agents, massive and granite-jawed, well-known to White House staff. (Those two always remind the President of the statues on Easter Island.) The door opens, and Chief-of-Staff Phil Powell is ushered in. He looks angry.

"Mr. President! What's all this about no speech tonight?"

The President points at the vacant seat in front of him next to Doug, and Phil sits.

Phil is very agitated. "And is it true that you have reinstated the military personnel that we replaced *two days ago?* These men will never allow-"

"Be quiet, Phil," the President says, and Phil shuts up. "Just sit there and listen to me. For a change."

Phil looks to his right at Doug, then cranes his head around to steal an appraising glance at the two agents standing behind him. He turns back to his chief with a confused look.

The President continues. "There will be no announcement today. I've changed my mind on all this. There will be no martial law on my watch."

"Sir, I thought we agreed to steer clear of that term-"

"Phil, I won't tell you again to hold your tongue."

"Yes, sir."

"You were very convincing, Phil. You made the best case that could be made for the actions that you suggested. And you had the staff – and me, convinced that you were right… that this was the only way. 'Safety through Sacrifice,' was the catchphrase you came up with. But the sacrifice we were about to inflict would have destroyed everything the nation is built upon."

"It's *temporary.*"

"Such actions are *never* temporary! And this is what troubles me about you, Philip – y*ou know history as well as I.* The precedent I was about to set would have damned the nation forever. And history would damn me with it. Not you. *Me!*"

"The nation is destroying *itself.* Every day there is-"

"Then it will destroy *itself.* I will not be the one to destroy it. And it'll be at least three years, and if I'm lucky, seven, before someone else gets that chance."

"Sir, may I continue?"

The President throws his hands in the air. "I never knew how to stop you, Philip."

"Is this about that stupid symphony?"

The President smiles, as if a little embarrassed. He looks down at the table. "Of course, it's not just because of a symphony-"

"All due respect, sir – I think it is. I heard what you said when it was over. How 'now I know what I need to do.' You said those words and I thought, 'what the hell is that supposed to mean?'"

"Let me try to clarify that," the President says, taking a moment to gather his thoughts and words. "I was ripe for it. See… I needed to come to a peace with myself about all this. And I prayed, I meditated, I had conversations with the few who are privy to all this. I was opening myself to try to come to grips, to have some decent, rational closure on all this. And then I heard that work by whatshisname, Englander. And I knew it wasn't mere coincidence."

Phil is appalled. "Sir! It was a piece of *music!* Allegedly. And one that seemed pretty generally unlistenable and hated by most of the people there! There were fights in the aisles! It was a bunch of *noises!* How could someone in your position let a bunch of discordant garbage influence your thinking process?!"

His colleague Doug has had enough. "PHIL!" Silence. "Control yourself." Oddly, the President seems unoffended by the outburst. He is deep in thought.

Phil sits back in his chair and sighs. "Sorry, Mr. President. I know you love your concert music. I guess the worth of that thing just eludes me completely. And its effect upon you – inexplicable."

The President decides he will try just once more. "See, Phil… that work is about freedom."

"Freedom, sir? Is that a joke?"

"No. Listen to me now. This whatshisname, this… Englander guy. He takes an orchestra of 100 people. And nobody plays the same thing. Everyone is in their own world,

234

with their own challenges and their own point-of-view but they acknowledge everyone else. See? Everyone is telling the same story at the same time, just relating it in their own way. And I never heard that 'discordant garbage' you describe. I heard a group of men and women, people of all kinds, coming together in good will to tell a story – the *same* story – but each in his or her own voice and honored by all the others. If you listened deeply, in some sections you could hear a hundred beautiful melodies going on at the same time. Each melody unique and precious, a whole world in itself that could stand on its own. *That's* my country, Philip. That's a symbol of my nation and my people, and what we must become to endure the future."

Phil makes a noise of disgust and looks out the window.

"And if a composer can do that – an uneducated, disconnected *nobody*, by the way, a man who another man just took bullets for, who sacrificed his *life* to keep him alive… a man who's had his home burned to the ground and his efforts sabotaged at every move he ever tried to make and still, *still* persevere and find his way through all the shit and into the light. If a composer can do that for music, maybe, just maybe, I can find the talent and grace, and the *people*, to help do that for my *country*. There are appalling injustices afoot and our people are all so different, but there is a *commonality*. We must find a way to exploit that commonness and bring health back.

"You see, Philip – there *is* no 'Safety through Sacrifice.' Such an attitude leads not just to defeat but to the worst *kind* of defeat – *self*-defeat – and in the worst way. We'll find a different way."

"This *was* the way," Phil didn't bother to try to hide the sneering derision in his voice. "We *had* the way. You lost your nerve."

The President studies his Chief-of-Staff with narrowed eyes. After a few moments, he holds out his hand to Doug. Doug hands him a single leaf of paper. The President takes it and puts it on the desk in front of Phil and spins it 180-degrees so that Phil can read it.

"Sign it," the President orders.

"What is it?" Phil asks as he leans forward to study the document.

"It's your resignation," the President says. "I wrote it myself. Sign it." Doug holds a pen out for Phil to take.

He ignores it. "I will *not* sign it."

"Last chance to resign."

Phil stands. "This is an outrage, I don't-"

"*Sit!*" The President barks. He nods at the two agents standing near the table and they take a step toward Phil – who wisely decides to resume his seat. Phil snatches the still-proffered pen, gives a cursory glance at the brief letter's content, shakes his head bitterly and scribbles his name on the line provided. He slams the pen to the desk and glares at his former boss.

The President once again gives the nod to his men. "You'll be escorted from the premises."

"There are things in my office that I-"

"Not today, Philip," the President clarifies. Phil stands, and the President looks up at him. "Thank you for your service. Now get out."

Part III

Why did we even bother? What good did it do?

Bran was thinking these words, but every one of the family and friends has had the same thought wracking their brains every day since the murder.

It's been almost two months since Matt's slaying, and the acute stage of grief has subsided into the chronic phase that shall never pass, only lessen.

What did they gain in trade for Matt's life? That's a terrible, even useless, way to think about it, but they all have so much now, so many dreams achieved – but the cost…

Yes, Bran is a famous composer now with more commissions on his horizon than he can possibly fulfill.

Yes, Jofi is hailed as a consummate musical genius that can now play or guest-conduct with any orchestra or ensemble in the world. He cares nothing for this.

Yes, Alma's vistas, too, are shining brighter than ever from her amazing talents spotlighted by her association with Jofi; and Jamaad is wealthy, busy, and among the brightest stars in his profession. This night, Jamaad is in Houston with Daisy Lee, busy about her work and career. And though she had been informed of the tragedy on the very day of her operatic debut, she sang with a broken heart but better than she had ever sung in her life. A true *prima donna*.

And finally, there are fresh impulses firing in all the arts, philosophy, even physics – which is finally developing rudimentary tools to incorporate consciousness and observation into the old matter-based conceptions.

Age-old and adamant barriers to this new kind of thinking and innovation are finally giving way to fresh insights. All this has followed abreast of Bran's colossal sucker-punch to the creative stasis of a century. The birth-pangs of a new era are stirring far and wide.

The family members are feeling the grief that a family feels when a loved-one departs, but it is Bran, and only he, who is wracked with guilt. This is a special kind of grief, less pure, corrosive.

Emma reaches over and takes Bran's hand and gives it a squeeze. He turns to her. He's had difficulty meeting her eyes since the tragedy and she knows this, so she touches softly his cheek to bring him back to her when he turns away, holds his gaze in her own, smiles, and again, it breaks his heart and he looks away. But he has no more tears. He sits and is sad.

They all get together every few evenings these days. Sit, mostly in near-silence. Have a little wine. Studio recordings have been suspended until they feel like recording again – not something anyone is in a hurry to do.

Alma now lives with Bran at his ex-Daisy home (they both find that place uncomfortable now), so at the mansion, there is often only Emma, Janet, Jofi, and Eric. It's been years since the place has been this quiet. In truth, it's *never* been so quiet.

Jofi was cleared quickly of any legal entanglements in the death of Fr. Preston Holt, the "mentally-disturbed priest who fled without authorization from his post as Assistant Pastor (formerly Pastor), of Holy Trinity Church in Ann Arbor, Michigan." That's how one account had it in the *Washington Post*.

58

It is Jofi who will take the lead in the group's healing, and it's why he's asked that friends and family be present this eve.

Jofi sits now at the head of the table. In front of him is a bottle of champagne on ice, and six glasses. He speaks, and his countenance is so severe it's almost grim.

"I will not be questioned about what I have to say to you." He waits a space. He wants that to sink in, and all acknowledge him with their unspoken assent.

"Matt is fine."

He waits for the subtle, inevitable hubbub to die down, the quiet glances back-and-forth, and speaks on.

"He is saddened by all the grief, and he thinks it has gone on too long. He's having trouble… moving on. And he *needs* to move on. It's not good for him, for any of us, that we're emotionally binding him to a world that he can no longer be part of. He won't move on until we can let him go in peace."

He notes the awe in his loved ones' faces, and he continues.

He looks at Emma. "Mom. Matt doesn't believe that there is anything left unspoken between you and him. He wants you to know that he woke up every day the most grateful of men that he was waking next to you. You lessened all the drudgery and annoyances of life, and you sent all the good things higher. He knows he will be with you again, but he doesn't want you to hasten to that goal. You are needed so badly where you are."

At those words, Eric starts to cry. Emma was doing pretty well through it all, but as badly as she feels her loss, it is Eric's grief that is so much harder for her to bear than her own, and she begins to cry as well.

"Eric?" Jofi says softly. "Your Dad has something for you as well."

The lad stops his crying and looks to his big brother with big red eyes still swimming in tears.

"You made your dad proud, and his biggest regret in all of this is that he had to leave you at such a young age and that he counts as a blessing every moment he spent with you. Your Dad needs you to know that he died a good death. He was never sick, or so old that he couldn't enjoy things. He died doing his job. For some men – for a man like Matt – that's a blessing. You've never brought dishonor to the people that love you, and Matt knows your heart well enough to know that you never will. He says to look to your brother and your mother and your aunt in times of need and they will never let you down."

"Either will we, kid," Bran adds and Alma nods agreement.

One might think that such words would start up the waterworks in the lad, but he sits, amazed, and when Jofi is done, Eric smiles at him.

Jofi turns to Janet, who turns away as if that might help avoid the hurt. "Matt said that you were the great heartbreak of his life. He nearly died of grief when you left this house the first time so many years ago, and when you returned, that joy was turned to remorse that he was never able to unburden, because he blamed himself for your troubles after your marriage. He knows you forgive him, and he begs you not to think poorly of him. He has never stopped loving you and never will."

Janet sits, looking down, pierced to her heart, tears plinking onto the table. Jofi turns to Alma. She is surprised.

"Me?"

"Yes," Jofi smiles. "Of course, you." She sits at attention. "Matt called you his daughter. He always wanted one, and he was so happy when you lived here. He said that having you here made him reconsider having one of his own because the odds of finding another like you were impossibly small. He said you brightened the end of his days."

No way to stop the waterworks in this lady. She weeps when she fails at a difficult crossword puzzle.

Jofi turns to Bran, who pulls away. "Oh boy. Me, too?"

"Matt said that if it weren't for you the joys of his last few years would never have happened. He's grateful. Matt bears you not a shred of ill-will that he died in defense of your life. Again – he died doing his lifework. He knows you'll make the best of what has happened and his only wish, in return for giving his life for yours…"

"Jesus man, *what!?*"

"…is that you give up your *guilt*. He knows you well enough to know that it's your nature to carry that guilt around, look at it straight in the face every day and never let yourself off the hook, but this is exactly the core of his request to you – that you stop that *right now*. Matt knows your high regard for him, but you know nothing of his high regard

240

for *you*. Show your love for him by doing his wish here. Start now. Live free. Make more Beauty. Come alive again for *him.*"

This is much more than even Bran, braced against the possibility, can bear, and he cries like a hurt boy.

But Jofi presses him still. *"You gotta do this Bran.* Matt needs to move on."

Bran just nods, not yet able to speak.

Everyone at the table looks wrung-out. Now Jofi concludes. "Matt also has words for Jamaad and Daisy Lee, and when next I see them I'll convey his communication to them."

Messages delivered, Jofi pops the cork on the champagne with remarkably little finesse and, divine simpleton that he sometimes is, manages to pour most of the instantly overflowing first glass all over the table. Stifling laughter, all wait politely while Jofi, finally, coaxes the remaining wine into six glasses, now distributed across the table (himself and Eric, too). Jofi looks to Emma.

"Mom?"

Emma raises her glass and forces a smile, then feels the falseness of the gesture. She puts her glass back down, lowers her head and communes with herself for a space. Now she raises her head up and this time her smile is genuine, and in a clear voice she intones –

> *"To my beautiful husband;*
> *to your loving father;*
> *to your perfect friend.*
> *To Matt."*

"To Matt," they declare in chorus, and drink of the wine together. And so, the real healing began.

No one ever asked Jofi how he knew all of this.

59

Everyone struggled to find their way to the 'new normal,' but Time has a way of taking care of that issue no matter our mindset or expectations.

By late-summer, seven months after Matt's death, Bran and Daisy have formally divorced, and he and Alma have married. Bran plans to sell the house (never again a *home)* that Daisy bequeathed him. When the house is sold Bran will offer Daisy the money from the sale. She will of course refuse. With the help of a local architect acquaintance, the couple will soon have a new home designed to their specifications on a vacant piece of lakefront-with-ten-acres within striking distance of Ann Arbor. It is under construction and due finished "before the snow flies," they are promised.

Jofi is conducting the National Orchestra in recordings of a Bruckner Symphony cycle. Jamaad has managed to get the producer credit and the cycle shall be released on the *Seraphim Media* label. No.1 is in the can and the Symphony No.2 is in preparation. Jofi does this with the counsel and blessing of Maestro Cavendish, who is secretly relieved to start building a quieter life, as he believes he has at last earned his place *"out* of the sun," as he put it to Jofi.

The recording studio is largely quiet these days, with Jofi and Jamaad spending so much time in Washington and Alma enjoying her life with her new husband. She's not sure if she'll ever return to the stage or studio. She loves being Bran's wife and spends much time with Emma and Janet.

Ah… the widow Emma, like a beautiful nun. Without Matt, her interest in the social scene is much diminished. She spends her days reading, playing the piano (never Bach), gardening, communing with her sons, sister, Alma, and a couple friends she might see on the odd occasion. She never seems bored. Graciousness is still her most obvious attribute.

Junior-varsity high-school quarterback Eric is feeling his oats these days and he has self-assumed the mantle of 'Man of the House' since Jofi is so often away, and he is sensitive to the needs of his Mom and Aunt Janet. He looks like a young, gangly version of Matt.

Janet's transformation from the tormented alcoholic to her more healthy current self has been extraordinary and heartening to all who know her. Matt's death caused her great suffering, but it purged a certain malignant part of her, and she's emerged from it all a calmer and more content woman. Matt's death has also brought her even closer to young Eric, of whom she is most protective.

My work, I feel, is finished here. I have essentially failed in my mission and I must come to terms with this. My main task – of finding Sam Morgan and bringing him into a relationship with Bran – this I have not been able to accomplish. Did the adversary get to him before I could? I can think of no other explanation. True, I found Bran, and his work was performed, but to what end? To what benefit? The revolution in the Arts and Sciences that seems to be underway may well have happened without the actions that terminated in my father's murder, it just might have taken a little longer. What else did the work accomplish? There is nothing I can discern. Now, I mark time and marvel at my uselessness and failure. I feel a lessening of myself within, a withering away. In fact, I pray for release. I have been gone for so long. I have been so long out of touch, and though I have been imprisoned in this body for almost 21 years, surely, I am still a stranger in a strange land. I pray now to return to my celestial home to bear my shame. If only my companion of ages, my dearest Metatron, would commune with me again and lend me the vision and grace to endure. I am so lost… so lost…
– from *Chronicles of Jophiel, Vol. II*

60

Young Jofi Fischer is a celebrated conductor, to be sure, but he is still in great demand as piano soloist. He has agreed to perform a concert of Schubert and Bach at the Folger Theater before the next set of Bruckner rehearsals to substitute for another luminary who had canceled her program.

The evening before Jofi was to depart for his concert in the nation's capital a wonderful and unexpected event occurs. Eric had just welcomed Bran and Alma who dropped in for a visit and the couple are relaxing, waiting for Jofi, and enjoying a drink in the great room while Jofi finishes packing. Alma has noticed that Jofi has been at that chore for quite a while and decides to see what is keeping him. She meets Jofi just as he opens the door to his room to finally join the others.

Jofi smiles a hello.

"Hi Jofi!" Alma chirps and leans in to peck him on the cheek, when Jofi suddenly snatches her by her shoulders and pushes her away at arm's length, and holds her there, gazing deeply into Alma's eyes.

"Jofi! You're hurting me!" Alma cries. "What's the matter? You look like someone slapped you!"

Jofi drops to his knees in front of his dear friend, grabs the front of her yoga pants and panties and pulls them down until his fingers are in her pubic hair. She gasps. With his other hand he lifts her top to the edge of her brassiere.

"My God! Jofi! What are you doing?" She is trying not to yell and alert the others.

Jofi ignores her and instead presses his face into her lower belly, dwelling there for a few long seconds and finally planting a kiss there. He looks up at her panicked face and he smiles. He rises.

Alma busies herself in recovering her composure and the proper arrangement of her clothes after Jofi's immodest invasion. *"Jofi!,"* she stage-whispers, "what were you *thinking?!"*

"It's a girl!" he says with the biggest smile.

"It's… it's a…" It is dawning on Alma. "It's a what now?"

"A girl. A girl baby. You're pregnant," Jofi says.

Alma looks like she just won the lottery.

"BRAN!" she cries at the top of her voice.

61

The next day, in D.C., Jofi was asked what he wanted to play in the indisposed pianist's stead, and he inquired about the program planned by the soloist. Being told this, he agreed to simply perform the same program—Bach and Schubert—maybe sneak in a piano piece by Bran as an inevitable encore piece. The librarian inquires, does Maestro Fischer require the piano scores? Maestro Fischer does not. He remembers. The recital, sold out, is that very evening.

The first piece on the program is the C minor Toccata by Bach. Jofi sails through the first section but half-way through the fugue the unthinkable, the unprecedented occurs – *Jofi makes a mistake*. His thumb goes for the F, but he just slightly overshoots it and it sounds the adjacent E along with it. He immediately ceases to play. He sits, stunned, staring at his open palms with a baffled expression and after a few moments stands, faces his audience and says simply, "I'm terribly sorry." And then he exits the stage.

There is a well-mannered little kerfuffle in the theater, but Jofi is fairly pounced upon by the less well-mannered producer on his way out of the hall, but he does not so much as acknowledge the producer's existence. Jofi simply makes a bee-line to his car, the producer screaming strings of obscenities at him from the parking lot as Jofi cruises away. The loud tirade stops abruptly as the producer recalls with panic that the man he just called a "lousy son-of-a-bitch" killed a murderer quite recently using only his baton.

Jofi drives to his hotel. The next morning, he cancels his orchestra rehearsal, claiming a health emergency. He explains that he needs to fly home to Michigan in the morning, and that progress on the Bruckner project shall be suspended.

On the plane home, Jofi can really feel it now. He feels himself separating from his body. He is slowly abandoning his earthly form. His prayer has been answered, and it shall not be long now. He tries to sleep.

He dreams of his mother.

62

Bran is waiting for Jofi at Metro Airport, about a half-hour from Ann Arbor on the way to Detroit. Bran pops the trunk and Jofi hoists his luggage inside and closes the lid. He opens the door to Bran's big ancient Lincoln Towncar and slips inside. It's cool and comfortable.

Bran looks terrified. "What's wrong with you, Jofi?"

"What do you mean?"

"The way you… I dunno… *dragged your ass* to the car. It's not like you. Plus, you're pale. You all right? Or what?"

Jofi wasn't prepared to explain so soon. He thought he could hide it. At least for a day or so.

"Plus, why are you home?" Bran continues with the third-degree as he pulls out into traffic. "You had another week there. Two more rehearsals, then the recording-"

"Yes, Bran!" Jofi is exasperated.

Bran gets all calm and tries again. "So… will you tell me what the hell is going on with you?"

"Yeah…" big sigh. "Just let me think a minute."

They are back on the freeway, and still, Jofi is mute. A few more minutes pass in silence and Bran says softly, "Spit it out, brother. This is *Bran."*

Jofi smiles in spite of himself. "I'm sorry, bro'. You're right," Jofi says. He tries to form the sentences but cannot. Finally he says, "Listen. It would be easier for me to just tell everybody together. Forgive me. I just need to do it like that. Okay?"

Bran shoots him an annoyed sidelong glance. "Yeah. Okay, I guess. Back at the mansion is pretty much everybody except Jamaad, who's still in Washington."

"Yeah… he called me. We talked."

"He's pissed?"

"Completely. I told him I'd clear things up with him today. He's flying back this afternoon."

"Wanna wait for him?

"Yeah. Let's do that. I'll ask Mom to make us all a little dinner. After that we'll talk."

Worried looks flash here and there across the dinner table as they eat of Emma's simple repast. Emma is downright jumpy. She can't eat; Jofi chooses not to. Emma waits until the last person (Alma) puts the last forkful of food in her mouth and without even waiting for her to chew says to Jofi, "Okay, so what's going on with you?"

Jofi motions with his head toward the great room, where they all move, sitting now in a semi-circle around the dormant fireplace.

"I have to tell you all something about myself," Jofi begins, noting a few smiles and sly glances. "We're always advised to have some discretion in this matter and work with as much anonymity as possible. This is difficult in my case, as so much of my work had to be done in the public eye. But you all need to know."

"Yeah," Jamaad says. "You're an Angel."

Jofi is startled. *"What?"*

"Like, tell us something we don't know, Jofi," Bran says. The men laugh good-naturedly, the ladies try not to, glancing furtively at one another.

Jofi feels cluelessly stupid and relieved at the same time. He smiles and puts his face in his hands and shakes his head.

"Dude," Bran says, "you told Alma, you told Janet-"

"Stop!" the two ladies cited cry out in unison. Jofi looks at them both with a smile.

"I mean," Bran explains, "they tried, but, Dude, they're *women!* Know what I mean?"

"O, shut up, Bran," Alma pipes, kinda-sorta kidding. Janet looks terribly embarrassed and is not even trying to hide it.

"Plus, there's just no other explanation for you, Jofi," Jamaad says. "It's such a crazy thing – none of us ever tell anyone. Who's gonna believe us? But crazy as it is it's still pretty much the simplest explanation of the wonder of you, my man."

Bran says, "Any other explanation is weirder than the Angel one. Believe me – we tried."

Emma has not joined in the fun. "But what's *wrong*, Jofi?" All are sober now in deference. Solemn, even.

Jofi's smile vanishes, too. "I have to go."

"To some other place?" Emma asks, hand to her heart, suddenly sick with premonition.

"No, Mom. I have to leave this body and-"

Emma's hand goes to her mouth. "O no," she whispers. "Not you… not you, too…"

Eric gasps. *"Jofi! What?"*

"I was playing a recital in D.C. … and I hit a wrong note."

"First and only. Ever." Bran surmises.

Jofi nods.

"Well, what does *that* mean?" Emma asks. "Is that such a big deal? I do it all the *time!*"

"Mom, in my case it means that I'm separating from my body. I can feel it."

All is quiet for a few heavy seconds and it all sinks in.

"How long?" Bran asks. "How long will it take."

"I dunno," Jofi replies. "Couple days, maybe less."

"Can't you stop it?" Emma is getting upset and poor Eric is crying, near panic.

"No, Mom. I have to go back. My mission is over. It was pretty much a failure. The little bit I accomplished – and at what terrible cost. I couldn't be more ashamed. But I have to face it. I need to go back to where I came from. And you know I'm not 'dying,' right?"

248

He doesn't know how to comfort his Mom. There *is* no way to do that.

"O, I don't know anything Jofi," Emma laments. "I suspected you were an Angel when you were a tiny baby. I knew before Angus died, but I couldn't tell him. He would never have believed me. But I don't know anything anymore…" And now she's crying.

Bran is sitting next to Emma and Alma is down the row. Alma gets up and goes to Bran and points him to her vacant chair. He gets it. He heads to her seat and Alma sits next to Emma. She takes Emma's hand and holds it. Emma doesn't even notice.

Janet, sitting on Emma's other side, asks, "Jofi honey, what can we do?"

"It would be nice to have you all around me," Jofi says. "Just there on the couch. I'll just lie there till I'm set free. I don't think it'll take long. I won't suffer at all or be any trouble."

"Set *free?*" Eric says. "What's *that* mean?!" He stands up and looks confused. Jofi rises and goes quickly to his brother. He embraces him and lets Eric cry his heart out on his shoulder. Janet and Alma do their best to bring some comfort to Emma, but no one is bringing any comfort to anyone.

63
The Ecstasy of Emma Fischer

Calmer now, the morning next, but no one had slept. Emma had sat all night in the great room, staring into the fireplace for hours after the fire had gone out. She sits there now. Eric tosses and turns in his bed, and Janet is making the morning coffee, determined to transcend her grief and somehow be a force for consolation among the family.

Jofi rises from his bed, greets Janet in the kitchen with a cheerful kiss on the cheek. Eric hears them stir, rises and joins the pair as Janet pours coffee for three. They hear Emma padding in from the great room to join them, re-tying her robe then running her hands through her enwildened hair to seem presentable. Her eyes are red and swollen. Janet pours a fourth cup.

After a light breakfast that Emma insisted on making, they dally there at the little table in the kitchen, enjoying the sun as it rises through the trees and transforms the bleak and dismal night into a more manageable daylight. The three oldest are tranquil, acceptance slowly making its way. Only Eric, who will not go to school today, is crestfallen beyond hope of pretending otherwise.

Eric and Janet excuse themselves to dress for the day and Jofi looks to Emma and smiles.

Emma smiles back, almost reluctantly. "What are you so cheerful about?" she asks.

"I have a present for you," Jofi replies.

Emma looks hurt and looks away from her son, tearing up. Just when she thought she had a handle on all this…

"It's a good thing, Mom. You'll like it."

"How are you feeling?" she asks, wiping at her eyes.

"Still good. I feel good," he says, rising from his chair. "Listen, I have to write a few letters. Some loose ends." He looks at the clock. "Say, three hours? See you before noon, okay?"

Emma smiles. "So my present is already here?"

"It's already here," Jofi says.

A few minutes before noon, as promised, Jofi left his room and sought out Emma, and he finds her sitting on the big armchair in his studio, of all places.

"Well, this is a rarity," Jofi says to his mom.

She looks at him and smiles. "I know. I never come in here. Well, almost never. But this is the heart of our home, for you. Isn't it, Jofi?"

Jofi nods. It's true.

"Have you come to take me to see my present?" she asks.

"Actually, you're in the right room and in just the right chair."

"Really? Well… should I close my eyes?"

Jofi beams her a loving look in answer, and he walks the few feet to his beloved concert grand, takes his seat on the bench and wiggles himself into comfort. Emma smiles. She is very comfortable and is viewing her son in profile about ten feet from her chair, Jofi directly in front of her and nine feet of piano stretching to her left.

Jofi leans forward, rests his hands over the keyboard, and begins to play.

Emma nestles into the big chair, closes her eyes and lets the music take her wherever Jofi might lead. After a few moments of Jofi's prelude Emma sits up, gasping, as if shocked. She remains in this tight suspense, almost as if she is about to flee the room, and only little by little she relaxes, ever so gradually as Jofi lets this strange music unfold. Another minute and she is sunken back into the folds of the big chair, eyes half-open, only her tight grip on the arms of the chair betraying her remaining tension.

Soon even this unease disappears and now, eyes closed, she appears asleep with only her rapid breathing betraying her taut engagement in Jofi's music, which has just changed dramatically in character.

Emma takes a deep breath, then another, then cries out! Bending forward and then thrashing back in her chair, twisting and crying out again and again as the arrows of Jofi's improvisation pierce her heart.

Gradually she calms… and at last she is still, her tear-streaked face glowing, shining as if with its own light, still subject, still enslaved by the spell of her son's strange recital as it continues.

After a space Jofi begins to sing, wordlessly, in accompaniment to his playing. His vocalizations are of an unearthly sweetness, and they begin a new effect on Emma.

She is breathing harder and more deeply, twisting in her chair, now thrashing slowly from side to side until at last she shudders, whimpering, finally spasming, crying out, again and again, until, exhausted, she swoons at long last into unconsciousness just as Jofi concludes his strange serenade.

She is awake now. After a brief struggle to get her bearings she wonders, *how long did he play? A minute? An hour? What just happened to me?*

Jofi is at her side, sitting on the arm of the chair leaning over with his forehead pressed against the top of his mother's head. He sits up.

"You okay, Mom?"

She looks up at her son and with a still-shaking hand reaches out to stroke his face.

"Jofi… what happened? … What did you *do?*"

"I played for you."

"You've played for me many times. But… but not…"

"I've never improvised before where anyone could over-hear. I realized it could be dangerous depending upon the circumstances."

"So you… you just made all that up?"

"Well… not exactly. I played… *you.*"

"What do you mean?"

Jofi considers how to frame this.

"Jofi. Tell me what just happened to me!" Emma's anxiety is returning. She is still disoriented and becoming very upset. Jofi hugs his mom's shoulders and explains.

"See… when popular composers write music, they write it for everybody to appreciate. Great composers write for a smaller more focused audience, and the appreciation is deeper and more personal. But there is a kind of music, the truest and most profound music, to which no earthly musician can yet attain, that is specific for an audience of *one*. Depending upon the intent and skill of the musician, such music can heal or kill, or produce any effect in between. Such is the hidden and divine power of sound."

"So you played only for me?"

"It would have had little effect on anyone else."

"But on me…"

"It was music that embodied all I know and love about you. I recall with the alacrity of a lightning strike every tender gesture, every act, every loving word from your lips. From my first home in the warmth of your womb, and the sweetness of your milk, to the struggles and the terrible tragedies which you have endured with me in my manhood, and with such grace. I wanted you to know how I see you. All I have known of earthly beauty has had its source in you."

Emma, exhausted, raises her head and looks upon her son with wonder. "You shot arrows into my heart," she whispers. "And the pain was so great… yet so sweet… that I could not wish to be rid of it."

Jofi stands and strokes his mother's hair. "Rest for a while, Mom."

She is already asleep.

64

Jofi abides until the next evening.

They are all together now. Jofi holding court lying comfortably on the big couch in the great room. There are many comings and goings among the six, many heart-to-hearts, everyone's goodbyes taking a different path, different words, same love.

Jofi can barely speak now. But he doesn't look ill. He looks peaceful, otherworldly. He's smiling through it all. There is no suffering here. Jofi is still the most beautiful creature any of them have ever beheld or ever shall behold. None of that has been diminished by his state. He is radiant.

It's just Jofi and Emma again, for a few quiet moments. The others are in the kitchen, sipping wine and talking softly among themselves.

"Mom."

"Yes, my dear."

"Did Dad know? About me? I mean, he knows now, but did he know before?"

"For years. He just pretended he didn't because you said you would explain when the time was right. He wanted to respect that."

Jofi managed a little laugh. "I really *was* going to tell you." A whisper is all he can manage now.

They gaze at one another in complete devotion and exchange a deep love smile.

"My Angel…" she whispers, stroking his flawless cheek. "The perfect light of my life." And she leans to kiss his brow, a long kiss, and when she pulls back to behold him she senses he is gone. He looks like he's sleeping, caught up in a beautiful dream…

Epilogue

I t's been precisely a year since Jofi's passing and Emma is hosting a memorial gathering this late morning at the estate. All the usual subjects and their friends will be in attendance. Other visitors shall include Daisy Lee (unaccompanied), Li Ming and his wife, and many other musician friends from the world over who have shared their art with the masterful departed one. No fans and no journalists.

Bran has just arrived and kisses Emma on the cheek. She looks good. She looks peaceful and full of grace. Suddenly Bran is enveloped by two strong arms around his chest from behind, squeezing the breath out of him.

"Let me go or I will *kill* you," Bran growls, and the assailant releases him. Emma shakes her head and decides to mingle.

It is Eric, natch, who breezes on by. He turns and points to Bran. "I know where you live, pal."

"Come heavy, kid," Bran calls after him with a grin.

"Hello, Bran." Another voice behind him. Bran turns and beholds the smiling face of Sir George Cavendish. It's been months.

Bran smiles and takes the maestro's proffered hand. "Nice to see you, Skip. I hope you've been well."

"I have so been indeed. And congratulations again on the birth of your daughter."

"Thanks."

"And good wishes to Alma."

"She and the baby'll be here soon. Daisy Lee is driving them over."

"Ah, Daisy. I read about her every week it seems."

Now they are joined by a lovely young woman who takes Sir George's arm and gives him a big smile. He kisses her cheek. "Ah… there you are, my dear. I want you to meet Bran Englander, the composer. Bran, this is Blythe."

She extends her hand, Bran presses it and smiles. She blushes. "It's such a pleasure to meet you, Mr. Englander," she gushes. "I *love* your work. And I can hardly wait to hear your violin concerto next season."

Bran bows. "Thank you." He turns to Sir George. "So, you're retiring!"

"And not a moment too soon," the maestro says.

"Have you found a new music director?"

"No…" the maestro muses. "With the way things are these days I believe they're looking hard for a certain 'type' of person to replace me. Extra-musical concerns abound and are holding things up."

"What do you mean?"

"Well, I think they'd like to find a one-eyed lesbian Eskimo in a wheelchair, but that's proved difficult."

Bran laughs. Blythe looks offended. "Oh, stop it, Sir George. *Really…*" And she storms away in high dudgeon.

"Ah," Bran observes. "Sensitive."

The maestro huffs.

"Skip, in what capacity does young Blythe attend you tonight? If you don't mind me asking."

"Yes! Of course! She is, ah… one of my ahh… students." The maestro clears his throat. "Yes."

Bran waits, with a slowly spreading smile.

"And she's, ah… my umm… my *mistress*, actually."

Bran nods and raises his glass of mimosa in a toast. "Maestro!" he says and takes a sip.

Blushing Skip says, "Yes. Thank you… *I say!* Is that a mimosa?"

They stroll to the bar together and Bran walks smack into Daisy.

"Bran!" she says.

Bran nods and turns to his pal Skip. "Pardon me for the moment, Sir George."

"Certainly." The maestro takes Daisy's hand and kisses it. "We'll talk later, my dear." She smiles after him and turns to Bran. Bran is spellbound. She's still Daisy, but even more so.

"She's a real beauty," Daisy says. "Your baby."

"Ah. Thanks."

"Have you been well? I was devastated to hear about Jofi and I'm so sorry."

"I'm good. You?"

"I'm good, too."

Bran smiles a sad smile and kisses Daisy on the cheek. She points to the corner of the room. "She and the baby are over there. Holding court."

"Thanks. See you later."

Bran heads that way, stopping here and there to briefly greet friends. He's amazed at all the music luminaries and the many people he does not know.

Alma spies him and breaks from the crowd. She greets her husband with a kiss and a smile, and they file back toward the crowd in the corner. Before they can get there, Jamaad intercepts them. Janet is with him.

"Hey," Bran greets them.

"Hey, you two. Listen."

"What's up, Jamaad?" Alma asks, cradling the infant near her cheek. "You look so serious."

Janet asks, "Have you had a dream about Jofi? I mean… with Jofi in it?"

"Because I have," Jamaad says, "and so has Janet. Have either of you?"

Both answer "Yes," at the same time. "Just last night," Alma said. "I told Bran this morning and he said the same. He had the same dream."

"I wonder if Emma has, too…" Janet wonders aloud.

"What was yours like?" Bran asks Jamaad.

"Well, it was last night. Just like you two. He said he was sorry."

"*Yes!*" Janet cries. "He told me the same thing. And that all his fretting and talk about his failure was for nothing."

"Yes." It's Emma, who sidles up unnoticed. "I had this dream last night also. Jofi said he was sorry for his lack of faith and wanted me to know."

Emma looks at the other four, who nod back to her in affirmation. Evidently, they all witnessed the same dream.

They're all silent for a moment thinking about this. Bran says, "I wonder what happened to him?"

"I don't know," Emma smiles. "But it was so wonderful to see him. I miss him so." She stretches out her arms to Alma and the babe. "May I hold her?"

"Of course," and Alma surrenders her precious package.

Emma snuggles the baby and smiles. "Do you have a name yet?" she asks.

"Yes! Finally!" Bran says. "Just last night we decided."

"It's been three months and the poor girl still doesn't have a name!" Emma laughed.

"Well, she does now! If it was a boy we were going to call him Matt," Alma says.

Emma kisses the baby. "That was nice. Thanks."

"But like Jofi predicted, she's a girl, so we took our moms' names and named her after *them.*"

"So… what do you call her?" Janet asks.

"My Mom's name is Samantha," Alma says.

"And my Mom's name is Morgen," Bran says. "It means 'morning' in German."

"So… Samantha Morgen Englander?" Emma says.

"Right!" Alma pipes. "We call her Sam."

Emma holds the baby so she can see her face.

"Well, hello, Sam Morgen," she coos. "Aren't you a beautiful little girl!"

ଈଓ

Jophiel in Literature and Lore

*A*ngels are found in all the world's major religions, and in many cases can be cross-referenced and the same beings found among various faiths under different names. Here in the West, most of Christian angelology derives from ancient Hebrew origins.

Jophiel (יוֹפִיאֵל in Hebrew) means *beauty of God* or *divine beauty*. Angelology traditionally has it that Jophiel is identical to the Angels Iophiel and Zophiel, and there are many other various spellings all referring to the same Angel.

The suffix –*el* indicates, in traditional Hebrew, *of God*. Therefore, Michael is *Micha of God,* Uriel is *Uri of God,* etc. So Jophiel is to be understood as *Jophi of God*.

In proper pronunciation, the –*el* syllable is pronounced distinctly. Therefore, Jophiel is not pronounced as *Jo-feel*. In English, it is properly *Jo-fee-EL*, with accent on the last syllable.

The ancient Hebrew guardian of the Torah (and wisdom itself), Jophiel is said to have taught 70 languages to souls at the dawn of creation. Why this was such a swell idea has not been explained. The Zohar lists Jophiel as a Great Angel Chief in charge of 53 legions of Angels. Jewish tradition says that Jophiel was the Angel who guarded the Tree of Knowledge and cast Adam and Eve out of the Garden of Eden when they sinned, and now guards the Tree of Life with a flaming sword.

C.E. Clement, in his book *Angels in Art*, names Jophiel as the teacher of Noah's boys, Ham, Japheth, and Shem. Heinrich Cornelius Agrippa and Thomas Rudd likewise name Jophiel as the teacher of Shem.

Jophiel is an Archangel of the Kabbalah and shows up in several well-known listings, including that of the early medieval theologian Pseudo-Dionysius's *De Coelesti Hierarchia (Celestial Hierarchy)*, a fifth-century work on angelology that has been influential in Christian theology. It's said that this work influenced Thomas Aquinas's writings about the nine choirs of Angels.

The *Calendarium naturale magicum perpetuum* lists Jophiel as the Angel of the *Sephira Chokhmah*, as do the *Key of Solomon* variant *The Veritable Clavicles of Solomon*, and the *Sixth and Seventh Books of Moses*, both latter works derived from the *Calendarium*.

Agrippa attributes Jophiel as the regent of Saturn, while Paracelsus assigns that Angel to Jupiter. Rudd attributes the science of the Zodiac to Jophiel along with the *Sephira Binah*. Athanasius Kircher names Jophiel as *Angelus pulchritudinis* – Angel of beauty.

According to Robert Ambelain, Jophiel is in charge of the second-highest rank of Angels, the Cherubim. John Milton, in his poem *Paradise Lost*, mentions that Zophiel is "of cherubim the swiftest wing."

Below is the *sigil* of Jophiel. In this sense, a sigil is the graphic representation of the essence of the Angel. One needs the 'keys' to properly understand the meaning of an angelic sigil, but it makes its mark on the viewer who simply contemplates it receptively:

There are only two Angels in the canon whose names do not end in –*el*. One of these is **Metatron** (מטטרון in Hebrew) traditionally, Jophiel's companion, who looms large in this book. Metatron is not considered '*of God*' like the other Angels because Metatron's origins are human. According to Jewish apocrypha, Metatron is the name Enoch received, after his transformation into an Angel. The book of Genesis is often cited as evidence of Enoch's bodily ascension into heaven: "And Enoch walked with God: and he was not; for God took him." Although Metatron is mentioned in a few brief passages in the Talmud, this Angel appears primarily in Kabbalistic texts. In that tradition, Metatron is the highest of the Angels and serves as the celestial scribe or recording Angel.

Here is the *sigil* of Metatron:

About Gerald Brennan

I was born on September 2, 1953, in Jessup, PA. At age two I moved to Dearborn, MI, where I lived with my family until my late teens. The eldest of six children, I went to Catholic school, and when my brain started working at about age 15, I left the Church, my youthful mind appalled by its many dogmas. Nor did the priests and nuns wish to indulge my curious nature. When we had philosophical questions, the answer was usually along the lines of "Shut up." It was in high school that I began to write down the music in my head.

Wandering in the desert for many years, I drank heavily, experimented with drugs, and studied music, science and philosophy. Though I never had any formal music education, living in Ann Arbor put many wonderful resources at my disposal, including many fine Steinway grands sprinkled merrily throughout the University of Michigan campus back in the day when there didn't need to be a lock on every door.

I became a good pianist in the following years, as well as composer. I had many musical adventures—breaking a Steinway grand playing Liszt at the University of Michigan music school, playing Liszt's American Steinway at the Smithsonian Museum in an impromptu recital that drew quite a wondrous crowd.

I became a National Public Radio affiliate producer with WUOM, WVGR and WFUM out of the U-M. I produced hundreds of weekly programs in my decade there—including *The Musical Theatre, New Music, New Releases, From the Monophonic Era, Music of Our World, Excursions* and *Nocturne.*

In 1980 I organized the Ann Arbor-based Sinewave Studios for the development and propagation of new art music. I produced about 20 concerts and conducted the

North American premiere of Karlheinz Stockhausen's *Für kommende zeiten* at the Detroit Institute of Art.

My writing career started in 1984 when I wrote and self-published a booklet on starting a classical record collection. Borders Books agreed to carry it, and it finally made its way into the paws of a publisher. They asked me to expand it into a sure enough book and thus was born *Classical Records, Starting Your Collection.* After it was published, I took it to the Ann Arbor News and asked them if they needed a music reviewer. Turned out they did, and so, all while I had the radio gig, I was reviewing the best acts in the world that came through town.

Before all that I worked in record stores, including the famous Liberty Music. I also sold pianos, moved pianos, sold sheet music, managed U-M's record and sheet music store, and wrote for various national music journals.

In 1998, I was headhunted by a visionary fellow named Michael Erlewine, who decided that it would be a good idea to get hold of every album in the world and put every bit of information about it into a database. Eventually the idea included taking a photo of the album and doing sound samples. They started with a core of a few music geeks and began by going through their own collections. The company Erlewine founded was called *All Media Guide* (www.allmusic.com), which became the world's largest repository of product data and editorial information about music.

Erlewine asked me to assume the post of Director of Content of Classical Music at AMG, to create a department that would be devoted to classical music. I jumped at it, and in four years my amazing staff and I, along with scores of excellent writers, amassed the data, created the classical website, and produced the giant reference book, *AMG Guide to Classical Music,* which I edited and saw published in 2005. My mission was accomplished; my staff was a well-oiled machine and easily the best and happiest of all AMG's departments. Then 'investor fatigue' set in among the shareholders and AMG was appointed a slick new president who knew little about what we did or why but was hired to sell the company at a good price to whomever, and fast. He instinctively disliked me and my open resistance to his schemes and I was fired. I had no hard feelings. I had completed my mission, and it was time to go.

Now I write music and books, make recordings, and give the rare recital.

Books include this one, also *Prince of Pines*, a dystopian male-adventure novel set in Michigan's Upper Peninsula; *The Complete Short Stories;* and *A Song of Blood and Ashes,* a vampire tale set in contemporary Ireland and Ann Arbor. Also, *There was this guy once…*, also *Classical Music & Recordings–a primer,* and *Views & Reviews - Chronicles from the Twilight of the Golden Age of Classical Music*

Musically, I've to date got 90 songs published in three *SongBooks*, several chamber and orchestral pieces, piano works, a full-length Broadway-style musical called *Penelope*, choral works, and a large orchestral piece known as *Sinfonia Matrix,* which requires some 80-octillion years to be heard in its entirety. Therefore, performance versions are extracted depending upon available forces, duration required and occasion.

Available CDs include *Mythos* (piano pieces based upon Greek myth characters, recorded in recital and in-studio), *Five Fantasy Nocturnes for piano, Campfire—The Burning Psaltery* (a phantasmagorical piece for an innocent 12-string psaltery), *7 Solo Songs from 'Penelope,'* and several CDs from the *SongBooks* recorded in studio and at home, by me and various performers.

Also available on CD is the electronically-based Ambient Music Series, which includes *Ambient Counterpoint, Grand Starbells, Monochrome Frescos, The Singing Moon,* and *Whisperings of Angels.*

All items detailed above are published by DreamStreet Press and available on Amazon or through DreamStreetPress.com.

OTHER BOOKS BY GERALD BRENNAN

PRINCE OF PINES

Pure unapologetic dystopian male-adventure, intelligent and well-crafted, with plenty of guns and good women.

THE COMPLETE SHORT STORIES

Contemporary tales in many different genres.

Song of Blood & Ashes

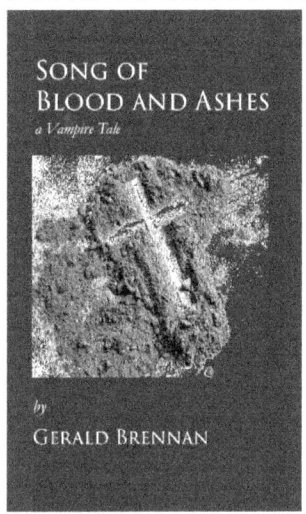

An ancient Vampire finally creates a protégé after centuries of searching. Blinded by her beauty and innocence, his choice was unwise. She loves a 'mortal' who does not reciprocate her affection. Her depraved appetites provoke a most horrifying catastrophe.

Classical Music & Recordings

This book is intended as an introduction to the species of art music which we call Classical Music.

VIEWS & REVIEWS

VIEWS & REVIEWS

Chronicles from the twilight
of the
GOLDEN AGE OF CLASSICAL MUSIC

&

by
GERALD BRENNAN

This book contains the original unedited versions of Gerald Brennan's previews, reviews, and interviews of the finest classical music soloists, ensembles, and orchestras in the world during what may well be looked back upon as the final flowering of Classical Music in the West.

THERE WAS THIS GUY ONCE...

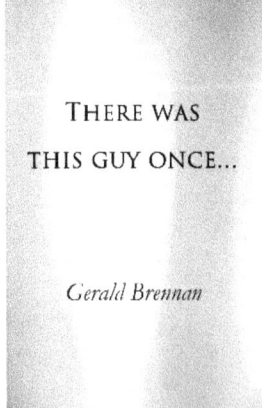

THERE WAS
THIS GUY ONCE...

Gerald Brennan

There is no plot but many characters. Not exactly autobiography, but a case could be made. This is a book about the people, influences, hopes, fears, and favorite things about my life as a composer, novelist, journalist, performing musician, and person.

www.ingramcontent.com/pod-product-compliance
Lightning Source LLC
Chambersburg PA
CBHW061518020726
47502CB00006B/2129